THE GARDEN OF SHARED STORIES

CLARE SWATMAN

B

Boldwood

First published in Great Britain in 2025 by Boldwood Books Ltd.

Copyright © Clare Swatman, 2025

Cover Design by JD Smith Design Ltd.

Cover Images: Shutterstock

A CIP catalogue record for this book is available from the British Library.

Paperback ISBN 978-1-78513-089-2

Large Print ISBN 978-1-78513-090-8

Hardback ISBN 978-1-78513-088-5

Trade Paperback ISBN 978-1-80656-113-1

Ebook ISBN 978-1-78513-091-5

Kindle ISBN 978-1-78513-092-2

Audio CD ISBN 978-1-78513-083-0

MP3 CD ISBN 978-1-78513-084-7

Digital audio download ISBN 978-1-78513-085-4

This book is printed on certified sustainable paper. Boldwood Books is dedicated to putting sustainability at the heart of our business. For more information please visit https://www.boldwoodbooks.com/about-us/sustainability/

Boldwood Books Ltd, 23 Bowerdean Street, London, SW6 3TN

www.boldwoodbooks.com

For Tom. I'd choose you, every time.

PART I

1

EMMA

It had been an absolute horror of a day when it happened: clients demanding the impossible, my boss taking her frustration out on me and then, to top it all off, someone stealing my home-made salad from the communal fridge. Now, as I stomped along the familiar path through the park towards home, I couldn't get the injustice of it all out of my head.

Luckily, the more distance I put between me and the office, the more the fury began to subside, gradually reducing from a raging torrent to a trickle, until, in its place settled an exhaustion so intense I thought my legs might give way.

I stopped dead in the middle of the path, suddenly desperate to sit down. To my right, a group of pre-teens were playing a rowdy game of rounders. To my left, a few metres away, was the rose garden, inside which stood the bandstand that only occasionally hosted any music, but was a popular choice for teenagers to smoke and snog, away from parents' prying eyes. It was empty right now though, so I hurried towards it. A cool breeze stirred the roses, and the sun hovered above the treetops like a large round of cheese as I sank gratefully onto the bench, closed my eyes, and tipped my face up towards the light. As the evening sun warmed my skin, the tension began to leave my body, draining away like bath water down a plughole. The light behind my eyelids glowed orange, and an occasional cheer from the rounders game drifted through my mind, barely causing a ripple.

In the old days, before Greg died, I would have wanted nothing more than to go straight home and off-load my worries and stresses of the day onto him. He would have done the same in return and, although he rarely let the little things get to him in the way I knew I often did, it always helped to know we had each other's backs, no matter what. But these days the only thing I had to hurry home for was another depressing meal for one, a glass of wine, and re-watching episodes of *Fleabag* until my eyeballs shrivelled up. It wasn't the most appealing or enticing thought.

In fact it made the space inside me where Greg should be swell a little more, so that I felt even emptier than usual. I swiped at my cheek and took a deep breath in and—

'Are you all right?'

My eyes flew open and when I turned my head there was a man beside me, watching me with a strange expression on his face. I hadn't heard him approach and I felt suddenly vulnerable, sitting there with a damp face and no idea where this man had sprung from. I looked away without replying.

'I'm really sorry to disturb you.'

I wanted to berate him for having disturbed me anyway, but I didn't have the energy so instead I gave a small nod and stared out across the gardens. I hoped he'd get the hint and move away, but I could still feel him there, and eventually I looked back at him, saying nothing.

'Sorry, I'm not a weirdo,' he said, with a small smile. 'I just hate seeing people sad. I should leave you be.'

I shook my head. 'It's fine. I'm fine. But thank you.'

He hooked his right ankle onto his left knee and spread his fingers across his calf. They were long and slender and, I couldn't help but notice, ringless. I glanced down at my own ring finger where the gold band I should have taken off months ago still sat, etching a groove into my skin. A reminder of everything I'd lost. I don't know why I did it to myself.

We sat in silence for a few minutes and I watched the rounders match in the distance, which seemed to have become more shouty since I'd sat down. A little to the left, a dog squatted in the grass, its owner waiting patiently with a green bag. I thought about Greg again, and how he would always laugh at people who carried bags of dog poo round with them, swinging from their belts like some kind of turdy treasure. Despite my sadness, I felt a smile spread across my lips, marvelling at how something as simple as a dog doing its business could bring Greg so vividly into my mind again, as though he was still right beside me.

'I haven't seen you here before,' said the voice.

The image of Greg popped like a balloon as I shook my head.

'I've not lived here long,' I said, more out of politeness than because I particularly wanted to start a conversation with this stranger. 'I'm just on my way home from a shitty day at work.'

'You too hey?'

I nodded, even though he wasn't looking at me. Then: 'You can tell me about it if you like. I'm a good listener. At least, that's what people tell me.'

What I really wanted to do was get up and walk home and lock myself away from the world again. But I didn't say that because I'm far too polite. 'I'm okay, thank you.'

'Fair enough.' He leaned forward and I caught a glimpse of his dark blond hair out of the corner of my eye as he lifted a small rucksack from the floor onto his lap. 'I know you've probably been told never to accept sweets from strangers, but would you like one?'

I glanced over at the bag he was offering me. It was a paper bag, blue, with yellow writing on it picking out the words 'Pic 'n' Mix' and I smiled again despite myself. I peered inside the bag and raised my eyebrows at him.

'Fizzy cola bottles, eh?'

He grinned, his teeth slightly crooked. Dimples appeared at the side of his mouth. I looked away again. 'What can I tell you? I'm a child.'

I laughed and stuck my hand inside, pulled out a fizzy worm and a cola bottle and popped the worm in my mouth. As I held it there a moment, letting the sugar fizz on my tongue, I tried to work out what it was that was snagging on my brain; what was slightly off about this moment. But I couldn't grasp it, and in the end I let it go and chewed my sweet slowly.

'God, I haven't had one of these for years,' I said.

'What?! You don't know what you're missing.' He held out the bag again and this time I chose a fried egg sweet.

'Sweets like this bring back memories,' I said, pressing the sweet onto my tongue.

'Good ones?'

Were they? Childhood images of me throwing up in the car after eating a giant bag of pick n mix my dad had bought me on holiday in Harrogate one year, my brother and I shovelling sweet after sweet into our mouths as we traipsed, bored, round Ripon Castle; hours spent agonising over whether to splash out on a 10 pence Wham! Bar, a twenty-pence piece clutched in my damp palm; Greg presenting me with a bag of Haribos for our first year of being together, slipping the ring sweet onto my finger and asking me to marry him.

'Mostly,' I said.

'Good.'

He set the bag down on the bench between us. 'Help yourself.'

'I'm fine, thanks.'

'Please. I can't stop once I start. You'll be doing me a favour.'

'Well, if you put it like that,' I said, diving in once more and grabbing a few soft chews between my thumb and finger, holding them in my palm.

It was unexpected, this moment. It wasn't often I spoke to strangers, and especially not to men. Since Greg had died more than two years earlier, I'd locked myself away from the world, and certainly didn't welcome chats with random men on the way home from work. Rachel, my best friend, said it was because I was terrified of someone asking me about Greg, but it was more than that. Since Greg died, I didn't feel as though I had any room inside me to take on any more people. What if I let someone in and they did even more damage? I'm not sure my poor, fractured heart could cope with that.

Yet there was something about this man that felt calming; that felt as though sitting in silence, chewing sweets together, was all that needed to be happening at this moment in time. It was a surprise.

I watched a bird hop across the patch of grass in front of us. The sun had dipped even lower now, behind the row of trees, and I shivered as a breeze made its way through the gaps between the slats of wood.

'Would you like to borrow my jumper?'

'Sorry?' I turned to find him holding out a blue sweatshirt. I was on the verge of saying no, on autopilot, when instead I blurted out, 'Thank you.' I took the jumper and slipped it over my head gratefully, the scent of washing powder filling my nose.

The kids were packing up their game of rounders now,

pulling on coats, picking up bags and heading in different directions across the park. I should probably be going home too. But something was holding me here a little longer.

'I'm Nick by the way. Nick Flynn,' the man beside me said, holding his hand across the gap between us. I looked down at it for a moment, then held my own out. As our skin touched I felt a jolt of something, like a spark of static, and I flinched. I wasn't sure whether he'd noticed anything. His skin felt cool to the touch, and something inside me felt odd, a little out of place.

'Emma Vickers,' I said, tucking my hands beneath my legs against the cool grain of the wood. 'Nice to meet you.'

'You too. So, you said you've just moved in round here?'

'That's right.'

'How are you finding it?'

I shrugged. 'It's fine.'

'You don't sound too sure.'

I sighed. I never talked about Greg. It hurt too much even to think about the hole he'd left inside me. Rachel told me it would be good to tell people about him, that talking about him, about how much he loved me, about the happy times we had together, would be much better for me than keeping everything all scrunched up inside. But somehow I just couldn't find the words. How do you tell someone that you've lost the person who made you you, without sounding like you've gone insane?

'Sorry, I don't mean to pry,' Nick said, and I realised I must have been quiet for slightly too long.

'No, it's okay,' I said. 'I lost someone and needed a fresh start.' It sounded so trite, so insignificant. And yet that one word, 'someone', contained everything.

'I lost someone too.'

'Oh?' I turned to face him and he was still looking down at the ground, not at me. When he did finally turn his head, there was a pain in his eyes that I recognised. 'My wife died. Two and a half years ago.'

I stared at him, at the dark glow of his eyes, the shadows on his cheeks in the fading light of the sun, and I saw him. Really saw him.

Sorry wasn't what he needed to hear, I understood that from the endless times I'd heard it from well-meaning friends and acquaintances. All it did, for me at least, was make me feel more alone than ever.

'It's shit, isn't it?'

His eyes widened and the corners of his mouth twitched upwards and I knew I'd said the right thing. He gave a nod and looked down at the paper bag of sweets on the bench between us, his long eyelashes creating spider-like shadows on his cheeks.

'Really shit,' he agreed.

I looked out into the garden, watching the roses bob in the gentle early evening breeze.

'I don't talk about it,' I said, slowly. 'My husband died and my best friend Rachel thinks I should talk about how I feel all the time, thinks it will help me come to terms with it. But I don't know how I can, because when I do it just makes me feel sad and other people feel uncomfortable.'

I felt him shift beside me, angle his body in my direction. 'Andy – that's my twin brother – says the same. He thinks I should try to talk it through because it would help me to move on. But I honestly just don't know how.'

'Me neither. How can you put into words how much you miss someone? How it feels every single day as though you need to remind yourself to get up, get dressed, carry on while all the time it feels as though you're being pressed down by a heavy weight?'

'Or that some days all you want to do is sit and wallow in your memories of happier times, while other days you can't let yourself think about them at all because it might break you completely?'

I looked at him. I felt breathless. My mum, Rachel, all my other friends, had tried and tried to get me to talk to them about my feelings, about how it would feel to move on and look for someone else, and I simply hadn't been able to. And yet now here I was, opening up to this man on a bench on a random March evening. I didn't know what it meant, but it felt good to have someone who seemed to understand exactly what I was going through.

Perhaps it meant nothing at all. And yet somehow, I felt sure it did.

'It's getting late.'

I looked out across the garden. Shadows had begun to fill in the gaps between the still-leafless trees. The sky was dark blue now, a band of buttery yellow outlining the horizon.

'I should go home.' I didn't move. I didn't want to, not yet, even though I knew I ought to.

'I've enjoyed talking to you. Will you come again, and meet me here?'

'What?' I peered at him, his face in shadow.

'I just thought... it would be nice to see you. You know, to chat, if you're passing again. But no pressure—'

'Yes!' The word was out before I planned it. 'I mean, sure. That would be nice.'

'Great, great.' He clasped his hands together, rubbing them like he was warming them in front of a fire. He stood, and I did the same. The gap between us remained, but it felt like there was something there, some invisible force pulling us together. I took a deliberate step back.

'Well, it was lovely to meet you, Nick Flynn.' His name felt strange on my tongue.

'It was lovely to meet you too, Emma Vickers.'

We hovered a moment, stuck in time. Then he bent down, picked up his rucksack and his bag of sweets and flashed me a smile.

'Same time Monday?'

'Same time Monday,' I confirmed.

Then he turned and stepped off the wooden platform, disappearing almost immediately into the shadows.

* * *

It wasn't until I closed my front door behind me and kicked off my shoes that I realised I was still wearing Nick's jumper. I pulled it off and hung it on the hook next to my jacket so I'd remember to take it back. My hand lingered on it for a moment, trying to remember the strange sensation I'd felt when my hand had touched Nick's, but it wasn't there.

I made my way into the kitchen and pulled a portion of chilli out of the freezer. Greg had been a stickler for sitting down to a proper meal every evening. After he died people brought me endless batches of home-cooked lasagnes, shepherd's pies, curries and home-made soup until my freezer was so full I was in danger of being crushed beneath an avalanche of frozen food every time I opened the door. But at the time, eating was the last thing I felt like doing, instead attempting to numb the pain of losing Greg by downing bottle after bottle of Pinot Grigio. Eventually, Rachel and my mum had stepped in and told me I needed to pull myself together.

'There's no point killing yourself as well,' Rachel said.

'Imagine what Greg would say if he could see what you're doing to yourself,' Mum said, a double-pronged attack.

And it was that, their tough love, that made me realise I

needed to look after myself. They were right, Greg would be furious if he could see me. Which was why I now spent my weekends batch cooking meals for the week ahead, and I was grateful for it every single evening when I got home from work.

As the chilli warmed and the rice cooked, I checked my messages. There was one from Rachel reminding me about a trip to the theatre on Sunday night to see our friend Angel in a show about feminism.

I tapped out a reply, telling her I was looking forward to it.

Would I tell her about my strange encounter in the park? We'd known each other since we were twelve years old and normally I told her everything. But there was something about what happened today that made me want to wrap it up and keep it to myself for a while longer.

Maybe it was just because I thought she'd leap on the merest hint of me being interested in someone. I mean, she loved Greg – everyone did – but as she always said, she loved me too, and she didn't want to see me sad for the rest of my life.

'You deserve someone to share your life with,' she always told me.

And no matter how many times I told her I just wasn't ready – and didn't know whether I ever would be – she kept hoping.

So no, I didn't think I would tell her about this just yet, however strange it felt to keep it from her. I'd see if anything came of it first.

I served up my dinner and took it through to the lounge. I might still try to eat a proper meal every night, but sitting at the table alone just felt too tragic, so I always ate in front of the TV – something Greg would definitely have disapproved of.

I pulled a tray from down the side of the sofa, sat down and switched on the TV. I'd been watching a series on Netflix, but as I forked chilli into my mouth, I couldn't concentrate on anything that was happening on the screen. Instead, my mind drifted back to earlier this evening and, specifically, to Nick.

What exactly was it about our encounter that had lodged itself in my mind? What was the feeling I'd had when I was with him for that brief time? I closed my eyes and tried to remember it, but it was elusive, and eventually I stopped trying.

Today was only Thursday, and we weren't meeting again until Monday. He hadn't shown any signs of wanting to give me his phone number or any other way of getting in touch with him, and I had no idea where he lived. Which meant that the only way of being certain of seeing him again was to turn up at the bandstand after work on Monday and hope he hadn't just been fobbing me off.

Something told me he wasn't.

It wasn't until later, as I was lying in bed and trying to get to sleep, that something else occurred to me. The thought that had snagged on my mind earlier, as I'd been sitting with Nick, finally revealed itself. And I wasn't sure what to make of it.

The sweets Nick had offered me were in a familiar paper bag.

A paper bag of 'Pic 'n' Mix'.

Exactly like the ones I used to get from Woolworths.

A shop that had closed down more than a decade before.

2

NICK

It had been a long time since I'd thought about any woman other than Dawn. We'd been together since sixth form, had a bond that we thought nothing would ever break, in the way that teenage sweethearts do.

But in the end, cancer had been the thing to break that bond. It had been stronger than us both. I still couldn't forgive it.

Sometimes, when I sat in the living room where Dawn died, or the kitchen where I used to cook as she chatted to me about her day, or the bedroom we shared for the eight years we lived together, I tried to conjure her in my mind. I closed my eyes and pictured her – blonde hair splayed out across the pillow; body curled into me on the two-seater sofa as we watched TV; scarf wrapped round her head when she lost her beautiful curls to the brutal chemotherapy, the dark circles beneath her eyes bruise-blue, her cheeks hollow. Still beautiful. Still positive.

Tonight though, I felt different. I felt as though, for the first time in two and a half years, something inside me had shifted.

And it was all down to Emma.

I couldn't explain it. From the moment I saw her on the bench in the bandstand, her red hair shining in the golden sunlight, I felt drawn to her. There was something magical about her, otherworldly.

Had she felt that jolt when we shook hands? I was fairly certain I couldn't have imagined it, but I couldn't bring myself to ask.

When we said goodbye I knew I needed to see her again, so I asked her to meet me there next week. It was the first thing I thought of, and it made perfect sense. No pressure. Just a chance to see whether the spark I felt between us was real.

I was so relieved when she agreed, but also knew I'd spend the next few days worrying about whether she'd turn up. I'd be disappointed if she didn't, and I wasn't sure whether I wanted to examine that too closely.

That night I met my brother Andy in the pub. I hadn't planned to mention it to him – after all, there wasn't really much to tell him apart from the fact that I'd chatted to a pretty woman for half an hour.

But in the end I didn't have to say anything, because the first thing he did was ask me why I looked weird.

'What do you mean, weird?' I said as we sat down at our usual table with our pints of Guinness. Our Thursday night pint had been a tradition for as long as we were both legally allowed to drink. A pint in our local, followed by a curry – chicken korma for me, lamb vindaloo for him. No one else came, it was always just the two of us. When Dawn fell ill, she insisted we kept up the tradition, almost pushing me out of the door every Thursday night and reassuring me that she was looking forward to the chance to sleep. After she died it was the last thing I wanted to do – but Andy knew it was exactly what I needed to stop myself from falling into the abyss of grief. So there we'd sit, pints in front of us, me staring morosely into the depths of the dark brown liquid, him regaling me with stories of his day. And slowly, the fog began to lift. Slowly, I began to tell him about my days too. About the things I'd seen, the things I'd heard. About my regular trips to the bandstand, Dawn and mine's special place for so many years.

He shrugged and wiped froth from his upper lip. 'You look... happy, I think. Well, happier than I've seen you since...' He stopped, not needing to name it.

I spun my pint round on the wooden table. 'Sidewinder' by R.E.M. was playing in the background and the sounds of the regular Thursday night drinkers buzzed around us. I tried to form the words in my mind, but Andy got there before me.

'Shit, it's not a woman is it? Tell me it is.'

I finally looked up. He was peering at me from over the top of his half-drunk pint, his gaze boring into me like a laser.

'Sort of.'

He took another mouthful then slammed his glass on the table. 'Who is she?'

I took a slow sip of my beer, trying to form the words to explain what had happened that afternoon. Andy watched me the whole time, the frown in his forehead deepening the longer he waited.

'It's probably nothing,' I said. 'I just got chatting to someone today.'

'Right. Who? Where?'

I puffed out my cheeks. 'At the bandstand.'

His eyebrows beetled upwards, his eyes widened, but he didn't say anything.

'I went there, as usual,' I continued. 'Normally it's empty, but today there was a woman sitting on the bench.' I swallowed. 'I sat next to her, hoping she'd leave. You know, let me have my space back. But she looked so sad that I just ended up asking her if she was okay.' I looked up at him. 'Turns out she'd lost someone too.

Someone special. We chatted a bit, you know. About Dawn, and her husband.'

Andy studied me thoughtfully, as though trying to work out what to say. He might have been my twin but I definitely couldn't read his mind right now.

'And what did she look like, this woman?'

I thought about her hair, glowing like fire in the sunlight. About her porcelain skin, the firecracker spark between us.

'She was pretty fit.' I grinned, and the mood was lightened.

'Good boy,' Andy said, holding his hand up for a high five. I smacked mine against it obediently.

'Seriously though, she was lovely.'

Andy nodded. 'You know this is the first time you've so much as looked at a woman since you lost Dawn?'

'I know.' I shrugged. 'It probably doesn't mean anything, but it's good to know I'm not dead inside.'

Andy leaned forward, pressed his hand against my forearm. 'Tell me you at least got her number?'

I shook my head. 'We've arranged to meet again next week.'

'Where?'

'Back at the bandstand.'

His eyebrows did their beetling thing again. I knew why he was so surprised. The bandstand was the place – apart from our home – where I felt closest to Dawn. Despite the graffiti, and the broken slat in the bench and the peeling paint across the roof, it had been a place that was always special to us. It was the place where we'd met and the place where I'd proposed. After her diagnosis – ovarian cancer, which explained why we'd struggled to get pregnant – we went there every week, just sitting on the bench holding hands as the rain hammered down on the rickety old roof, or the sun shone through the gaps in it, or a freezing wind chilled us to the bone.

Even now, I still went there at least once a week, just to sit and think about her, to remember her. Which was why the bandstand being the place where I'd met Emma was such big news to Andy.

'I know,' I said. 'It just felt like the right thing to do. I can't explain it.'

He stood suddenly and I looked up at him. 'I'm going to get us both another pint and then you're going to tell me everything. And I want every single detail about the woman who has miraculously brought my little brother back to life.'

I watched as he disappeared towards the bar and tried to work out what I was going to tell him about a woman I still knew next to nothing about.

* * *

Hours later, back home alone and full of beer and curry, I lay on the sofa and stared blindly at an old episode of *Frasier* I'd seen dozens of times. It had been one of Dawn's and my favourite shows, and we could recite almost every word of every episode. Today, Daphne was still oblivious to the fact that Niles was in love with her – an early episode – so I turned the sound down low and let it wash over me.

I felt strange tonight. Out of sorts in a way I couldn't quite put my finger on.

But I also felt another emotion, one that I couldn't seem to shake. Guilt.

How could I be thinking about another woman when Dawn had died only two and a half years ago? We'd been together since we were sixteen, had both only ever loved each other. Now, here I was, aged thirty-one a widower of less than three years – and thinking about someone else.

'You know Dawn would want you to be happy, don't you?'

Andy had said earlier when I told him over the poppadoms how I felt.

I shrugged. 'Not this soon though.'

Andy pressed his hand against mine. 'It's not that soon, Nicky.'

I'd asked if we could talk about something else after that, and sure enough our chat went back to the usual moaning about work, him telling me what my nieces had been up to, and something funny Mum had said last night.

Now, my mind returned to Emma. She was just a sketch in my head at the moment, a pencil drawing, no details defined or filled in. And yet I couldn't seem to stop thinking about her. About her all-encompassing smile, the way it drew you in no matter how much you resisted; about the way she'd looked when she told me about losing someone, the pain in her eyes a reflection of my own. About the way her gaze burrowed into my soul.

I didn't know what this meant or whether it would lead anywhere. But I did know that I was glad I'd arranged to see her again.

* * *

The weekend dragged by, but by the time Monday arrived I felt energised and giddy in a way I hadn't for a long, long time. I couldn't imagine I was 'over' losing Dawn, but it felt refreshing not to wake up feeling as though I'd been crushed beneath a heavy blanket of grief.

At five o'clock, however, I started to wonder whether I was simply setting myself up for disappointment. What if Emma didn't turn up? What if she'd just been humouring me, and hadn't given me a single thought all weekend?

But then again, why wouldn't she have just said so?

Most days when I walked to the bandstand, I was buried so deep inside my memories of Dawn that I barely saw my surroundings. But today, despite low-lying clouds and a hint of damp in the air, I noticed the kids on skateboards, the couple walking hand in hand ahead of me, the dog barking at a pigeon. Blossom had begun to sprinkle the branches of the trees with colour, and snowdrops and daffodils bowed their heads along the edges of the paths. I felt lighter, as though a darkness had lifted and shown me the world again.

Just before I saw the bandstand I stopped dead. My legs felt weak and my belly squirmed with nerves. Would she be there? I closed my eyes, tipped my head up to the clouds, and took a deep breath. This was it, the moment of truth.

I turned the corner.

It was empty.

I knew it had been a possibility that she wouldn't come, but now that it had come to pass, I didn't quite know what to do. I glanced around. I was a couple of minutes late, but perhaps she was later. I cast my gaze across the park, hoping I'd spot her scurrying towards me, bag banging against her hip. But there was no sign of her.

I reached the bandstand and lowered myself onto the bench. The trees above my head rustled in the breeze and a leaf blew in and skittered around my feet. And then—

'Hello,' a voice said.

'Oh, I didn't see you coming!'

'I'm so sorry I'm late, I had to finish something for tomorrow and it took longer than expected,' she said, sweeping towards me in a cloud of musky perfume and sitting on the other end of the bench.

'It's fine. I'm glad you're here.'

'Of course,' she said. I looked at her, her hair wild around her face, her cheeks flushed, and the first word that came into my head was *radiant*. I looked away.

'How was your weekend?'

She shrugged. 'You know. The usual. Theatre with Rachel on Thursday night, sat on my own with a glass of wine and *Spin the Wheel* on Saturday, farmers' market on Sunday. Mediocre.' She looked up. 'Lonely.'

My belly fizzed. 'I know what you mean,' I said. 'Pretty much the same for me apart from the TV show. *Jonathan Creek* for me.'

She frowned. 'God, I haven't seen that in years. I didn't even know it was still on.'

I looked out across the park, watching as a young couple struggled with the rain cover on their pram. I hadn't even realised it had started to rain.

'So,' Emma said.

'So?'

'What do you want to talk about?'

'Oh, I...' I stopped. What did you talk about with a woman you'd only just met, who you didn't know, and who you felt guilty about being wildly attracted to?

'Want to talk about your sugar addiction?'

'What?'

She smiled, her face lighting up again. 'The pick n mix.'

'Oh yes.' I smiled back. 'I am partial to a fizzy cola bottle.'

'Well you're in luck because I've brought the snacks today.' She opened the bag on her lap and dug around inside, then pulled out several packets of sweets, one at a time, laying them on the bench between us. 'Tangfastics, Fruit Pastilles, Maltesers and...' she pulled the last one out with a flourish '...blackcurrant and liquorice in case you want something a bit more grown up.'

'Blimey, you don't do things by halves do you?' I said, picking up the Tangfastics. 'Can I open these?'

'Go for it,' she said with a wave. I opened the packet and held them out to her. 'You choose first,' she said. I pulled out a few then handed them to her, and we both sat quietly chewing for a few moments. It was strangely relaxing.

'So, you said this place was a special to you,' she said, finally.

'It is.'

'Want to tell me about it?'

Did I? Usually I hated talking about Dawn to anyone who'd never met her. Nothing I said ever conveyed how much she'd meant to me, how much we'd shaped each other.

'This was the place I met Dawn,' I said, tipping my head back and fixing my gaze on the peeling paint of the ceiling. 'We were only sixteen, just babies, and we went to different schools. But we used to come here and hang out in the evenings, me and my mates, and one night she was here with some of her friends and – well, that was it. I couldn't see anyone else. It was all about her.' I stopped, remembering the moment I first saw her. The way she consumed my thoughts from the moment I laid eyes on her; the way she shone.

Could it be something about this place, some sort of super-natural force surrounding it, that meant it would always be the place where magic happened? I shook my head. *Don't be so ridiculous.*

I turned to look at Emma. 'Dawn was the love of my life and I haven't really felt alive since she died.' *Until now*, I wanted to say, but it was too much too soon.

She raised her eyes to meet mine. 'What happened?'

'She had ovarian cancer. We thought she was pregnant. We were trying to get pregnant, had talked about nothing else for months and months. We'd even picked out names and colours for the nursery, had talked about what our future child might be like. Would they have my eyes or Dawn's? Would they be tall, short, skinny, blonde, or dark? It was all we could think about and we couldn't wait to be parents. But then... well, Dawn was unwell for quite a while, it turned out the bloating and the sickness were not, in fact, to do with forming a new life, but taking one away.'

'I'm so sorry.'

I nodded, my words stuck in my throat.

Emma looked back out at the park again and I did the same. The dampness had turned to a light drizzle. 'Greg died in an accident at work.' Her voice was quieter than before, and I had to lean close to hear her properly. 'He was a tree surgeon and fell from his harness. He... he died on impact.'

'Oh, that's horrendous,' I said.

She gave a little shake of her head as if to say, *I don't want to talk about it*. 'It was bad enough coming to terms with that, but in the first few weeks after his death I tortured myself with the words I'd said to him as he left that morning. "Maybe I should find someone who gives a shit about having a baby with me, then."'

She sniffed and wiped her hand across her cheek. 'Sorry. I don't talk about this very often.'

'You don't need to apologise for anything.'

She shook her head. 'Anyway. This house is my fresh start. I thought I wanted to stay in the house where we'd lived together, but in the end it was too hard, seeing all the places that reminded me of him.'

'I still live in the house where Dawn died.' I looked up at her. 'Do you think that's maudlin?'

'Not in the slightest. It's whatever works for you.'

A shout from the park distracted me and I looked away to watch a group of children on bikes passing. I waited until they'd gone before I spoke again. 'They remind me of me when I was that age.'

'Who does?'

I nodded towards the park. 'Those kids.'

She looked out across the grass and a frown flitted across her forehead. 'It's a nice place to hang out.'

'It is. Although this rickety old thing has seen better days.'

Emma looked round her. 'I don't know. I think it looks pretty good.'

'I'm particularly fond of the graffiti down there that says, "If you can read this, fuck off." Very eloquent I feel.'

'Almost Shakespearean.' She grinned and picked up the Haribos. 'More sugar?'

'Love some, thanks.'

We sat silently chewing for a while longer. The rain had stopped now but the low cloud made it feel chilly and I shivered.

'Would you prefer to go somewhere warmer?' I said.

'Are you cold?'

'A bit.'

'Oh, that reminds me,' she said. She leaned down and pulled something out of her bag and presented it to me. 'Your jumper. Thank you for lending it to me.'

'Oh thanks.' I'd forgotten I'd lent it to her, and it smelt of the outdoors, a flowery, heady scent. I pulled it over my head and felt instantly better.

'You said you're lonely?' I said.

'Sometimes.' She didn't look me in the eye. 'I see my friends, but it's little things. You know, when you're watching something together and laugh at the same things, or want to ask the other person a question and you forget they're no longer there until the question has almost formed on your lips.' She traced her finger over the worn grain of the wood. 'Sometimes I wake up in the morning and for a few minutes I forget that Greg is no longer there and I roll over and see the empty side of the bed and it makes my stomach lurch.' She looked up at me. 'Do you know what I mean?'

I nodded, a lump in my throat. 'I do.' I swallowed. 'Perhaps you've got the right idea, moving to a new home. Because sometimes being in the same room as we were together makes it even harder when a memory comes crashing in.'

A bolt of something jolted through me then, my entire body fizzing. When I looked down at the space between us, her hand was resting on top of mine.

It was only there for a few seconds, but when she pulled her hand away, I felt odd. Almost empty, as though she'd taken a part of my soul with her.

What the hell was that?

'So have you seen anyone else, since Dawn died?'

I shook my head. 'No. Andy – my brother – thinks I should. And a couple of mates have tried to set me up with friends, but I just haven't been ready. I was starting to think I never would be.'

She smiled sadly. 'Same here. Rachel even set me up a profile on Tinder but I haven't looked at it since.'

'What's that?'

'What's what?'

'Tindle, or whatever you said.'

She gave me a strange look, small creases lining her forehead. 'Are you teasing me?'

I shook my head.

'You really don't know what Tinder is?'

'I really have no idea.'

It was her turn to shake her head now. 'Wow, I didn't think there was anyone left in the world who hadn't heard of Tinder. It's a dating app. You know, where you put your details in, say what sort of person you're looking for, what you're like, and hopefully someone you like the look of likes the look of you too.' She pulled back a bit and squinted at me. 'Is this really not ringing any bells?'

I held my hands out and shrugged. 'What can I say? I'm an old-fashioned kind of guy.'

'You really are. A relic almost.' She smiled. 'It's nice. So what else do you like doing, apart from eating sweets and moping around this place?' she said.

'I play the violin,' I said.

'Are you any good?'

I shrugged, suddenly shy. 'I'm not bad. I've played here before.' She looked round her at the run-down space, her eyes wide. 'Believe it or not it was actually used for concerts, years ago.'

'That's pretty cool.' She reached her hand out and pressed it against the cool metal strut. 'It's almost as though the notes and songs are trapped somewhere in the fabric of this place, waiting for someone to hear them again.'

'That's a nice way to look at it,' I said.

'Will you play for me one day?' Her face reddened, as though she realised what she'd just said a fraction too late.

'I'd love to,' I said. Dawn had always loved listening to me play, and the thought of playing for someone else made me feel strange. As though I was cheating on Dawn, perhaps. But Dawn wasn't coming back, and I had to at least try to move on, to make a new life for myself. Not to mention that the thought of seeing Emma again filled me with a feeling of hope, and excitement. 'I'll bring it with me next time.'

'Will we meet here again next time?'

Next time.

'It seems as good a place as any, don't you think?'

She nodded. 'I do.'

It was getting dark again now, and even the jumper Emma had returned to me wasn't quite enough to keep the chill away.

'Do you want to go for a quick drink?' I said, before I could change my mind about asking.

'Oh. I'd love to, but I've actually got to get back tonight,' she said.

I tried to ignore the disappointment that settled in my belly like a stone. Was she fobbing me off, or did she genuinely have to go?

'No worries.'

'Honestly, I do,' she said, as if she could read my mind. 'But it's been really lovely to see you again. Are you free on Thursday?'

'I...' I hesitated. Thursday was sacred, mine and Andy's curry night. And even though I knew he'd be happy to forgo it if it meant I was meeting a woman, I wasn't sure.

'Can you make Wednesday instead?' I said.

'Wednesday it is.'

She got up then, and I did the same. We stood facing each other, eyes locked. I didn't know what to do. Should I hold out my hand? Would she expect a hug? Before I could agonise any longer, she leaned forward, pecked my cheek and smiled.

'See you Wednesday,' she said. I held my hand to my burning cheek as she turned and left. It wasn't until she disappeared into the darkness of the park that I realised I should have offered to walk her home.

3

EMMA

I hadn't exactly been lying when I told Nick I had to get back tonight. Work was manic and I had quite a bit to do before tomorrow.

But I also needed to process what had just happened. What did it mean, for example, that in the two years since Greg had died I hadn't felt able to properly open up to Rachel, or to Mum or even my counsellor, and yet when I was with Nick, the words seemed to come easily, the desire to talk about Greg and the accident strong. Perhaps it was simply that he understood because he was grieving too.

Except I couldn't deny that there was something more between us than simply having lost a loved one. And I definitely couldn't get away from the fact that every time Nick and I touched it felt as though there was an explosion somewhere inside me. I'd never felt anything like it, not even with Greg, who I'd loved so much.

Did Nick feel it too?

I couldn't be sure, but I felt certain he did.

I didn't turn round to see whether Nick was following me but instead scurried towards the park gates. I was planning to head home but as I emerged onto the high street I pulled my phone out of my bag and saw a couple of WhatsApp messages from Rachel, asking what I was up to. Despite previously wanting to keep this to myself, I was suddenly desperate to talk to her about it.

I tapped out a reply.

EMMA

Are you free for a drink?

Three dots immediately appeared.

RACHEL

Hell yes! The Crown?

I replied:

EMMA

See you there.

As I entered the wine bar, quiet on a Monday night, I hoped Nick wouldn't see me here. I wasn't sure how far away he lived and was suddenly aware he might pass by here on his way home. I didn't want him to think I was lying to him.

I bought two glasses of Pinot Grigio and settled at a table away from the speaker. It only took Rachel fifteen minutes to get there. She gave me a hug then sat, downing half her glass of wine in one go.

'I needed that,' she said, wiping her hand across her mouth. 'The little buggers were doing my head in tonight, thank God you messaged.'

It was still astounding to me that my best friend, who I'd known since we were twelve years old, was a mother. I still remembered her sobbing her heart out when she found her first boyfriend Carl snogging Mandy Johnston at the school disco; I could remember the smell of vomit when Gary McDonald dumped her and she drank her body weight in vodka to drown her sorrows. And I could still picture the pure joy on her face when she'd met Iain, Greg's best friend, three months after Greg and I had got together. They were smitten, and it felt like the four of us were the luckiest people alive to have found each other. All for one and one for all.

Now, I still saw the pair of them regularly but when it was the three of us it felt odd, like a car trying to drive with three wheels.

And although I knew Rachel tried not to moan about the kids too much around me, aware that Greg and I had tried for a couple of years to have a baby, I loved hearing her talk about these little creatures who were the perfect mix of two of my favourite people in the world.

'What have they been up to now?' I said, taking a sip of my wine.

'Oh, just the usual. Aiden thought it would be funny to do a poo in the bath, and Harry screamed the house down about it. Can't say I blame him, sitting in a shit soup with his little brother.' She grinned. 'Thank God for you and your well-timed messages pleading with me to meet you urgently. I left Iain to mediate.'

'I mean, it wasn't urgent...' I started.

'It was *very* urgent. At least Iain thinks it was and that's all that matters.'

I laughed.

'Anyway, enough of all that nonsense. Tell me what you've been up to. You look lovely, have you been somewhere nice?'

I felt a smile spread across my face. 'Maybe.'

Rachel's eyebrows shot up beneath her fringe. 'Oh my,' she whispered.

'What?'

'You look...' She screwed her face up while she searched for the word she was looking for. '*Happy.*'

'Do I?'

She leaned closer and squinted at me. 'I haven't seen this look on your face for such a long time. Are you... Have you been on a *date?*'

I felt my face burn and Rachel gasped. 'Right, tell me everything, Vickers.' She sat back and crossed her arms.

'I...' I started, unsure where to begin. 'He's called Nick.' She waited. 'We met in the bandstand in the rose garden, after work.'

'Today?' She sounded surprised.

I shook my head. 'Last week.'

Her eyes widened. 'And why are you only just telling me this now?'

I picked at a hangnail on my thumb, unable to meet her eye. 'I don't know. I didn't... I wasn't sure whether it was anything.'

'And now you are?'

I shrugged. 'Not really.'

Rachel leaned forward and waited for me to meet her eye. When I did I saw nothing but kindness in them. 'You know I adored Greg, Ems, but I can't tell you how good it is to see you even thinking about someone else. Greg would want this for you. I know he would.'

'I know,' I said, even though I wasn't so sure.

'So are you seeing him again, this Nick?'

'We're meeting on Wednesday.'

'Where?'

'The same place.'

She frowned. 'The bandstand? Why on earth are you meeting there again?'

I shrugged. It was hard to explain. Quite apart from the fact that it was clearly an important place for Nick, it felt as though it was the place we were meant to be. For now, at least. And if I was honest, I was worried the spell might be broken if we tried to meet somewhere else.

'It just felt like the right thing to do,' I said. 'Anyway, the rose garden is pretty.'

'Fine. But promise me you'll go somewhere else next time? Somewhere a bit less... bird-shitty.'

'Assuming there is a next time, you have my word,' I said.

Rachel held her glass up and I clinked mine against it. 'Here's to the possibility of new beginnings,' she said.

'Only a possibility,' I said.

She rolled her eyes. 'If that's the best I'm going to get then I'll take it.'

* * *

As I walked home a couple of hours later, I thought about what Rachel and I had talked about. She'd wanted to find out more about Nick – check out his Instagram and Facebook accounts, see what else we could find out about him.

'But I only know his name. I don't even know where he lives or what his job is,' I said.

'That'll do for now,' she said.

But in the end it wasn't enough, and we couldn't find any trace of a Nick Flynn around thirty years old who looked or sounded anything like the man I'd just met.

'Are you sure he told you his real name?' she said.

'I don't see why he wouldn't. But I'm not surprised he's not on social media. I mean, he didn't even know what Tinder was.'

'How can he not? Does he live in the Dark Ages?'

I grinned. 'Not everyone lives their entire lives online you know.'

'Most people who say they don't are lying though.'

Now, as I let myself into the house, the mystery of Nick was on my mind. Who was this man who had taken up residence in my head and seemed unwilling to leave? What was it about him that had successfully pierced the barrier I'd constructed around myself over the last two years?

I thought about the way my body had reacted when our skin touched, and I shivered. I hadn't mentioned it to Rachel, but as I hung my coat on the peg by the front door, I felt the same feeling again, almost as though he was here, right beside me.

I went straight upstairs and threw myself onto the bed and stared up at the ceiling. Greg hadn't lived in this house with me and, most nights over the three months since I'd moved in, I wondered whether I'd made a mistake, leaving the home Greg and I had built together. In the old house, I could conjure him whenever I wanted – the pair of us curled on the sofa watching TV together; the places where we'd had sex when we'd first moved in, not bothering us at all that we had to rough it on the bare floorboards, hardly a stick of furniture in the place; the small box room he'd commandeered as his weights room that always had a slight undertone of sweat; the ridiculous oversized coffee machine that sat on the worktop that we'd always bickered over whose turn it was to clean.

At the time I'd thought it would be easier to live somewhere where the memories didn't come flooding in at unexpected moments, flooring me with a sucker-punch. But now I wasn't so sure. My bedroom didn't hold any memories of Greg. It held nothing but me, and my things, and sometimes, I worried I was forgetting about him.

Tonight, though, it did have an advantage – because when thoughts of Nick buzzed around my head, the way they were doing right now, at least I didn't feel like I was cheating on Greg.

I turned my head towards the empty space beside me and felt a lurch of sadness.

Was I doing the right thing, meeting Nick again? Should I shut this down before it went any further?

Maybe. The trouble was, I didn't really want to.

* * *

I was equal part nervous and equal part excited about seeing Nick again. There was less doubt this time about whether he'd turn up, but in a way that made it even more nerve-wracking. Because that meant this was something different for both of us.

A step away from our pasts, and towards the possibility of a new future.

It had been a rough couple of days at work and I'd hardly had a moment to breathe. But now, as I walked through the rose garden towards the bandstand, my legs felt shaky and my breath was short in my chest.

What would we talk about today?

Would we arrange a proper date?

Did I want to?

I stepped up into the bandstand. I was a few minutes early and he wasn't here yet so I took the opportunity to look out into the park and take a few deep, calming breaths. I closed my eyes and let my shoulders drop, my breathing deepen, and my heart rate slow.

'Hello.'

My eyes snapped open. 'You've got to stop sneaking up on me,' I said, as Nick sat on the bench beside me. He lay a bag and what looked like a violin case carefully on the ground.

'Sorry. I didn't mean to.'

'It's okay. I was just doing some deep breathing.'

He nodded but didn't say anything.

'It's good to see you,' I said.

'You too.'

He sounded distant, and I wondered whether he felt as guilty as me about us meeting. I didn't know how to ask him.

'How's your week been?'

He shrugged. 'Fine.'

'Are you going to play today?'

'Sorry?'

I nodded at the case beside him. 'The violin.'

He stared at it as though surprised to see it there. 'Right. Maybe in a bit.'

We fell into silence. Had I done something wrong, or upset him somehow? I couldn't think how. Perhaps we should just call this a day now and—

'Sorry, I'm a bit distracted today.'

'You don't need to explain anything to me.'

He shook his head. 'I didn't think about it when we arranged to meet. But today... it would have been Dawn's birthday.'

'Oh.' I stood up, my bag snagging against my thigh. 'I should leave you to be here alone. We can do this another day.'

'No, please stay,' he said.

I looked down at him. 'I don't want to intrude. I know how much this place means to you.'

'Honestly it's fine. I'd like you stay – if you want to?'

'Sure,' I said, lowering myself back down uncertainly.

He looked down at his feet, his trainers clean and unmarked. 'I forgot.'

'Sorry?'

He took a deep, shaky breath, his shoulders rising up and down slowly, and turned his head to look at me. 'It's her birthday today and I only remembered after we arranged to meet.'

I got it. The guilt you felt the first time you forgot an important date, or didn't realise it straight away. 'It doesn't mean you've forgotten her, you know,' I said, gently.

He shook his head. 'I'm sorry. You don't need this... this—' He swept his hand in an arc as if indicating everything around him, then drew himself up so he was sitting straight. 'We don't need to do anything. I just wanted to take a minute.'

'Hang on,' I said. I'd had an idea. I rummaged in my bag and pulled out a little plastic bag and held it in the air. He looked at it and frowned. 'I know this sounds weird, and I promise I don't usually carry candles around. But it was someone's birthday at work this week and these are some of the candles we didn't put on his cake, and because I never clear my bag out they're still here and...' Stop waffling, Emma. 'Anyway, why don't we light a candle for Dawn? For her birthday?'

He stared at me without saying anything and I worried I'd got it wrong. Was it completely inappropriate?

Finally he held out his hand and I gave him the bag. He studied it, then looked back at me.

'Thank you,' he said.

He took the box of matches out of the bag as well as two candles, and handed one to me. I held it as he lit it, then lit his own. They both burned quickly, and I kept hold of mine until it was about to scorch my fingers, then threw it into the floor where it sizzled out. Seconds later, Nick did the same.

A woman walking past gave me a strange look and I smiled at her.

'They burned quicker than I expected,' I said.

'It was a lovely thought. Thank you.'

'We can do another one if you like?'

He shook his head.

'Do you want to tell me about her?'

He shook his head again.

'I think it's time I started talking about something else,' he said.

'Do you *want* to talk about something else?'

He closed his eyes briefly, then fixed me with a look. 'Yes. I actually think I do.'

'Well then. What do you want to talk about, Nick Flynn?'

He tucked his hands under his thighs and leaned forward. 'I don't know. Tell me something about yourself.'

'What, like my job, my date of birth? My star sign? My inside leg measurement?' A smile flitted across his lips and I found myself smiling back.

'If you like.'

'Fine. But I warn you, I work in HR and it's unendingly dull. And I don't believe in star signs.'

He raised his eyebrows. 'What, you don't think that a twelfth of the population of the world is going to experience the same thing this month? That's shocking.'

'I know right. How could I?'

His eyes sparkled as he looked at me, and I had to look away. I hoped he didn't notice my face flaming.

'Okay, come on. What else? Where would you most like to go in the world?'

'That's easy. Australia.'

He nodded. 'Good choice.'

'What about you?'

He screwed his face up. 'I don't know. New York maybe.'

'You've never been to New York?'

He shook his head. 'Nope. I didn't get on a plane until I was twenty-four and even that was only to go on a trip to Germany with the kids from school.'

'Sounds horrendous.'

'Ah they're okay really. Most of them anyway.' He blew air out through his lips, his cheeks puffing out. 'Teenagers get a bad rap most of the time.'

'Yeah, you're probably right. I mean, we were all teenagers once right?'

'Exactly.'

'What about your family?' I said.

'Ah, now you're asking.' He rubbed his hand over his face. 'Andy's the best. He's four minutes older than me but it feels like a lifetime. He's always been there for me, would put his life on the line for me, if need be. I'd do the same for him, of course.' He stopped, gathering himself. 'Mum's okay.' I waited, while he took a deep breath. 'But I can't forgive her for always sticking up for my father over me or Andy.'

'Is he still around, your father?'

He gave a tense nod. 'Yeah. Which is why I don't really see either of them any more.' He looked at me. 'He's just not a very nice man.'

'I'm sorry,' I said, not wanting to push for more details, and he shook his head and looked away again. We sat in silence for a moment. I was surprised to find that I wanted to keep talking to him, to dig deeper into what made this man tick. What did he like to eat, what was his favourite film, what music did he listen to, what football team did he support? But before I could ask any of those things, he asked me something.

'What's the best thing that's ever happened to you, Emma Vickers?' My heart stopped and I turned to look at him. I wanted to say 'meeting you' but I knew that would sound ridiculous. Besides, what about Greg?

So instead I looked away and shrugged. 'I'm not sure,' I said.

I could feel him still watching me, but I kept my gaze trained on the ground.

'What about the worst thing then?' His voice was soft and it made something in me open up, suddenly want to tell him things. Before I could think about it too much, I found myself telling him about Greg, and how it had felt when he'd died. How I'd been empty and numb for months, but that the worst part of it was that I would spend nights lying in bed imagining him lying at the bottom of the tree, in pain, unable to move. How I pictured him calling for me, and knowing he wasn't going to make it out of there alive. 'I tortured myself about that for months,' I said.

'How did you stop?'

'I'm not sure I ever did. Although Rachel helped. And counselling.'

'Ah, counselling. Andy thinks I should have that.'

I looked at him sharply. 'You haven't had any?'

He shook his head. 'I didn't really see the point. I mean, Dawn got ill, she had treatment but it didn't work, and then she died. I don't really blame myself or anything, because there was nothing either of us could have done to change it. I just feel sad, and there's nothing anyone else can do about that either.'

'But...' I started, but didn't know how to carry on.

'What?' he said, a frown creasing his forehead.

'I just...' I sighed. 'I don't know. I just think it's important to have someone neutral to talk to, to process your feelings.' I was a fine one to talk.

'I did process them. What else is there to say?'

'What about the baby stuff? Don't you think it would have been good to talk about that, at least?'

He froze and I wondered whether I'd overstepped the mark. I mean, I didn't really know this man very well. How would I feel if the situation was reversed and he was pushing me like this? I was about to apologise when I realised he was saying something. I leaned in closer to hear him.

'I have dreams sometimes,' he said. His voice cracked and he cleared his throat and looked up at the roof. 'I wake up in a sweat in the middle of the night and realise I've been dreaming about a baby crying, and I couldn't get to it, and I'd been shouting for Dawn to come and she wasn't there.' He swallowed, and looked down at his hands in his lap. 'I'll never stop feeling guilty for not realising that something was wrong with Dawn earlier, rather than being so sure the symptoms she was experiencing were because she was pregnant.'

I didn't know what to say. Telling him it wasn't his fault, that he isn't a doctor, that he wasn't supposed to know what the symptoms of ovarian cancer were, wouldn't help, because I knew that he wouldn't believe it. Why would he, when I didn't believe people when they told me I shouldn't feel guilty about Greg's death? When I tortured myself that he fell from that tree because he was upset about what I'd said to him as he'd left that day, that he was distracted?

So instead I put my hand on the bench between us, and our fingers touched in a spark of electricity. 'I'm sorry you couldn't have a baby,' I said, simply.

'Me too,' he whispered.

* * *

I had no idea know how long we talked for, but by the time we'd covered the fact that he'd been mildly bullied at school for playing the violin and that subtitled films were his favourite 'but not for any pretentious reasons', it was starting to get dark. I shivered, goosebumps prickling my skin.

'So what's next?' he said, as I rummaged in my bag for my cardigan and tugged it over my arms.

'Next?' I said.

'You said you don't particularly like your job or your boss. So why stay?'

I considered his words before answering. 'It's just been easier, to stay,' I said carefully. 'And my boss isn't that bad, just a bit mad sometimes.' The truth was, the thought of trying to find another job while I was still in the depths of grief had felt like attempting to climb a mountain without a scrap of equipment. But now, I could see that Nick was probably right, and that a new job should probably be next on my to-do list.

'I don't know. I need to get the house sorted first. I mean, I've been there three months and there are still boxes that need unpacking in the smallest bedroom.'

He nodded. 'Ah yes, I know that feeling,' he said. 'I put off clearing out Dawn's things for a long time. But I got it done in the end and you will too, when you're ready.'

'Moving was harder than I thought it would be,' I admitted. 'Leaving the place that Greg and I had bought together and buying this house, it's been a lot...'

He nodded. 'Is it nearby, where you live now?'

I nodded. 'Just down the road, on Cherry Tree Close.'

There was a moment's silence and when I looked round Nick had a surprised expression on his face, his skin a little flushed.

'You live on Cherry Tree Close?'

'I do. Why?'

'I live there too.'

I stared at him. The close was only small, about a dozen or so houses. And although I hadn't met all the neighbours yet, it seemed strange that we hadn't at least seen each other in passing in all that time.

'How weird,' I said.

'It is.'

'Perhaps we leave at completely different times every day.'

'Maybe. I don't remember anyone moving in recently though.' His voice sounded tight. 'Must be going mad. Which number are you?'

'Number five.'

His face drained of colour and he scooted away, moving across the bench as far away from me as he could get.

'Is this a joke?' he said. He looked round, his eyes wide. 'Is Jeremy Beadle about to jump out on me?'

'What do you mean?'

'You live at number five, do you?' There was an edge to his voice that I didn't understand.

'Yes. Why? Nick, what's going on?' He looked furious, but my mind couldn't seem to work out where this conversation had so quickly gone off track.

He stood, picked up his bag and clutched it against his belly. 'I think I'm going to go now.'

I stood too. 'Wait! Tell me what's happening here. Please.'

'Number five Cherry Tree Close is *my* house. I've lived there for eight years.'

* * *

Time stood still. Oxygen was sucked out of the air. Everything around us stopped moving, the world suspended.

'But... how can you?' I stammered.

'Because I do. And I assume you already know that, which means I've clearly misread this whole thing.'

'But... no! Of course I don't know that. I... I don't know what to say.'

His gaze was fixed on me, his eyes wild.

'Please, sit down and talk to me.'

He hesitated for a moment, not moving. Then in one swift

movement he threw his bag back down and perched on the very edge of the wooden slats at one end of the bench. I sat too, right at the other end, as far away from him as possible.

'So, we both live in the same house, apparently,' I said. I was trying for light-hearted but it fell flat. I squirmed beneath his glare. 'Maybe there are two number fives,' I said. 'Maybe, you know, when they built the houses, they used some strange numbering pattern, some weird superstition, like on those housing estates where they don't build a number thirteen in case it brings bad luck. That must be it, right?'

He shook his head. 'I'm fairly certain there's only one number five.' His voice was flat. I was tempted to get up and leave him there, but he looked so upset I couldn't bear to just walk away. Besides, there must be some perfectly reasonable explanation for this. We just needed to work out what it was.

I had an idea. 'Hang on.' I opened my bag and pulled out my phone and scrolled back through my camera roll until I found the photo I was looking for. I held it out and he stared at it with a confused look on his face.

'What the hell is this?' he said.

'Just look at the photos,' I said.

He glanced down at the phone as though it was a bomb that was about to explode, and his frown deepened. 'This is my house,' he said.

I turned it round and looked at it. 'Are you totally sure?'

'Absolutely. I laid those paving slabs myself.'

I peered at the mossy path leading up to the front door and turned the phone to face him again. 'This path here?'

He nodded, and looked at the photo more closely. 'Although they look much more worn and old here.'

I turned it back to look at it again. My mind was all over the place, trying to find a reasonable explanation for what might be happening. The only answers I could come up with were either that there were two houses that looked exactly the same on two different streets with the same name – or that Nick was mentally ill.

'Anyway, what the hell is that thing?'

I looked up. 'What thing?'

'That... computer thing in your hand.'

I looked down at my iPhone, then back up at Nick. He seemed deadly serious, and suddenly I felt a little afraid. I glanced round. A man was walking past with his pug on a lead, and a couple strolled a little further away, chatting. I was okay, I wasn't alone with him.

'This is my phone, Nick,' I said gently.

He held his hand out. 'Can I have a look?'

I hesitated. What was the worst that could happen? I handed it over and watched as he poked at the screen. The photo of my house on the day I'd moved in glowed from the screen, then disappeared, the screen turning black.

'I've never seen anything like this,' he said.

'It's just an iPhone,' I said. It wasn't even a new one.

'You see, you're saying that as if I should know what that is, but I've never heard of it.' He crossed his arms.

'I...' I stopped. 'I honestly don't know what to say. I mean, these are pretty ubiquitous.'

He looked down at it again and held it up to his face. 'I don't get it. Is it a camera or a phone?'

'It's both. Look.' I gently prised the phone from his hands and swiped my fingers across the screen, which sprang back to life instantly. Surely he was going to laugh at any moment and tell me he was only kidding. But he just kept staring at the phone in wonder and the more he stared the more my anxiety grew.

'Can I ask you something?' he said.

'Sure,' I said.

'Don't freak out, but what year do you think it is?'

'What year?'

He nodded.

'It's 2019,' I said.

He didn't reply for a moment, and I held my breath, wondering what on earth he was going to say next. Was he about to admit he was mentally unwell, that he lived in some sort of fantasy world? I tried to marry this up with the Nick I'd been speaking to over the last couple of weeks, and it just didn't seem to match. But then again, how else could this strange behaviour be explained?

'It's 1999,' he said.

I stared at him. How did I respond to that?

'What do you mean? What's 1999?'

'Today,' he said. 'Right now. The year I'm living in is 1999.'

4

NICK

Emma was staring at me, a look of terror in her eyes. I couldn't blame her.

'I know you might think I've gone mad,' I said, and she gave a small nod. 'But listen to me. This photo, this house. It's mine. I live there right now. And you say you do too. And that *thing* – that phone thing. It doesn't exist, where I live. But you seem to think that's weird.'

She continued to stare at me, not speaking. I ploughed on.

'Remember when I didn't know what you were talking about when you were telling me about dating the other day? You called me a relic. But what if... what if I'm not a relic, what if I'm simply living twenty years in your past?'

Emma leapt up and backed away from me.

'You're not serious?' Her voice trembled.

I needed to try and explain what I meant before she got up and ran away.

'I know it sounds impossible,' I said. 'It *should* be impossible. But if you assume we're both telling the truth, can you think of a better explanation?'

Emma froze for a moment as though torn between going and staying. Eventually, she sank back down onto the bench again.

'But... how?' she whispered.

'I don't know. But the more I think about it, the more it makes sense.'

'Really?'

A thought occurred to me then. I opened my bag and handed her my Nokia phone.

'This is my phone. It's the latest model.'

Emma turned it over in her hands, prodded it. It sprang to life, the date and time glowing from the grey screen: *2nd April 1999.*

She dropped it as though it was on fire and it clattered onto the bench and bounced onto the floor. I bent down to pick it up, cradling it in my hand.

'Why don't you try and ring me?' I said.

'What?'

'I assume that fancy computer-camera-phone thing makes simple phone calls as well?'

'Of course it does.'

'Try and ring me.'

I watched as she swiped her finger across the screen of her phone, then I read out my phone number. I held my breath while we waited for it to connect.

The number you have dialled has not been recognised. The tinny voice rang out, and when Emma ended the call we both sat in silence for a moment. Then she shrugged.

'You could have just given me a wrong number.'

I nodded. 'I could have done. I don't know what else to suggest.'

She looked at me, her expression hard to read. 'Try and ring me.'

She read her number out and I tapped the numbers on the keypad carefully, checking it before I pressed the green dial button. We both waited, watching as my phone tried to connect. And then: *The number you dialled has not been recognised.*

We stared at it for a few seconds, taking in the implications. Although there was a chance that there was simply a problem with the phone network, or we'd both given out our numbers wrong, it was pretty clear to me that it was more than that. I hoped she'd realised the same.

Finally, she looked at me.

'My God,' she whispered. Her eyes were wide.

'I know,' I whispered back.

The world still turned, lives still went on around us. But something in this tiny bubble in which we were sitting had shifted. She ran her fingers through her hair and her eyes were wild. 'This should be impossible. This *is* impossible.'

'And yet here we are.'

She nodded. 'Here we are.'

* * *

I'd spent most of my life either studying maths – at school, at university – or working in the field of maths and logic. I understood how the world worked, how time is a continuous moving thing, that there is no chance that it can move backwards, or that two people living in different times can ever be together.

And yet, unless one of us was seriously ill or playing some elaborate hoax, then that's exactly what appeared to be happening right here. The question was, what did it mean?

'Did you feel a jolt when we touched?'

Emma turned to me, her face pale. 'Every time. I thought it was just me.'

I shook my head. 'It felt like more than the usual attraction. To me at least.'

'It did to me too. It felt kind of... other-worldly.' She shook her head. 'That's not right. It's almost impossible to describe.'

'Impossible's the word.' I sat forward and dropped my head down. The floor was covered in bird poo and litter, and one of the slats of the bench was loose beneath my thigh. 'Tell me what you see,' I said.

'What I see?'

I looked at her. Her face was stricken. I knew how she felt. 'Tell me what the bandstand looks like, to you. Tell me what you can see in the park. What the weather's like. Anything.'

She looked away from me and cast her eyes around her. 'The bandstand is painted white and the railings are dark green. There's a bit of graffiti up there—' she pointed to the roof above my head '—but other than that it's in pretty good nick.' She looked out across the park. 'It's still light but it'll be dark soon. There's a threat of rain. There's a rose garden all around the bandstand, and although only some of them are in bloom at the moment, I bet in the summer it looks spectacular. There are a couple of men over there by that tree doing some sort of tai chi, and a few kids in the play-ground over there.' I glanced to where she was pointing but said nothing. She looked back at me. 'You see the same, right?'

I shook my head, then looked up. 'The roof here is covered in graffiti, and there's barely any paint left on the wood or the metal. This bench,' I said, patting the rickety slats, 'is in danger of falling apart and I'd be amazed if it didn't have woodworm or dry rot or something,' I looked out across the park. 'It's a bright evening and the sun has only just gone behind the trees. There's no rose garden, I can't see anyone doing any kind of tai chi but there are a couple of kids kicking a football around.' I looked back at her. 'I can't see a playground either.'

We stared at each other as the implications of what we'd just discovered sank in.

The impossible seemed, somehow, to be possible.

'I've got an idea,' I said, picking up my rucksack. I stuck my hand in the front pocket and pulled out my keys. The keyring was a small, foldaway pocketknife. 'I'm going to go over there and etch something in that tree.'

'What will that do?'

'You'll see.' Before she could ask anything else I stepped off the bandstand and marched across to the tree a few metres away. I reached as high as I could and carved each of our initials and the date into the bark, big enough to see from the ground. I folded the knife back into its case and turned around – and stopped dead. Because the bandstand was empty. I looked around to see where Emma had gone but she was nowhere to be seen. I ran back and leapt onto the platform – and there she was, sitting on the bench, staring at me.

'Where did you go?' I said, breathless.

'I was here all the time,' she replied, her voice a whisper. 'But I couldn't see you either.'

'You mean...'

'We're only together inside this bandstand.' She stood. 'Wait here and you'll see what I mean.'

Sure enough, the moment she stepped off the wooden slats of the bandstand floor, she disappeared, as if she'd never been there at all. Would she come back? I glanced down and noticed she'd left her bag, which was a good sign. I could hardly breathe as I waited. It felt like she'd been gone for ages. But I had no way of seeing what she was up to, or of knowing whether she was going to return.

Finally, just as I began to think she'd given up on me, she reappeared, her face flushed.

'"EV and NF, 2nd April 1999",' she said, excitement in her voice. 'It's there, Nick, the etching on the tree.'

'My God,' I said. I laughed out loud as it hit me. 'I can't actually believe this.'

'Me neither.' She sat back down beside me and I held my hand out and pressed it against her arm. The moment we touched a spark shot through me and I could see the same had happened to her. I pulled away and then did it again, and the same thing happened again.

'This is mad,' she said.

'You're telling me.' I tried it one more time. 'It's like the air around us is charged,' I said, as a jolt went through me. 'Like atoms and the atmosphere and God only knows what else have caused some sort of weird chemical reaction and created this... this time slip where only you and I exist.'

She gasped, making me jump. 'That explains the sweets!' she said, clapping her hand over her mouth.

'What do you mean? What sweets?'

'The sweets you had, in the Woolworths bag.'

'What about them?'

Her eyes widened. 'Woolworths closed down in 2004. I knew there was something weird about it when I saw them.'

I rubbed my face with my hands. I needed a drink, but I didn't have anything with me and I wasn't going to risk leaving yet, not before we'd worked things out a little more. What if the time slip disappeared and we never saw each other again?

'Do you want to know anything?' she said.

'Like what?'

'Anything about the future. What life is like in 2019?'

Did I? I'd never really thought about it before. When Dawn

had been diagnosed with cancer, I wondered whether we would have done anything differently if we'd known it was coming. Whether we would have made more of our lives if we'd known how little time we had left together. But the truth was, I didn't think we would have done. We were happy as we were. Knowing what was coming was more likely to have ruined things for us than improved them.

'I'm not sure,' I said. 'Why don't you start by telling me what the hell you do with that weird phone thing? It looks like something out of *Star Trek*.'

She laughed. 'It's so bizarre to think how normal it's become to have one of these,' she said, holding the camera/phone/computer in her hand. 'These have only been around about eight or nine years, but even kids have them.'

'But what do they do? I mean, I can see they take photos. But what else are they for?'

'Everything,' she said, simply. 'Honestly, it's amazing. Let me show you.'

She swiped her finger across the screen and typed in some numbers and the screen sprang to life. She tapped a square in the corner of the screen.

'This here is how you access the internet.' I watched as she typed in 'time slips' and the page filled with lists. She tapped on one and a website loaded. It was incredible to see, and I knew I was staring gormlessly but I didn't care.

'And look at this,' she said, clicking on a little pink square. 'This is Instagram.'

'What's that?'

'It's a social media site where people post photos and follow each other.'

'So you can literally just look up anything at any time, no matter where you are?'

She shrugged. 'More or less.'

'Jeez.' I looked round. 'But where's the modem? I mean, how do you get the internet connection out here in the middle of the park?'

'It's all on 4G. Or 5G. Or a wireless internet connection if you're in range of one.' She looked at me and laughed. 'Your face is a picture.'

'It's just...' I trailed off. 'It's like magic, to be honest.'

'I guess it is, really. I mean, I've never really thought about how it works, I'm only ever really bothered that it does. But when you think about how little time twenty years is, it feels mad that things have changed so much.'

'Can I have a go?' I said.

She handed it to me. I turned the phone over in my hand. The case was smooth, an Apple sign on the back. I held it up next to mine. 'And to think I thought my phone was hi-tech.'

'I suppose it is compared to everything that's come before.'

I tapped the screen the way she had but it remained blank.

'I can't see anything,' I said.

She took it from me and it sprang back to life. She handed it back and it went dark again.

'It looks like it's defunct wherever you are.'

I laid both phones down on the bench and let out a long sigh. 'This feels really freaky.'

'It really does.'

I twisted my body so I was facing her. 'I must seem like a dinosaur to you. And—Oh!' A thought had just occurred to me, something I wasn't sure I wanted to think about too much.

'What?'

I shook my head. 'Nothing.'

'Come on, it clearly wasn't nothing. What have you just realised?'

'How old are you?' I said.

'I'm thirty-seven,' she said. 'Why?'

'I'm thirty-one. Which means in 2019 I'll be fifty-one. That's... that's pretty old.'

She shrugged. 'It's not that old.'

'I bet you wouldn't date a fifty-one-year-old.'

'I would if it was Brad Pitt.'

'Brad Pitt's in his fifties?!' I shook my head. 'God that's weird.'

'How old is Prince William?' Emma said.

I frowned. 'I'm not sure. About fifteen I think.'

'He's married with three kids now.'

'Wow.'

'Oh, and is Our Price still a thing?'

'Yes. Don't tell me that closes down, too?'

She holds her hands out. 'When people stop buying CDs and streaming music it all falls apart.'

'What's streaming?'

'It's when you listen to music through the internet.'

'So, no more CDs?'

She shrugged. 'Hardly any. But vinyl makes a comeback if that's any consolation.'

'It is a bit.' I stared out into the park, my head spinning. The kids playing football had packed up and gone home now, and the twilight was beginning to pull across the sky, pushing the spring sunshine away. Shadows loomed and I shivered.

'Let's not talk about the future any more.'

'Sorry. It must be freaky.'

I shrugged. Emma pressed her hand against my arm and as the usual spark juddered through me, I turned to her. 'I'm not sure what this is or what it means that it's happened, but I'm glad it has. I'm glad to have met you.'

'I am too.'

5

EMMA

You wait two years to meet someone you can imagine a future with, and then they live twenty years in the past.

Of course they bloody do.

Nick and I talked endlessly that night, telling each other stories from our lives, about our likes and dislikes. I learned that he loved rummaging for treasure in charity shops, that he preferred baths to showers, that when he was eight he spent three months in hospital with a mystery infection, and that he supported Ipswich football team because his grandad did but had always been hopeless at playing football. I told him about my love for musicals, how I collected a programme from every one I'd been to see but always felt sad that I hadn't gone further with my own acting career; I told him how Rachel and I loved to go to the cinema and watch sad films, but that Rachel always tells me I'm cold-hearted because it takes a lot to make me cry; and that I used to go horse-riding until I fell off and broke my leg at the age of eleven and never got on a horse again. We steered clear of talking about the twenty-year gap between us, and just focused on getting to know one another, as though everything was normal.

Later, as it got chilly, he told me a bit more about Dawn.

'Everyone loved her,' he said, smiling sadly. 'She had such a big heart and I'm sure everyone only invited us to places because they liked her so much and I was just a tag-on. I remember this one time just after we got married, and she took me to a work do with her – she was a carer in a nursing home a few miles away from here. The old people adored her, but one of them, Marjorie, seemed to take an instant dislike to me from the moment I arrived. She was rude to me all night, gave me daggers across the room that were so sharp that I could almost feel them on my skin, and she turned away if I tried to speak to her. It didn't bother me particularly, but Dawn was really upset. She loved Marjorie and she really wanted her to like me. So before we left at the end of the evening, she went over to have a word with her. She was over there for a few minutes, and when she walked back over she had a huge grin on her face. "Marjorie wants to speak to you," she told me, so I dutifully went over, expecting the old woman to apologise to me or something. But when I got there and sat down beside her she looked at me and said, in a voice that carried across the entire room, "You're far too pleased with yourself young man. You need to be a bit more grateful that you have such a wonderful woman and stop standing around looking so bloomin' smug about it."'

I laughed. 'Oh dear,' I said. 'Sounds like she got your measure.'

'That's what Dawn said,' he said, chuckling.

'Greg was the same,' I told him. 'He was the life and soul of any room, people always seemed to like having him around, were drawn to him. Sometimes when I was next to him I felt invisible.'

'I'm sure you could never be invisible,' he said.

I was about to object when he added, 'You're too beautiful to be invisible.'

I felt my face flush and when I looked at Nick, his cheeks were pink too. 'Sorry,' he said. 'Too much?'

I shook my head. 'No. It was a lovely thing to say. Thank you.'

Neither of us wanted to leave that night, but it was getting cold and dark – in both our worlds – so we agreed to meet up again the following day.

'But what if you're not here? I mean, what if whatever this is —' he flapped his hand around in the air '—isn't here?'

'I don't know. But unless we stay here for the rest of our lives then we don't really have a choice but to risk it.'

We'd left shortly afterwards, together this time, and as we stepped off the small platform of the bandstand, Nick disappeared. I held my hand out but it just swiped the air where he had been. I shivered.

Now, back at the house where I now knew he also lived, I felt strange. It was as though there were ghosts living alongside me here, and I could almost feel the presence of Nick beside me. What was he doing right now, in 1999? Was he standing right here in the hallway thinking about me, or was he in the kitchen, making dinner? Or perhaps he was in the front room watching TV, or in the bedroom, asleep. I shivered. I probably shouldn't be thinking about him in the bedroom.

I dropped my bag in the hall and trudged towards the kitchen at the back of the house. The kitchen here was modern, dark blue cupboards and low-hanging lights, so it definitely wouldn't be the same kitchen Nick had back then. But he was here in this space nonetheless, cooking, eating, laughing, living. Loving.

I sat on one of the bar stools and placed my phone on the worktop in front of me. I thought about the conversation Nick and I had had when we'd realised what was going on. At what point had I decided to believe him when he said we were living twenty years apart? At what point had disbelief and horror become the realisation that he was telling the truth? I also let myself think about the moment when he told me I was beautiful, and I held it to my chest for a moment as a warm feeling flooded through me. It had been a long time since anyone had said something like that and I wanted to savour it, just for a moment.

My phone flashed with a message and for a ridiculous second my heart flared in the hope that it might be Nick. But of course, even if he was somewhere out there in the world, he wouldn't be able to contact me.

The screen showed me it was Rachel, asking if I wanted to go to hers for dinner.

I thought about the chaos of her home – the two boys running rings round her, Iain cooking dinner, the TV blaring, and wondered whether I could face it tonight. But then I pictured the alternative – a lonely night on my own watching TV with a glass of wine and some toast, surrounded by the ghosts of the past, and I told her I'd love to.

Twenty minutes later, I was in Rachel's kitchen, glass of wine in hand, trying to hear her over the shouts of Harry and Aiden who appeared to be having some sort of sword fight with plastic light sabres.

'Anyway, you're very quiet tonight. How did it go with Nick?' she said as Iain ducked behind her and kissed the top of her head. My heart clenched with a stab of jealousy which I pushed away immediately.

I shrugged.

'It's okay, Iain knows about him,' she said.

'Honestly, Ems, I'm really happy for you,' Iain said. 'And I know Greg would be too.'

I felt my face flush. 'Thanks. But it's... it's not that.'

Rachel stopped what she was doing and squinted at me. 'Ems? What's wrong?'

'I—' I started. But whatever I was about to say was drowned out by a crashing sound followed by a stunned silence.

'Boys!' they both yelled simultaneously. Behind me, Aiden and Harry were standing surrounded by shards of broken pottery looking like butter wouldn't melt in their mouths.

'Sorry, Mummy,' they chorused as Rachel bent down.

'Bollocks, that was the vase my mum gave me for my birthday,' she said, picking up the largest pieces.

'I'll clear this up,' Iain said, smoothly stepping in. 'Why don't you two go in the other room and talk?'

I threw him a grateful look, and Rachel and I scooted out of the kitchen as quickly as we could.

'That's better, we can actually hear ourselves think,' Rachel said as she slid the door to the living room closed and the racket from the rest of the house melted away. 'Now, sit down and tell me what's going on with you.'

A sense of dread thumped in my belly, but I did as I was told and perched on one end of the sofa. Rachel settled on the other end and tucked her legs beneath her.

I hadn't wanted to talk about what had happened with me and Nick. I'd planned to tell her that everything was fine, that Nick and I had got on and that we'd arranged to see each other again. No need to mention the small issue of us being twenty years apart. But one look at Rachel's face and I knew I couldn't keep it in any longer. I needed to talk about it.

'I met Nick again.'

'Yes, I know that.' She waited and I squirmed in my seat. Finding the words for this was harder than I'd imagined.

'We got on really well,' I continued slowly. 'We talked a lot, about Greg, and about his wife.' I stared at the rug in front of me, at the small red stain across the corner where one of the boys had spilt a Fruit Shoot. A stray piece of Lego was nestled against the leg of the coffee table. I turned to look at Rachel who was giving me a look I couldn't read. 'We found something out. Something... unusual.'

A frown creased her forehead and she folded her arms. 'Is he ill or something? Because I'm not sure you should—'

'It's not that,' I said, cutting her off. I rubbed my hand over my face and took a deep breath. 'He lives in 1999.'

She stared at me, a pink blush creeping up her cheeks. 'I have no idea what you're talking about.'

I sat back against the sofa, tipping my head against the wall behind me and staring at the ceiling. Then I told her everything that Nick and I had found out today. I didn't dare look at her as I spoke, scared of seeing any judgement in her face, and when I finished I waited for her to say something.

She didn't speak for a long time but when she finally did it wasn't unexpected. 'Are you feeling okay?'

I lifted my head and looked at her. 'I know it sounds completely mad,' I said. 'I know it does and I don't blame you for not believing me. But there's literally no other way to explain what happened today.'

She pressed her hand against my arm, and I looked down at it, remembering the jolt every time Nick and I had touched. It was as though some sort of chemical reaction was occurring, something that connected us through the years, the decades. I didn't have enough knowledge of science or anything else to understand it. All I could be certain of was that it was true.

'Do you want me to arrange for some more grief counselling?'

'No!' I said, pulling my arm away. 'This isn't about Greg, or about grief, or anything like that. This *happened*.'

'I know why you might want to believe that, but it's impossible, Ems. You know that, right?' She shuffled towards me and tucked her finger under my chin, turning my head so we were looking right at each other. 'I'm worried about you.'

'You don't need to be.' I felt a pressure building behind my eyes and I knew I was on the verge of tears. I so desperately wanted her to believe me, and yet I didn't blame her for thinking this was my mind playing tricks on me. Because I'd be exactly the same if the situation were reversed. An idea occurred to me then.

'Come with me.'

'What?'

'Tomorrow. Come with me when I meet Nick and I'll show you.'

She paused for a moment, clearly torn between agreeing and telling me I needed help.

'Please,' I said.

'Okay.' She sighed heavily. 'For you.'

'Thank you.'

'And now,' she said, hauling herself up to standing, 'I think you really need to eat.'

* * *

The following evening I arrived at the park gates a few minutes early, pacing up and down as I waited for Rachel. I had no idea whether this was going to work – there were so many things that could go wrong – but it was the only thing I could think of to try.

'Hey.' I jumped at Rachel's voice. I must have looked scared because when I spun round she held her hands up in surrender. 'It's only me,' she said.

'Sorry.' I smiled, a weak attempt at trying to relax.

We set off into the park, falling into step.

'I need to apologise to you,' she said.

I glanced at her. 'What for?'

'Not believing you.'

'I don't blame you.'

She shook her head. 'It was wrong of me to dismiss you like that. It's just... you know I worry about you, don't you? Since Greg.'

'I do.'

'I just wanted to be sure that this wasn't all some elaborate trick your mind was playing on you.'

'So are you saying that you believe me now?'

I stared down at our feet, which were walking in perfect unison. Suddenly, Rachel's stopped moving. When I looked back at her she was just standing there, staring at the bandstand. She met my eye. 'I don't know, Ems. But I really *want* to believe you.'

I nodded.

'Come on then,' I said. 'Let me show you.'

It was slightly warmer today and the park was busier, kids kicking balls around, couples soaking up the last of the sun's rays, sharing picnics and throwing frisbees and laughing. I kept my eyes fixed on the bandstand and wondered whether Nick would be there, and if he was what he could see. What was the weather like for him? Was he nervous?

I stopped just before we stepped up onto the platform. There was someone else there, a man, sitting on the bench on his phone.

'Is that him?' Rachel whispered.

I shook my head and turned to face her. 'I'm not sure what to do.'

There had never been anyone else here before. If I went and sat down now, would the time slip not work? Or would this person just see me sitting there talking to myself? Could *they* see Nick? There were so many questions I couldn't answer about how this worked.

'Let's wait until he's gone.'

We walked away, heading back along the same path. We took a couple of loops round, checking on each circuit whether the bandstand was empty. As time ticked by, anxiety knotted in my belly. What if Nick thought I wasn't coming and left? Would he ever come back or would he give up on me?

Eventually, after a torturous fifteen minutes, the guy on his phone left. I took hold of Rachel's hand. 'Come on,' I said, pulling her urgently. We stepped onto the bandstand and stopped. There was no one here.

I spun round a couple of times, but there was no sign of Nick, or anyone else.

'Oh,' I said, slumping onto the bench.

Rachel sat beside me and took my hand gently without saying a word. I knew she was just trying to be kind and not say *I told you so*, but I wanted to make her understand.

'I promise you he was here, before,' I said. 'He was sitting just there, where you are, and we just talked, as normal.' I wiped my eye. 'I'm not making this up, Rach. He's not a ghost. I know he's not.'

She smiled at me and stroked her thumb across my hand. 'The mind does weird things sometimes, especially when it's suffering. It's not unusual.'

'I...' I stopped. I wanted to tell her she was wrong, that Nick was real, that we'd had this real connection. But I could see why she didn't believe me, and there were no words to properly explain how I'd felt when Nick and I had been together.

And besides, what if she was right? What if this really was all a figment of my imagination, and Nick had never really existed?

I stood, my legs shaking. 'Can we get out of here?'

'Of course we can,' she said. She held my hand as we stepped off the bandstand and onto the grass, and kept hold of it as we walked back along the path in silence. But as we passed a tree, it struck me.

'I can prove it!' I said, stopping in my tracks.

'What?' She looked at me, confused.

'Come with me,' I said, dragging her towards the tree. We stopped just in front of it, and I pointed at a spot on the bark about two feet above our heads. She squinted up, then looked at me.

'What's this?' she said.

'You can see it?' My heart thumped with excitement.

'Those letters? Of course.'

I gasped. 'Nick wrote them, yesterday.' I pointed at them. 'Look, it's our initials and the date.'

She peered more closely at the carved initials and traced her finger over them. I held my breath as I waited for her to realise I was telling her the truth. But instead she turned to me with pity in her eyes and said: 'Are you sure you didn't just see these on here and think they were a sign?'

'No of course not,' I said. 'Nick carved these while I was sitting over there. I swear.'

She looked back at the letters. I could feel frustration curdling at the base of my belly.

'I don't know,' she said.

'What do you mean you don't know?' I said, trying to tamp down a dart of fury.

'I just mean...' She stopped. 'Listen, I know you really want to believe this, but I worry about you. I mean, this...' She waved her hand towards the tree trunk. 'This could have been written at any time. It could have been written today.'

I stared at her but she wouldn't meet my eye.

'You think I'm making this up,' I said. It was a statement, not a question.

'I just...' She shuffled her feet, then finally met my eye. 'Listen, Em, I want to believe you. I really do. But you know how this sounds, don't you? I mean, you must do. And with everything that's happened, no one would blame you for wanting it to be true.'

I felt tears prick my eyes and I swiped my hand across my cheek.

'This isn't grief, Rachel,' I said. 'I promise you, this really happened. This is real. I... I don't know how else to prove it to you.'

I watched as a look I couldn't read flitted across her face.

'Let's go back,' I said, suddenly, grabbing her hand and pulling her behind me.

'Back where?'

'To the bandstand,' I said, urgently. 'I'll prove to you this is real.'

I could feel her reluctance, but she let me drag her along anyway. And when we arrived back at the rose garden, we both stopped.

'What now?' Rachel said, rubbing her wrist. The skin was red and I felt guilty.

'Nick and I were here, in the bandstand together, when he went to etch that in the tree,' I said, my words tumbling out over one another in their urgency. 'But when he stepped off here into the park, I couldn't see him any more until he got back inside the confines of the bandstand. So what if it's only when the two of us are alone together in there that we can see each other?'

'Right...?' Rachel said, her mouth twisting into a question.

I ploughed on. 'What if he's in there right now?'

'Well I mean...' Rachel stuttered.

'In a minute I'm going to go inside and look. And if he's there, I'm going to ask him to do something, just for you.'

'What do you mean?'

'I'm going to get Nick to prove this to you in the same way he proved it to me.'

'Emma, I really don't need you to do this. Please, let's just go.'

I shook my head. 'No, Rach. I need you to believe me and this is the only thing I can think of to show you once and for all. Please? For me?'

She looked as though she was going to say something else, but then seemed to change her mind and let out a long puff of air. 'OK. For you.'

'Thank you,' I said, clasping her hand. 'Now, go and wait by the tree. I'll come and find you when I'm done.'

And before she could say anything else, I turned and stepped into the bandstand.

* * *

'You're here!'

Nick was standing beside the bench, looking as though he was ready to leave.

'I'm so sorry,' I said. 'I... I came before but you weren't here so...' I trailed off.

He frowned. 'What time were you here?'

'I'm not sure. About twenty minutes ago?'

He scratched his chin. 'I was here then.'

I nodded, unsurprised. 'I think it was because I was with Rachel.'

'Your friend?'

I nodded. 'I told her about you—' I felt my face redden but carried on '—and of course she didn't believe me so I wanted to show her, I wanted her to meet you so that she knew I wasn't making this up. So we came together and you... well, you weren't here.' When I stopped, Nick was watching me with a curious expression on his face. 'What?' I said.

'I was just thinking,' he said, slowly. 'We don't really know how any of this works – or why. All we know is that it does work. We know that we can't see the same things out there.' He gestured towards the park. 'And we know that we can only see each other when we're inside this thing together. But maybe that's another "rule" of this, that other people can't see us.'

'And when we're with other people, we can't see each other either,' I finished.

'Blimey,' he said, sitting down heavily. 'This is a lot to take in.'

'It is.' I looked down at him, at his handsome face, his clean-shaven chin, the dimple in his cheek, and sat beside him.

'What?' he said, rubbing his hair self-consciously. 'Have I got something on my face?'

'No,' I said. 'I wanted to ask you a favour actually.'

'Oh?' He arched an eyebrow.

'Rachel's waiting for me, out there.' I pointed to the tree, and he glanced over and quickly back again. 'She doesn't believe me, about you, and I wanted to prove to her that you're real. That it's not just the grief making me go doolally.'

'So how can I help?'

'I need concrete proof.'

He nodded. 'And I assume you've had an idea?'

'I have.' I told him the idea I'd come up with. He considered it for a moment, then nodded, dug out his pocket knife, and turned to me. 'Back in a minute,' he said. Then he got up and disappeared into the park.

While I waited I looked over at the tree. Rachel was sitting on the ground, her back leaning against it, and I looked away before she noticed me. Even though I knew I wouldn't see Nick there, it still felt strange to me, to know he was both here and not here at the same time.

Just as I was beginning to wonder whether Nick was ever coming back, he appeared in the opening.

'I did it,' he said, his eyes shining.

'Thank you,' I said. I glanced behind me. Rachel was still there. 'Do you need to get going soon?'

'Not yet.'

'Can you give me five minutes?'

'Sure.'

I picked up my bag and jumped off the bandstand, and raced towards the tree. As I approached, Rachel stood up, shielding her eyes from the sun.

'What's happened?' she said, squinting at me.

I stepped round her and peered up at the tree trunk at the place where Nick had carved his and my initials. And then I spotted it and my heart leapt.

'Look at this,' I said, my voice a whisper.

Slowly, Rachel turned, and peered up at the trunk. She reached out her hand and ran her finger over the brand-new carving that had appeared since we last looked, just below the other one: *Rachel, April 2019*. It looked worn, as though it had been there for some time.

As though it had been there for twenty years.

I waited, my heart in my throat, as she took it in. Then slowly, she turned to face me. 'Oh my God,' she whispered, her cheeks reddening. 'This is... it's *mad*.'

'You can see it?'

She looked back at the tree, then back at me, then shook her head. 'I can't get my head around it. It *can't* be real.'

'But you know it is, right? You believe me?' I so desperately needed her to.

She looked back at the initials and then back at me. 'How can I not? But—' she looked stern '—you do understand that this doesn't change anything, right?'

'What do you mean?'

A frown flitted across her face. 'I know you really like this man, Ems. But he... it's—' She stopped. 'It's completely impossible.'

'I...' I'd been about to say I didn't really like him, that he was just a man I'd met, but I stopped myself. Because Rachel had always been able to read me, often better than I could read myself, and I knew she was right. I didn't know what was going on here, or why. All I knew was that, for the first time since Greg had died, I was thinking about another man. I *liked* another man.

'Oh, Em,' Rachel said, and suddenly her arms were round me. I let my head rest on her shoulder and my tears soak into her jumper. When I pulled away, she pressed her hand against my cheek. 'Is he still there?'

I nodded.

'Go back to him. But promise me something.'

I nodded.

'Don't go falling in love with him, will you?'

I smiled. 'I'll try not to.'

* * *

Nick looked up as I stepped back inside the bandstand, a question on his face. 'She believes me,' I said. I didn't tell him about her warning.

'That's great,' he said, as I tucked my bag under the bench. When I looked back at him, he seemed thoughtful.

'You okay?' I said.

'Yeah, I'm fine,' he said, unconvincingly.

'Come on, tell me.'

He gave a small smile. 'Am I that easy to read already?'

'You must be.'

He sighed. 'It's nothing really. It's just... I feel a bit sad that you've got someone to talk to about all of this and I... well, I haven't, not really.'

'What about your brother?'

'Yeah, I guess. I just... Andy's brilliant, but he's a real straight down the line guy. You know, black is black, white is white. I just don't think he'll believe me, even if I could prove it to him the way you just did with Rachel.'

'You never know,' I said. 'He might surprise you.'

He looked at me and I shivered under his gaze. 'Yeah, he might.' His gaze became more intense and the shiver turned into a swirling in my belly as he reached his fingers towards mine, which were resting on the bench between us. I held my breath as they slid closer, and then, finally, with a crack and a feeling like being hit by lightning, he curled them round mine. The outside world receded, the sides of the bandstand shrinking around us so that it was just the two of us here, in this one moment in time.

I imagined closing the gap between us and pressing my mouth onto his, the feel of his lips warm and soft against mine and—

'Do you mind?' he said, breaking into my thoughts.

'This?' I said, indicating our hands, and he nodded. 'No,' I said, simply. 'It's nice.'

'Good.' He moved slightly closer and I could feel the heat from his thigh. My skin where our hands touched hummed and crackled with a feeling, soft and gentle like TV static turned down low. We sat for a moment and watched the world go by. It had all been such a whirlwind over the last few days I'd hardly had time to think. But now, sitting here, hands intertwined, I allowed myself to imagine what it might be like to be with another man.

Greg and I had been together for almost a decade. We'd been very different, but we balanced each other out and it worked. He grabbed life by the horns, never let anything faze him or get him down. Sometimes it was exhausting, but it was good for me when I was younger. Greg helped me to grow, come out of my shell and see what the world had to offer me. He always described us as two sides of the same coin, and that was how it felt, most of the time.

Other times, I found his lust for life exhausting, and craved some downtime. He loved being with other people, said yes to any invitation. Sometimes, I wished it could just be me and him. Because the times when it was – the times when he was usually restless, wondering what to do next – were my favourite times.

After ten years together Greg and I knew each other inside out. I knew that he preferred his coffee with cream and liked tea so strong a spoon could stand up in it; I knew what side of the bed he liked to sleep on, that he would always choose to take the stairs rather than the lift because when he was eight he'd got stuck in a broken-down lift and wet himself; I knew when he was sad or stressed and that he believed that nothing he ever did would ever be good enough to please his father. When he died, I couldn't imagine ever wanting to speak to anyone again, let alone meeting and getting to know someone completely new.

And yet now here I was, sitting with this man I knew very little about, having feelings I never imagined feeling again. Although I didn't know him well yet, being with Nick already felt calmer than being with Greg had ever felt. There was an energy about him that was soothing, gentle, and I wanted to get to know him better.

'I've been trying to work out whether there's any way we can control this,' Nick said, suddenly.

I looked round at him. 'What do you mean?'

He rubbed his face. 'Have you thought about what this means, that this is happening to us?'

'Of course,' I admitted.

'Me too. A lot. I keep thinking that it makes no sense, that things like this don't happen outside science fiction films. And yet here we are.' He looked at me. 'Do you ever think perhaps we were meant to find each other, for whatever reason? That the universe wants to bring us together?'

I stared at him. 'This is exactly what I've thought,' I whispered.

He smiled. 'Well, if we're right, then surely there has to be a way for us to actually make it happen. I mean, it would be a pretty cruel twist of fate if the universe let us meet but then kept us apart forever, wouldn't it?'

I smiled. 'And have you worked it out yet?'

He shook his head. 'Not yet. But I hate not knowing whether I'm ever going to see you again every time we part. There *has* to be a way.'

I looked down at the bench, my fingers worrying at a loose piece of wood. 'I have had an idea,' I said.

'Go on.'

I raised my eyes to look at him. 'I could look for you in 2019.'

'No.' The word shot out like a bullet.

'But—'

'No, stop.' His voice was harsher than I'd heard it before and I stiffened. He softened. 'Sorry, Emma. But I've already thought about that and it's a definite no for me.'

'But why? I mean, I know you said you'd be older than me, but it would only be fourteen years and that's not much.'

He shook his head. 'It's not that.' He let out a long breath of air, his cheeks puffing outwards from the effort. 'What if some-

thing terrible has happened to me in the last twenty years or...
what if you can't find me at all?'

It took a moment to realise what he meant. 'You mean, what if
you've died.'

He nodded. I swallowed.

'I wouldn't have to tell you.'

He shook his head. 'If you looked and you found out something bad, I'd know. And I can't live with that. I just can't.' He took
my hand again, the usual spark jolting me. 'Promise me you won't
look.'

He looked so distraught I had no choice. 'I promise.' I
attempted a smile. 'But you'd better come up with a better idea
soon, because we can't keep this up forever.'

'I'll do my best.'

6

NICK

I thought about what Emma had said all the way home. I thought about it while I was in the shower, while I ate dinner and as I tried to fall asleep, staring up into the darkness until well into the early hours.

I knew I'd made the right decision telling Emma not to look for me in 2019. Knowing anything about the future felt dangerous, as though it could unwittingly make me live my life differently. Even knowing that I will eventually sell this place because in twenty years' time Emma is living in it felt wrong.

The truth was, for the first time since Dawn had left me, I was finally coming back to life. When I was with Emma, the parts of me that had curled up and died after losing Dawn began to turn their heads back to the sun, to unfurl. At last, I could see a reason for living again.

I couldn't look for her right now in 1999 because she would be seventeen years old and everything about that scenario was wrong. But apart from all that, I couldn't get the thought out of my mind that, if I *had* still been around in 2019, I would definitely already have found Emma. The fact that I hadn't hung over me like a dark cloud.

The trouble was, I couldn't see any other way for us to be together.

I sat up and switched on the bedside lamp, the room flooding with light. The wardrobe door hung slightly open and the empty coat hangers inside made my stomach flip over. It had taken me a long time to get rid of Dawn's things, and for months after she died I would stand at this wardrobe and inhale the lingering scent of her. Eventually, when it faded, Andy had suggested it was time to let someone else enjoy her clothes, her jewellery, her things, and I knew he was right. We'd spent a whole day sorting through everything, bagging up the things I agreed to get rid of and putting everything else into a box to keep close by.

Handing those bags over to the charity shop was one of the hardest things I've ever done, but Andy reminded me that her things were not where Dawn was. Rather she was in my memories. My heart. My soul.

I climbed out of bed and kneeled down to pull a box out from underneath. It was only a small one, just a few nick-nacks and things I wanted to keep close to me. I used to look at it at least once a day, but I realised now that, since meeting Emma, I'd barely given it a thought. Guilt stabbed me. Did that mean I was forgetting Dawn?

I lifted the lid from the box and spread the first few items across the duvet. There was the note she'd written me during her last couple of days, a short message that I'd read so many times I knew it off by heart.

Promise me you'll live your life. Find love, see the world, play in the concerts. Grab it all by the hands and whatever you do, do NOT grieve for me for more than a year. I absolutely forbid it.

My hands shook as I let my eyes slide over the words again. All the times I'd read it before I never dreamed I'd be doing any of those things. I dropped it and picked up a photo; my favourite of Dawn, her blonde hair shining in the sunlight as she sat reading a book, oblivious to the fact that I was looking at her. My heart clenched and tears stabbed behind my eyes. I sniffed and picked up the next photo. It was taken after she started her treatment, just after she'd shaved her head. I'd come home early and found her sitting in the bathroom, surrounded by blonde curls, looking up at me with eyes wide. She looked utterly beautiful and I'd wanted to capture her bravery so she'd lifted her chin and let me take a photo with my digital camera.

I was about to put everything back in the box when something caught my eye and I picked it up with trembling hands. It was a little toy sheep that Dawn had bought when we were trying for a baby. We'd agreed not to buy anything at all, not wanting to tempt fate. One day Dawn had come home and I remembered the light in her eyes as she pulled this little yellow sheep out of the plastic bag. 'I'm sorry, I couldn't resist it,' she'd said, and we'd tucked it away in a drawer for later, not realising at the time that later would never come. That, in fact, three months after that moment she would receive the devastating news about her cancer that would rip our lives apart.

I threw the sheep back into the box, replaced the lid and slid it back under the bed. This wasn't the time to look to the past. I needed to think about what to do right here and now. How to solve the problem that I'd started to fall in love with someone who was living in a different time.

I stood back up and opened the curtains, the sun bright against my face.

Outside, the street was quiet, all the other houses closed up, their inhabitants still asleep. The front garden was shades of grey in the early morning air, and a light mist hung in the air. My Ford Focus had a layer of condensation speckling the windscreen and I watched as a fox sprinted across the close and dived into the bushes.

Did Emma see the same, or had the view from here changed by 2019? Did she stand in this room and look out and try to picture me? I turned to face the bed. Was she here right now, asleep? Was she thinking about me, wondering the same things?

I checked the clock beside the bed. Almost 7 a.m. Andy would be up soon and I really needed someone to talk to.

I showered and dressed, then went downstairs to the kitchen and filled the kettle. The phone was on the wall in here. I thought about Emma's phone – what had she called it, an iPhone? – and all the things she'd told me it could do. I had a mobile but the landline was still what I used for everyday calls. Would that change soon? It was weird to think that Emma knew all the things that were to come, but for me they were a complete mystery, like something out of *Dr Who* or *Tomorrow's World*.

I picked up the phone and pressed the button for Andy's number which was stored in my phone. I heard it ring and imagined Andy and Amanda looking at each other in confusion, wondering who was calling this early.

It rang and rang. I was about to give up when a voice came on the line.

'Oh hi, Amanda.' Bugger. 'Sorry to call so early.'

'Hi, Nick. Is everything all right?'

'Yes, yes, it's fine. Sorry.'

A silence. Then: 'I guess you want to speak to Andy?'

'Yes please.'

There was a clatter and footsteps and I waited, staring out at the back garden, the spindly tree that Dawn and I had planted and that we'd hoped we'd get apples from one day. I shivered.

Would Emma pick apples from this tree later this year?
Would she—

'Nick. Everything okay?'

'Hey, Andy. Yeah.'

'Right. You know it's quarter past seven right?'

'Yep. Yes. Sorry. I wanted to catch you before work.' I swallowed. 'Sorry for cancelling on you last night.'

'It's fine. I never want to stand in the way of true love.' I could hear the smile in his voice.

'Are you free tonight?'

'Tonight? I guess so. I mean, I'll check.'

'Great. Will you let me know?'

'Yeah sure. But...' He stopped. 'Is something wrong, Nicky?'

'No, honestly, I'm fine. I just need to talk to you about something. Nothing serious,' I added, in case he thought I was dying.

'Okay. Well let's assume we're meeting at the curry place at the usual time unless you hear from me, okay?'

'Sure. Thanks.'

When I hung up I stood for a moment, frozen. I hadn't decided exactly what I wanted to tell Andy yet. All I knew was that I needed to try and explain to him what was going on and hope he didn't think I was going mad.

Unless I was?

I had no idea how I was going to get through a day of teaching, but I had to try. Perhaps it would be good for me, to have a distraction. But first, I needed to find something out.

I made a coffee and drank it while I packed my bag, then left to walk the fifteen minutes to the school where I worked. It was quiet here this early, and I waved to the cleaner as I passed and headed past my classroom and to the school library. The librarian hadn't arrived yet so I made my way straight to the science reference section. I ran my finger along the edge of the shelf... *The Mysteries of Time, Reality and Time, Simple Physics Explained*.

I was a maths teacher and I dealt in numbers and logic. I had no way of explaining what was happening between Emma and I, so I hoped one of these books on this shelf might give me some clues. I pulled out a couple that looked vaguely helpful and took them to a desk and sat down.

Much of it was impenetrable, long sentences with explanations about cosmic strings, theories and black holes that made my head ache. But some of it seemed promising, and I read as much as I could, scribbling notes on a pad as I went, trying to make sense of it all.

I don't know how long I was there, but when I heard the library door open I looked up and blinked.

'Mr Flynn?' The librarian looked confused to see me here. I stood and gave her a vague smile and gathered up the books and stuck them in my bag before she noticed what I was reading. I checked my watch: 8.45 a.m.

'Sorry, I need to dash,' I said, hurrying. It wasn't until I got to my classroom that I realised I hadn't checked the books I'd borrowed out of the library. I'd have to go back later and apologise.

I turned to my class, who were screeching chairs across the floor and chatting to each other, and clapped my hands.

'Right, let's get going.'

* * *

The day had dragged by, but finally it was time to meet Andy. I arrived early and sat at our usual table, my leg bouncing up and down nervously. When the waiter asked if I wanted a drink I ordered a beer and drank it quickly, hoping to temper my nerves.

'You look like you haven't slept for a week,' Andy said, sliding out the chair opposite me and sitting down.

I rubbed my hand over my face. 'It's been a busy day.'

He ordered himself a beer and another one for me, then folded his arms over his chest and sat back.

'Come on, out with it. Is this something to do with that woman you've been meeting?'

I let out a long breath and flipped the beer mat over and over. I couldn't look him in the eye so I stared at the tablecloth.

'Sort of.'

Andy didn't say anything. I swallowed, then looked up at him. He was watching me with a worried look on his face. 'Have you... Do you believe...' I started, but I had no idea how to say what I needed to say.

Andy leaned forward and rested his elbows on the table.

'Nicky, what's going on? It's not like you to be so tongue-tied.'

Instead of replying I reached down for my bag and unzipped it. Andy's gaze felt like it was burning me as I pulled the books out and lay them on the table. I pushed them towards him and he picked the top one up.

'*The Mysteries of Time*,' he read out. He picked the other one up. '*Reality and Time*.'

He lowered it and looked at me. 'What are these?'

'They're from the school library. Physics books. Sort of.'

'Right. I suppose my question is why have you got them and why are you showing them to me?'

How was I going to explain this? It was clearly insane. If Andy came to me and told me what I was about to tell him I'd be worried about his state of mind. But I needed to get it out there.

'You know this woman I've met? Emma.'

'Yes.'

I flipped the beer mat over and over again, the tap, tap, tap drilling into my brain. I took a deep breath.

'She lives in 2019.'

I didn't know whether I'd expected Andy to laugh in my face, or get angry, or tell me I was being ridiculous. What I hadn't expected from my loud and opinionated brother was the complete and utter silence I was now greeted with. I felt dizzy and realised I'd been holding my breath.

'Aren't you going to say anything?'

He didn't get a chance to reply because the beers arrived, and the waiter stopped by the table.

'Hello, you two, I thought you'd abandoned me when you didn't come yesterday.'

'Ah sorry, Abdul, but you know we'd never leave you for long.' Andy flashed him a smile and Abdul grinned back.

'Well good. The place wouldn't be the same without you. The usual?'

Andy glanced at me and I nodded. 'Perfect thank you,' he said.

He waited until Abdul had left then turned to me and shook his head. 'I don't know what to say.'

'That makes a change.'

He nodded his head in acknowledgement. 'That's true. But seriously, Nicky. What are you talking about?'

'I know it sounds completely insane but I really need you to listen to me.'

He nodded without speaking.

'Emma and I, we've realised that we live twenty years apart.' I felt my face flush but carried on. 'We didn't realise at first, of course. But she knows things about the future, and she has this phone, like a computer, that she carries round with her that fits in her pocket.'

Andy studied me for a moment and rubbed the stubble on his chin. He leaned forward onto his elbows. 'Sorry, are you saying that, because this Emma has some sort of futuristic phone, that you think she lives in the future?' Andy took a gulp of his beer and wiped the froth away with the back of his hand.

I shook my head and took a sip of my own beer. 'No, not just that. It's hard to explain. When she touches my skin, there's this weird spark between us, like deep down inside me. But when we're not inside the bandstand together, we can't see each other. We don't exist, except in there.'

'I don't think—'

'The tree!' I interrupted, desperate for him to understand. 'I took my knife and I carved our initials on the tree. And when I got back to the bandstand Emma went to look at the tree and our initials were still there.'

Andy's forehead folded into a crease. 'And you believe her?'

'What do you mean?'

'Well, presumably you told her you were carving something. And then she said she saw it. But you have no proof that she wasn't just seeing it today. In 1999.'

'I know but—' I started.

'Nicky,' Andy said, reaching for my hand and covering it with his own. 'I love you, and I know you desperately want to believe that this woman is something special. But I think she's conning you.'

'No!' I snatched my hand back and scraped the chair back across the floor away from him. The people a couple of tables away glanced at us then back at their dinner. My heart pounded in my chest and my whole body shook.

'Woah, calm down,' he said, holding his hands up.

I didn't move, torn between wanting to stay and try to explain, and wanting to get out of there. My chest felt tight and I struggled to breathe.

'You don't understand,' I said. Tears pricked my eyes and I blinked them back. Abdul hovered nearby, steaming dishes balanced on a tray.

'Sorry,' Andy said, smiling at him. He turned to me. 'Come on, Nicky. Please sit back at the table. Let's eat and talk about it. I promise to listen.'

I didn't want to make a scene, so I dragged my chair back to the table and waited as Abdul served our food. Neither of us looked at each other, and I was relieved when Abdul finally left us to it. I spooned curry and rice onto my plate and pulled a chunk of naan bread off. My appetite had vanished.

'I'm sorry,' Andy said. He was watching me across the table with an expression on his face that I couldn't read.

I shook my head. 'I know how it sounds. I do. But I promise you she's not conning me, and I promise this is nothing to do with missing Dawn.'

'Then why don't you explain and I won't interrupt. I promise.'

'Okay.'

Over the next fifteen minutes, between mouthfuls of curry and gulps of beer, I told Andy everything. All the things Emma and I had struggled to believe ourselves but had realised had no other explanation than the one we had finally settled on. 'Plus she told me the carving looked old, like it had been there a long time,' I finished.

Andy wiped the last smear of sauce from his plate with a piece of naan and chewed it slowly. I waited for him to say something.

'So,' he said, swallowing and dabbing his mouth with his napkin. He threw it on the table and looked at me. His eyes were serious. 'These books.'

I glanced down at the library books, whose existence I'd forgotten about until then.

'What about them?'

'Do you believe they hold the answer?'

I shook my head. 'Not really. I just didn't know what else to do.'

'Because the situation is impossible?'

Anger flared through me again. 'You still don't believe me.'

'I didn't say that.'

I looked up, surprised. 'What then?'

Andy rubbed his chin thoughtfully. 'Honestly? I have no idea. But I do know that you obviously do believe this, and I agree there does seem to be something strange going on here.'

'So you don't think I've gone mad?'

He shook his head. 'Not completely. But—' he held his finger up to stop me speaking '—I do think there must be some other, more likely explanation for what's happening. And I'm going to help you find it.'

'I've thought of everything. You know me. I'm logical. Sensible. I don't believe things easily.'

'I know that. Usually.'

'But?'

When his eyes flicked away from me I knew what he was going to say. 'You still think this is grief talking, don't you?'

He shrugged. 'I honestly don't know, Nicky. I just don't think we should rule it out, that's all.'

I nodded. I hadn't convinced him yet, but it was a start.

* * *

Even though Emma and I had worked out that the bandstand was the only place we could see each other and be together, I still got a knot of anxiety in my chest every time I approached it and saw there was no one there. What if this was it? What if whatever wormhole had temporarily existed here had closed up and we'd never be able to see each other again?

The relief I felt every time I stepped up onto the raised floor of the bandstand and saw Emma waiting for me was so intense it could have knocked me over.

Today, as I walked through the park in the blazing sunshine, I was thinking about what I wanted to talk to her about. I'd been trawling through the books I'd borrowed from the school library but they hadn't helped me at all, so a couple of days ago I'd gone to the main library in town to see if I could find anything on the internet. I remembered Emma telling me that she could access the internet wherever she was on that phone she carried around and wondered what that would be like – would it make life easier or would it be really intrusive?

I'd spent a couple of hours searching for information about time slips, time travel and anything else I could think of. And although most of it had been hopeless, supporting the theory that time slips were believed to simply be a made-up plot device for novels and films, I did come away with one thing to suggest to Emma.

'Hey,' she said, standing as I stepped into the bandstand. It was a warm evening where I was, but she was bundled up in a jacket and scarf. Her hair was pulled back in a ponytail, and her cheeks were pink as though she'd run here. I stood still for a moment, unsure what to do next.

She stepped towards me and the air shifted.

'It's good to see you,' she said. She nodded at my bare arms. 'You're making me feel cold.'

'It's a beautiful evening here,' I said. 'I wish you could see it.'

'So do I.'

We sat down, a couple of feet apart. Above our heads – or at least my head – the leaves rustled in the breeze, and beams of sunlight poked through the holes in the roof. Emma looked grey, tendrils of hair whipping round her face in the strong wind. Her hand rested on the bench between us, and I reached out tentatively and wrapped my fingers round hers. As our skin touched, she gasped. 'I'll never get bored of that feeling,' she said, a smile spreading across her face. Our fingers were threaded together, hers cold to the touch.

'You brought your violin,' she said, nodding down at the case I'd rested by my feet.

'I did.' I smiled. 'I realised I forgot to play it for you the other day and I never like to break a promise.'

'Will you play it now?'

'Right now?'

She shrugged. 'There's no time like the present.'

I had so many things I needed to say to her, things to tell her. And yet she was right. There really was no time like the present, especially when you had no idea whether you'd have a future. I leaned down and picked up my violin case and clicked it open. As I saw it nestled there in the blue velvet, my stomach rolled over, and my hand hovered above it, unsure.

'What's wrong?'

'I haven't played this since...'

'Since Dawn died,' she finished, gently.

I nodded, swallowed down the lump in my throat.

'If you can't, it doesn't matter.'

I shook my head. 'No. It does matter.'

I needed to get over this, move on. Carefully, I cradled the neck of the violin, lifted it, then tucked it under my chin. I picked up the bow, took a deep breath, then started playing. I didn't look at Emma, just stared out into the park as I dragged the bow back and forth across the strings. It sounded slightly out of tune, but I didn't want to stop. I hadn't decided until I started what I was going to play, but as soon as the notes began I knew exactly what to play. 'I Don't Want to Miss a Thing' by Aerosmith, a song Dawn had loved and that I'd learned the violin part for especially to play to her. I wasn't sure whether Emma would recognise it.

A couple walking past hand in hand stopped to listen and I flashed them a smile. Beside me, I felt Emma shift. With every note I played I felt a something fill my chest, a feeling I hadn't felt in a long, long time. And as I reached the final note and brought the bow to a stop, I held my breath for a few seconds, letting the last notes slip away on the breeze. The couple clapped, then turned and walked away, deep in conversation.

'I had no idea you were so good,' Emma said beside me, and for the first time since I'd taken the violin out of its case I met her gaze. Her eyes twinkled and a smile played on her lips.

I lowered the violin onto my lap. 'I used to be. I'm pretty rusty now.'

'It sounded pretty incredible to me.' I jumped as she lay her hand on my arm, a warmth spreading through me. Would I ever get used to the jolt that passed between us every time we touched? Would it make it impossible for us to ever be together in a more intimate way or...

I felt a heat rise in my cheeks. 'Thank you,' I said. 'It felt pretty good to play. Especially here.'

She nodded but didn't ask any questions for which I was grateful. We sat quietly for a moment, watching our own views. I imagined stepping across the invisible line that ran between us, separating us. If there was a way for us to do it, what would it be like in her world? How much could things really have changed in twenty years? Would I feel like an alien, a relic? Emma had called me that one day, before we realised what was happening between us. A relic.

'What are you smiling about?' Emma's voice interrupted my thoughts and I turned to look at her.

'I was just wondering what it's like where you are.'

She wrapped her arms round herself and shivered. 'It's bloody cold.'

'It looks it. It's a lovely day here.'

'I want to be there with you.'

'I want you to be too.'

A silence fell. Then: 'I wonder what I'm doing today?'

I frowned. 'What do you mean?'

She blinked slowly at me, then shrugged. 'I was seventeen in 1999. I wonder what I was doing right now.'

A stone lodged in my belly. Of course I'd realised how young she'd be right now, but I hadn't really thought about it in any kind of detail. I moved away and rubbed my arm where her hand had been.

'What's wrong?' she said.

I shook my head. 'I just... it feels wrong. You're a *child*.'

'But I'm not.' She stood up suddenly and did a twirl. 'Look. I'm thirty-seven years old and a proper grown-up.' She smiled at me, her lips wide, and I had a sudden urge to kiss her. She sat down and leaned towards me without touching me. 'It's all right, Nick. Even if we never find a way to be together, whatever this is between us right now, it's all right.'

'I know,' I said. And I did, really. And yet I couldn't completely shake the thought of her seventeen-year-old self being here, in my present day.

'Why don't you tell me about your music.' She nodded at the violin that still rested on my lap.

'There's not much to tell. I've been playing the violin since I was six years old because my mother played and she wanted me to. My father didn't care because nothing I ever did was good enough anyway, and he thought I should be playing something more manly like drums or guitar.' I shrugged, remembering the first time he'd come to hear me play. I'd been terrified, standing at the front of the school assembly, my violin trembling in my arm until I thought I might drop it. When I played I felt so happy, but the moment I finished and sought out my parents my heart dropped. Because while my mother was clapping and cheering with pride, my father just sat there, arms folded, staring at me, a smirk on his face. I pushed the memory away. 'What about you? Do you play any instruments?'

She shook her head. 'No. I always wish I had but I was more into drama than music. I was a bit of a show-off.' She smiled. 'I was in plays at school, but I'll never forget my first proper part, in the open-air theatre across the other side of this park. I played Cecily Cardew in *The Importance of Being Earnest*.'

'Did you? Wow! When was that?'

She frowned, the crinkles in her forehead making her look unbearably cute. Suddenly, she gasped. 'Gosh, I think it was then – I mean now!' She shook her head. 'I mean, I think it was 1999! Yes, it was, because I was the youngest member of the cast and very young for the part, and it was in the papers at the time and Mum cut it out and stuck it to the fridge.' She stopped, breathless, and looked up at me. 'What? Why are you looking at me like that?'

'I...' I started. 'Sorry. I was just—it seems weird to me, that you have a memory from childhood, but for me it hasn't even happened yet.'

'Yeah. It is weird isn't it.'

I didn't want to think about it too much. I wasn't sure I wanted that knowledge. Even knowing about something small that happens just a short time in my future felt wrong.

'Actually I have something to tell you,' I said, leaning down and placing my violin back in its case.

'Have you? What?'

'Hang on.' I reached for my rucksack this time and took out the pieces of paper I'd printed at the library. 'I found some things out.'

'What sort of things?'

I smoothed the top piece of paper and stared at it, the words blurring. 'I went to the library and did some research about time slips and time travel.'

'Right?'

I glanced at her. I hoped I'd read this situation correctly. The last thing I wanted to do was be too intense and scare her off. I'd been so certain, but now I was saying it out loud I felt nervous, unsure of myself. I cleared my throat. I was a teacher, I could do this.

'I was trying to find out what scientists know about time slips. I wanted to know what the explanations were for the phenomena, and how they were believed to occur.' I picked up the first sheet and squinted at it. 'Many people don't believe time slips are possible. But we know they are because we're living one, so I was looking for explanations on how they *would* work, rather than whether they *could*.' I glanced at her, then back down at the paper in my hands. 'One explanation is that they're caused by electromagnetic fields which produce hallucinations in the brain. But we know this has to be more than a hallucination, otherwise we're both going mad. Another possible explanation is that travelling at a certain speed can cause time to slow down, but unless we can work out how to travel faster than the speed of light then that didn't seem to be helpful either.' I cleared my throat again. 'Have you heard of cosmic strings or wormholes?'

She shook her head.

'Well, it seems like they're both a sort of defect in space-time which, if they warp, might be able to create paths that loop back in time.' I lowered my hands into my lap and looked at Emma. 'I wondered whether that could be the explanation for what's happening here.'

'You really are a teacher, aren't you?' Her smile softened the words, but I still felt myself flushing.

'Sorry,' I said.

She shook her head. 'I'm only teasing. It's brilliant. But I don't see how this helps us?'

'Neither did I, at first.'

'But now you do?'

'I'm not sure. Probably not. I mean, scientists have never been able to deliberately recreate a time slip as far as I'm aware. But then they've never experienced what we're experiencing either, so I thought, maybe, we could use our knowledge of that to help us.'

'I'm listening.' She closed the gap between us and I felt the buzz of electricity through my jeans from the press of her leg against mine. It made it hard to focus.

'We don't know how or why this is happening, just that it is, right?'

She nodded, a tendril of hair coming loose and sticking to her cheek. I wanted to brush it away but resisted.

'I've been trying to think of a reason why it's happening here, in this bandstand, and the only thing I could come up with was that we've both lost someone we love, and that we both live in the same house. So I wondered whether they could be the things that are causing a connection between us.'

Emma frowned. 'But even if that's true, how does that help us?'

I cleared my throat. 'What if we could do something in the house that could somehow connect us there? Find some way that we could be together there, as well as here. It wouldn't be perfect, but it would be something.'

Her eyes widened, her lips parted. 'I love the idea,' she said. 'But I honestly don't see how we could recreate this, however much we want it to happen.'

'But what if we could? What if there was something we could try? Would you do it?'

'Of course.'

Thank God. I wasn't reading this wrong.

'So, what are you suggesting? Do we need to concoct some sort of spell, or a weird ceremony?' she said, a smile playing on her lips.

I shook my head, trying to stay focused. 'My idea is actually simpler than that. Basically, as far as I can work out, a wormhole is a sort of short cut between two different parts of space and time. There's clearly some unexplained force pulling the two of us through a wormhole here, in this bandstand, so what if we were able to create an artificial wormhole in the house?'

Emma frowned and tilted her head to one side.

'How do you suggest we do that?'

I took a deep breath. This was it. The moment I'd find out whether she thought my idea was a good one – or completely insane.

'I wondered whether, if we did exactly the same thing at exactly the same time in exactly the same part of the house, we might somehow be able to override the natural timeline, and it would let us be together there as well as here.'

Emma studied me for a moment and I held my breath. I was

no expert (clearly), but I'd given this a lot of thought, and it was the only possible thing I could think of for us to try. All my research pointed towards the idea that the principle of a wormhole relied on creating a time difference between the two ends of the 'tunnel', then bringing those two timelines together in space. And while they had also talked about travelling faster than the speed of light in order to achieve this, I hoped that our experiment might just push the natural phenomenon to work without that added complication.

Finally, she let out a breath. 'Oh my God,' she whispered.

'Is… is that a good reaction?' I said.

Her face broke into a grin. 'Yes!' she said. 'I think… I mean, obviously I have no idea whether it will work but it's better than any idea I've got, so it's got to be worth a try, right?' Her eyes were bright.

'Right,' I said, shivering with excitement.

'So what do we have to do?' she said.

'Well, first we'll have to sync our watches, then we'll need to work out exactly what we're going to do in the house, and where,' I said. 'I also wondered whether we could give each other one item that belongs to the other one, just to see if it helps to strengthen the connection. I—' Something in her eyes made me stop in my tracks. 'What?'

'If this doesn't work, we need a backup plan,' she said softly.

'Yes, of course,' I said, disappointed that she already seemed to have decided it wasn't going to work. 'We can arrange to meet back here again tomorrow, no matter what happens.'

'That's one idea.' She shifted a little and her arm grazed against mine and I buzzed with electricity. 'But I was thinking of something else we could try too.'

She moved even closer until I could see the flash of green in her eyes, a smudge of lipstick above her top lip, and suddenly my heart was beating so fast and so hard because I knew what was about to happen and I wanted it more than anything else in the whole world.

I held my breath, and then we moved towards each other.

Our lips touched.

It was an explosion; my whole body felt as though it had been set alight, fireworks going off inside my belly and across my skin, every nerve ending tingled and jangled. A feeling like gentle static made my lips fizz and I snaked my hand round the back of her neck and pulled her closer.

It was as though I was outside my body looking down, and yet I couldn't have felt more present.

It was like nothing I'd ever experienced before.

It was like magic.

She moved away. I could still feel her breath on my lips and her hand on my thigh and I could barely breathe.

'Jesus Christ,' she whispered. 'Was that—'

'I can't—'

We both laughed, and it broke the tension. I shifted away slightly so I could see her clearly, and she was looking at me, searching my face.

'That's the first time I've kissed anyone since Greg,' she whispered.

'And me since Dawn,' I said. I felt breathless.

I'd never even considered kissing anyone else since Dawn had died, let alone imagined what it would actually be like. In fact, apart from drunken snogs as a teenager, Dawn was the only woman I had ever been with. I'd assumed that kissing someone else, touching them, would feel like a betrayal, as though what Dawn and I had shared had meant nothing to me, when it had meant everything.

But that wasn't how it felt.

Instead it felt as though I'd simply found a space inside me for Emma to fill; new experiences, nestled alongside the old ones.

Emma shivered.

'Are you cold?' I said.

'Freezing.'

I reached around her shoulders and pulled her gently towards me, and she pressed her cheek against my chest. I wondered whether she could hear the skittering of my heart.

We sat like that for a few minutes, not moving. I wanted to talk to her, ask her how she felt about what had just happened, but I couldn't find the words.

So I said nothing and just held her.

And right then, it was everything.

7

EMMA

My hands shook as I opened the notes app on my phone and read the list again. It didn't seem like much, but it was all we had. For now, at least.

Kissing Nick had been an explosion of chemicals, like fizzing candy going off in my mouth, a chemical reaction it was impossible to describe. My whole body tingled afterwards and the truth was I could have sat there in his arms forever.

But all good things must come to an end, and eventually, the cold got the better of us both. Plus, of course, we desperately wanted to give our idea a try. Because if we could work out a way of being together away from the bandstand, then it really would change everything.

I'd felt giddy and anxious with expectation as Nick and I had both checked our lists – mine on my phone, his on a piece of paper torn from a notepad which fluttered in a breeze as he clutched it.

'So, our watches are synched, we're sure of that are we?' I said. Goosebumps had formed on my arms and I shivered.

'Perfectly,' he said.

'And you're ready?'

'As ready as I'll ever be.'

We stood for another moment. I studied his face in the dimming light, the contour of his cheekbones and the slight shadow of stubble on his chin, and I longed to reach out and touch his lips again. But it was time to go.

'Hopefully see you later then,' I said.

'Hopefully,' he said gently. Then he turned and jumped off the bandstand and disappeared like a popped bubble.

I hurried home through the gardens, where the rose bushes shivered in the unseasonally cold spring breeze, and out into the park. We had almost an hour before our plan began and there was no way I could eat anything. My stomach was in knots. Instead, as soon as I got home I poured myself a glass of wine and ran a bath and sat in it, warming up. As water lapped at my sides and steam rose around my face, I tipped my head back and closed my eyes and tried to imagine Nick sitting in the same place. He'd said he preferred a bath to a shower, but did he spend hours soaking in it, full to the brim with bubbles the way I did, or was he quick and efficient? There were so many everyday things that I didn't know about this man, and I knew that if we couldn't get our experiment to work, they'd probably remain a mystery forever.

I hauled myself out of the bath and hurriedly dressed. We'd agreed to put our first item on the list into action at seven o'clock, and my phone told me it was nearly time. I clipped my damp hair off my face, then hurried down to the kitchen and opened the back door. It was dark now and the wind had got up even more. I picked up the empty wallet Nick had given me as his personal item ('sorry, it's all I really have on me', he'd said, as I'd handed him one of my favourite MAC lip glosses) and clutched it in my left hand as I stepped onto the back step. I wrapped my cardigan more tightly round me.

Three minutes to go.

The garden was peaceful tonight, most of the trees still bare of leaves. A dog barked a few gardens away and I could make out the quiet whine of a distant motorbike.

My stomach was in knots, and I wondered how Nick was feeling. What if this worked, and we somehow found a way to be together? What if, against all the odds, we succeeded in beating the laws of physics?

It seemed futile. But we had to at least try.

I checked my phone again, the screen glowing brightly in the darkness. One minute.

Thirty seconds.

And then.

Time.

We'd agreed we would both stand here on the back step for five minutes, in exactly the same place, to see whether we could recreate the feeling I'd had that he was somewhere in the fabric of the house just after we'd first met. 'Should we do anything else while we're there?' I'd asked.

'I don't see that there's much point,' Nick replied. 'Just make sure you've got your feet in the right place, hold my wallet in your hands, and see what happens.'

I looked down now and checked. Feet a foot apart, a couple of inches from the front of the step, a foot from the left. I shuffled to the right slightly and planted my feet firmly.

Then I clutched the wallet to my chest and closed my eyes.

I felt weak with nerves. I pressed my hands into the door frame behind me to steady myself, and waited, heart thumping wildly.

Something brushed against my skin and I flinched. But when I opened my eyes, there was nothing there. I reached my hand out and swiped it through the air in front of me. Could I feel the crackle of something? Did the air feel different, charged?

I held my breath and listened. I had no idea what I was waiting for. If this did work and we did manage to cross time, what would it feel like? When Nick and I were together in the bandstand everything felt normal until we touched. Would I simply feel his presence, or was I able to conjure him somehow?

I checked my phone. Two minutes had passed.

I inhaled deeply, exhaled slowly. Right now, Nick was standing in this exact spot, twenty years in the past. Perhaps if I just concentrated harder, really focused on his presence, we'd make the connection. It had to work. It had to.

I closed my eyes and waited, the wind whipping through my cardigan, creating goosebumps on my skin.

But nothing happened, and when I checked my watch again, five minutes was up. I was reluctant to move from the spot, just in case, but eventually I had to. Disappointment lodged in my chest like a heavy weight as I stepped back into the kitchen and closed the door behind me.

I wished I could ring Nick and ask him how it had felt for him; whether he'd felt anything at all. But instead I had to make do with checking the list and trying the next thing we'd agreed.

7.10 p.m.: Sit on the sofa in the living room, with your back against the wall by the door. Try to be roughly one metre away from the door. Stay for five minutes.

I topped up my wine and walked through to the living room. We'd worked out we had our sofa in the same place, up against the wall with the window to the left, so I sat right in the middle and tucked my feet up underneath me, Nick's wallet in my lap. I tried not to think too hard about what might or might not

happen, watching the clock tick closer and closer towards
7.10 p.m.

And then, it was time.

I placed my hands on top of the wallet, palms down,
scrunched my eyes shut and willed Nick into being. Tried to
picture him in exactly the same spot doing exactly the same
thing. Hopeful, waiting.

Nothing.

7.13 p.m.... 7.14 p.m.... Still nothing. Not even a slight tremor or
crackle in the air.

7.15 p.m....

Five minutes was up.

I sat for a moment, letting the realisation that it hadn't worked
– again – settle. Then I looked down and checked my notes once
more.

7.20 p.m.: Sit at the table in the kitchen, facing the window.

7.30 p.m.: Stand in front of the sink in the upstairs bathroom
and stare into the mirror. Stay for five minutes

7.40 p.m.: Lie on the bed in the main bedroom.

Despite the mundanity of our actions, all the talk of cosmic
strings and wormholes had given me some hope that this really
could work. That we really could somehow achieve what scientists had so far failed to achieve.

How naive we'd been.

But I couldn't give up, not yet. I owed it to Nick to at least try
to complete the list, and so for the next half an hour I dutifully
made my way round the house, to the kitchen, the bathroom and,
finally, the bedroom. And it was here, as I lay on the bed and

stared up at the ceiling, that I let myself properly think about Nick. I tried to imagine him here, lying beside me. Imagined a life where we were here, together, in this house. I stretched my arm out and let my hand rest on the other side of the bed: the side where Greg had always slept, and the side Nick had told me he slept on too. The stone of disappointment was mixed with a feeling of guilt that, in all of this, Greg had barely been on my mind. He'd been my whole life for so long and yet now here I was, not only thinking about another man, but letting him fill all my thoughts.

I turned my head to the empty space. A tear trickled down my face.

Time was up. It was over.

It hadn't worked.

And I needed someone to talk to.

* * *

'The boys wanted to see you, can you nip up and kiss them goodnight?' Rachel said as I stepped inside her house half an hour later.

'Course.'

I ran upstairs and into Aiden's room. A night light glowed dimly on the bedside table and all I could see was a head peeking out the top of the duvet. I sat on the end of Aiden's bed and he peered at me bleary-eyed.

'Aunty Emma,' he said, his words blurry with sleep.

'Hey, sweetie,' I whispered. 'I've just come to kiss you goodnight.'

He smiled, but didn't reply, so I leaned over and planted a gentle kiss on his warm forehead, then left him in his dream world. When I got to Harry's room, it was a different story. He was wide awake and sitting on top of his duvet, and when I walked in he said, 'Can you read me this?' He had a Peppa Pig picture book in his hand and a smile so wide I couldn't resist. So, although, I desperately wanted to get back downstairs to tell Rachel everything that had happened today, I sat and read his book to him, laughing when he corrected me, and loving the feeling of his hot little body pressed against me. I loved these boys with every bone of my body, and spending time with them had helped with the sadness I felt about not having children of my own. They'd helped mend my broken heart and I'd never forget it.

By the time the story was finished, Harry was half asleep, so I tucked him in, kissed him softly and crept out of the room.

Downstairs, Rachel was sitting at the kitchen island, a glass of wine waiting for me.

'They're out for the count,' I said, pulling myself onto the stool.

'You're so good at that,' she said. 'They always try it on for me. Maybe I should hire you as a sleep nanny every night.'

'I'd be happy to be here every night,' I said. 'I adore them.'

'I know you do,' she said, pressing her hand against mine. She knew how much I'd wanted a baby of my own. That was another one of the reasons it had been so utterly devastating when Greg had died – because we'd thought we were on the cusp of a great new adventure, but instead our chances of having a baby had died with him as well.

She pulled her hand away and slid my wine towards me. As I put the glass to my lips, she said: 'So, what's happened?'

I let the cold liquid sit in my mouth for a moment before swallowing. I'd thought about how to tell Rachel about the last few hours all the way here, but now the moment had come, I wasn't sure where to start.

'We kissed,' I said, in the end.

Rachel's eyes widened. 'Oh my *God!*' she said. 'This is big news!' She gasped. 'Oh, but... but he's...'

I nodded. 'I know. It's not ideal, what with him not actually existing.'

'Except he might.'

I nodded in agreement. 'He might.'

Rachel glared at me, a look I couldn't quite decipher.

'What?' I said. 'Why are you giving me that look?'

'There's something else isn't there?'

I sighed and twirled my wine glass round on the worktop, watching the liquid slosh up and down the sides. 'Sort of. I...' I took a gulp of wine and met her eye. 'We tried something. A sort of experiment.'

Rachel frowned. 'What sort of experiment?'

'You know we live in the same house, right? I mean, I live in the house Nick used to live in.'

'Of course.'

'Well, Nick did some research about time slips and it's... well, it's complicated. Obviously. But we thought there might be a way we could override linear time and be together, in the house.'

'Riiiiight?' She sounded confused. 'So what did you do, some sort of weird ritual in the garden or something? Ooh, or did you drive your car really fast during a lightning storm like Marty McFly?'

I shook my head. 'If only it were that easy,' I said, smiling. 'No, sadly it wasn't quite as exciting as *Back to the Future*. Nick explained that scientists reckon wormholes work by sort of bending time back on itself. And the only other way of doing that that we could see – apart from travelling faster than the speed of light – was to try and force the time portal into existence in the house by being in exactly the same positions as each other at exactly the same time.'

Rachel let out a long breath of air. 'And I guess from your face that it didn't work?'

I shook my head sadly. 'No.'

She let out a long breath, her cheeks puffing up with the effort. 'I'm so sorry, darling. But did you really expect it to?' Her voice was gentle but I bristled at her words anyway, defensive.

I sniffed. 'I hoped I might at least feel something. You know, a presence, a change in the air or something. But there was nothing.'

I picked up my glass and downed it, and Rachel did the same.

'And have you given any more thought to looking for him?' she said. 'Now, I mean, in 2019?'

I shook my head. 'I've had a quick look on Rightmove to find out when he sold the house, but nothing else.'

'And?'

'It was sold in 2006.'

She nodded. 'Is that it?'

'Yep. I can't do any more because Nick's worried that if I look for him and find out something terrible has happened to him in the last twenty years, it will ruin his life.' I shrugged. 'So I promised him I wouldn't.'

'But what if he doesn't know you're looking? Then even if you did find out something bad, you wouldn't have to tell him.'

'That's what I said. But he still said no, because he'd be able to tell.' I took a gulp of wine. 'The trouble is I think he's right, too. What if I *did* discover he'd died, or was really ill, or something equally as terrible? Because if he was still alive, why wouldn't he have come to look for me? And if I found out for certain, how on earth could I carry on as if nothing had happened?'

Rachel pressed her hands against mine and squeezed them. 'Ems, I know what you're saying. But if you *don't* do this, then there's absolutely no chance of being with him anyway, so what difference does it make?'

I pulled my hands away and put them in my lap. I knew Rachel was right. And yet I knew Nick was too.

Which meant I was stuck.

'Why did this have to happen to me?' I said, burying my face in my hands. When I looked back up Rachel was topping our glasses up. 'I just want to be happy, Rach. Is that really too much to ask?'

'And I want that for you too. But you can't have a relationship with someone you can only see when you're in the middle of the park.'

'I know.'

'So maybe it's time to start looking for someone else – now that you know you're ready for something?' she said gently.

I felt a tear trickle down my cheek and I swiped it away. 'I don't want anybody else,' I whispered.

* * *

I could tell from Nick's face the moment I stepped into the bandstand that he'd had no luck last night either. I slumped beside him on the bench, arms folded, and stared out into the park. It was warmer tonight and there were a few people taking evening strolls. I hoped none of them would come anywhere near us and disturb our peace.

'That's that then,' I said.

I saw his head turn towards me from the corner of my eye, but I didn't look at him.

'I'm sorry it didn't work. But just because that failed, it doesn't mean we should give up.'

'Doesn't it?'

I heard his sharp intake of breath. 'Do you *want* to give up?'

I shrugged. I knew I was being belligerent, but it was easier than admitting how frustrated I felt.

My skin sparked as he pressed his hand against mine and I stared down at his long fingers, his neat nails.

'I'll leave you alone if you like.'

'No!' The word exploded out of me, and I finally looked up at him. His eyes were open, his expression soft. I shook my head gently. 'I'm sorry, I know I'm being an arse.' I twisted my hands around in my lap. 'I just don't know if I can do this any more, knowing it can never go anywhere.'

'It's—'

'The thing is, it's killing me, not being able to speak to you,' I interrupted before he had a chance to say anything. I just needed to get it out there. 'When something happens, I want to text you, or ring you, and laugh about it, or ask you something, except I can't and I never will be able to because you're not there.' I twisted to face him, and took his hand in mine, threading my fingers through his as my skin fizzed. 'Except you are, somewhere. Just not with me.'

'I'm sorry.'

'It's not your fault. I just want... I want to do all the things people do when they first meet. I want to kiss you. I want to talk on the phone for hours. I want to go on a date.'

'Then you should.'

'What?'

His gaze burned into me as though he was searching deep inside my soul. I wondered what he would see there. 'You should do all of those things. You deserve all of those things.'

I stared at him. 'What are you saying?'

'I'm saying that you should go on dates with other people. You should find someone who can make you happy. You deserve that.'

I felt as though the air had been sucked from me. 'Is that what you want me to do?'

'It's not what I want for me. But it's what I want for you, yes.'

I snatched my hand away and tucked it beneath my thigh. I watched a bird fly from a nearby bush and land on the metal railings beside me. It stared at me for a moment, then flew away. I turned back to Nick. 'But I'm falling in love with you,' I said, my voice quiet.

I hadn't planned to say it, but once it was out there I knew it was true. I *was* falling in love with this man, and it was killing me.

He didn't reply and I felt my face burn. Had I got this totally wrong? Was he about to get up and walk away and never come back to this place again? Should I laugh, pretend it was a joke, or—

'Emma?'

I looked up. Nick was watching me. 'Sorry, did you say something?'

A smile spread across his lips. 'I said I'm falling in love with you too.'

'You are?'

'Yes. But—'

'No. No buts. Buts are never good.'

He shook his head. 'I know. I never imagined loving anyone again after Dawn. But—' he gave me a look '—you know this is impossible, right? *We're* impossible.'

I blinked, my eyes burning, and sniffed. Of course I knew that. Of course I hadn't imagined that he might say he'd found another way for us to be together, that somehow he'd unlocked the secret that no scientist has previously been able to unlock. That would be crazy.

'I know,' I said, my voice cracking.

I knew it, and yet I didn't want to believe it.

8

NICK

It's one thing doing the right thing. It's entirely another thing to like it.

'But you've only just met this girl,' Andy said.

'I know.'

I couldn't even explain to myself the connection I felt when I was with Emma after just two weeks of knowing her, so how could I begin to explain it to Andy, or anyone else? It wasn't at all surprising that he couldn't understand how wretched I felt about telling Emma she should date other people – especially as he still seemed to believe she was some sort of liar or con artist.

'Well, I think it's a good thing.' He plonked a mug of strong tea in front of me and sat down. I'd come immediately to Andy's after leaving Emma. I hadn't wanted to leave her, but we couldn't stay in the bandstand forever and eventually it had started to get too cold for both of us. I'd felt bereft the moment we stepped off the wooden platform and she disappeared as though she had never even been there at all. I'd needed someone to talk to, and Andy was always the person I turned to, even if he wasn't the most romantic person in the world. He understood me. And he understood how sad I'd been for the last two years.

'It doesn't feel like a good thing,' I said, taking a sip of the scalding-hot tea he'd made me.

He didn't get a chance to reply before the door flew open and a bundle of energy flew into the room.

'Uncle Nick!' My youngest niece Ella raced to my side and I lifted her onto my lap where she beamed up at me.

'Hello, gorgeous girl,' I said, kissing the top of her head. She smelt of lemon shampoo, a comforting scent I could have breathed in all day. She wriggled around on my lap and peered up at me through her too-long fringe.

'The tooth fairy's coming tonight,' she said, giving me a gappy grin.

'No way, look at you,' I said.

She stuck her tongue through the space where her tooth had been and crossed her eyes.

'I have to wrap my tooth in a tissue and then the tooth fairy will leave me some money.'

'And how much does the tooth fairy bring these days?'

'Ten pounds,' she said.

I raised my eyebrows and glanced at Andy.

'Er, I don't think that's quite right, is it, Els?' he said.

She looked at him. 'That's what Daisy in my class got.'

'I don't think she did,' Andy said. 'I think the tooth fairy gives the same to everyone, and that's fifty pence.'

'But she *did* get that much, she told me,' Ella said, crossing her arms. She looked so like her dad when she did that I wanted to laugh out loud.

'I suspect Daisy is telling porky-pies,' Andy said, standing and holding out his hand. 'Now come on, let's get you to bed otherwise the tooth fairy won't come at all.'

'But I want to stay with Uncle Nick a bit longer.'

'Not tonight, sweetheart. Come on.'

Ella let out a long huff and reluctantly slid off my knee onto the floor. Her pink pyjama legs had ridden up to her knees and her dressing gown hung off one shoulder.

'Night, Elly-Welly,' I said as she took Andy's hand.

'Night, Uncle Nick-Nick,' she said.

I heard them run up the stairs. I could hear Ella's big sister Imogen arguing about something, and I took a gulp of tea and smiled sadly. Andy was my big brother by four minutes, but he'd always been my protector, and it had always felt like the age gap was much bigger than that. His family were so precious to me, and I loved spending time with them all.

But sometimes, being with them made my heart hurt too. Because it reminded me of everything that Dawn and I hadn't been able to have.

Everything I'd lost.

'Sorry about that, 'Manda's got them all under control now,' Andy said, sitting back at the table a few minutes later.

'She's a trooper that one.'

'She is.' He shook his head. 'Honestly, ten quid. Does she think we were born yesterday?'

'You can't blame a kid for trying.'

He grinned. 'That's true. Shows entrepreneurial spirit, I suppose.' He stood again. 'Do you want a beer?'

'Go on then.'

He pulled a couple of cans from the fridge, handed me one, then sat down again. It was dark outside and the kitchen light shone above our heads like we were on stage.

'You're getting thin on top you know,' I said, clicking my can open.

'Fuck off,' he said, his hand flying to his scalp.

I grinned. He knew I was teasing – we were both lucky to still have thick heads of hair, but I knew Andy was paranoid about looking old. 'Anyway, I don't want to talk about me. We need to sort out this mess you've got yourself into.'

'I know.' I sighed. 'I don't see that there is any way to sort it though.'

'So, you're still totally convinced that this Emma lives in 2019? There's definitely no other explanation?'

I stared at him. 'I'm completely certain.'

He held my gaze, then shook his head. 'Well then, tell me about her.'

I closed my eyes and tried to think of the words to describe Emma. 'She's...' I opened my eyes. 'She's amazing,' I said, my voice cracking. 'It's not just that she's beautiful, although she is. She's got this amazing red hair, and piercing green eyes, and she's funny and sad at the same time, and she likes sweets, and music and theatre and...' I stopped, spinning my can round on the table, and looked at Andy. 'You know, when Dawn died I never thought I'd even want to imagine a future with someone else. And yet now I've met Emma and we've talked for hours, we've shared so many things I never thought I'd share with anyone else apart from you. She's... Meeting her has helped to mend my broken heart, Andy, and it feels magical.' I swallowed. 'Except now we've discovered that we can't be together.'

'Jesus, Nicky. I had no idea you were this serious about her.'

'I am. I think...' I shook my head. 'I *know* – I'm falling in love with her.'

'And does she feel the same way?'

I nodded sadly.

'I don't know what to tell you,' Andy said. 'I mean, this is insane. You know that, right?'

'You think I'm insane?' A beat of anger thumped in my veins.

But Andy shook his head. 'Not you. This situation. It's insane and, if what you say really is true, it's completely impossible.'

'You're telling me.' I decided to ignore the implication that he still didn't believe me.

'So what are you going to do about it?'

I shrugged. 'Both of us have thought about nothing else. But we've run out of ideas.'

'So you say you can only see each other in the bandstand?'

I nodded.

'And she lives in your house?'

I nodded again.

Andy screwed his face up, thinking.

'No,' I said.

He looked at me. 'No what?'

'I know what you're thinking.'

'You don't.'

'You're wondering why I don't ask her to look for me in 2019.'

He nodded. 'Okay, I was wondering that.'

'It's not an option.'

'It's not ideal. But if she really is in 2019 then it *is* an option.'

I sighed. 'Emma's already suggested it. She said if she went to look for me and found me then the age difference would only be fourteen years and that wouldn't be so bad.'

'And she's right. And it strikes me that unless you can do some complicated physics that no one else has ever managed to do, then it's your only solution.'

'Because if I was still round then, why wouldn't I have gone to look for her?'

Andy didn't reply for a while and I wondered whether he'd heard me. But then I saw the moment that realisation dawned, and he puffed out his cheeks, leaned back in his chair and stared up at the ceiling.

'Fuuuuuuck, Nicky.'

'I know.'

When he looked back at me, his eyes were sad. 'You have to let this go now, for your own sake. You do know that, right?'

'I do. And that's why I told Emma to go and find someone else. To date. To have some fun.'

'And what did she say?'

'She said she didn't want to.'

'And you?'

'It broke my heart,' I said. 'But I don't see that there's any choice. I have to let her – and myself – be happy.'

* * *

I brushed the dirt away and placed the yellow and orange gerberas carefully on the grass, then sat down.

'Hi, my love,' I said.

I always felt embarrassed talking to Dawn's ashes, but today I found I didn't care. I had so much I wanted to say to her.

The grass was damp beneath my bum and a cool breeze weaved its way through the trees and headstones. I rubbed my arms, wishing I'd brought a jumper, and smoothed my hand over the small plaque in the ground. The inscription was still crystal-clear: 'Dawn Flynn. Wonderful wife and much-missed daughter. September 1966–October 1996. Fly high, my darling'.

I cleared my throat.

'I'm sorry I haven't been to see you for a while. I've brought your favourite flowers, liven the place up a bit.' I swallowed down a lump in my throat. Coming here was so hard and yet comforting at the same time. I'd never been under any illusions that Dawn was actually listening to me, which was why I'd always felt so awkward talking to her. But after the last few weeks I'd begun to realise that anything was possible, and if there was even a small chance that she knew what was going on in my life, I owed it to her to explain myself.

'The house still feels weird without you. Even though it's been almost two and a half years, I still keep expecting you to walk through the door at any moment, throw your shoes and bag in a heap and run through to find me.' I smiled sadly to myself. 'I miss you, D.'

A dog barked in the distance and voices floated over the wall of the crematorium, and I waited a moment to gather my thoughts.

'The thing is, D, something's happened. Something unexpected. I've met someone. She's called Emma and we met at the bandstand. I go there every week, do you know that? It's where I feel closest to you, closer than I do here...' I sniffed. 'Anyway, one day she was just there and we got talking and I told her all about you. And the thing is...' I let out a long breath. 'The thing is, D, I really like her. Except something weird has happened. Because she...' I checked behind me to make sure nobody was listening, then turned back to her headstone. 'She lives in 2019.'

A beat where nothing moved, not even the blossom on the trees. I held my breath to see if there would be any sign Dawn had heard me. I don't know what I was expecting – a single ray of sunshine, or a bluebird to land on my shoulder or something? But apart from a solitary Topic wrapper drifting across the grass behind Dawn's gravestone, there was nothing.

I really didn't know what had happened to me recently.

'Anyway, I know it sounds ridiculous. It does even to me and I'm experiencing it. But I just wanted to tell you, you know. Because I still can't get used to the fact that when something momentous happens, something amazing, you're not here to share it with.'

I sat for a moment longer, wondering whether to say anything else. On the way here I'd imagined telling Dawn everything – about the things Emma had told me about the future, about the kiss we'd shared, about Andy telling me I should date someone else. All of it.

But now I was here I wasn't sure I really wanted to share everything with her any more. I wasn't sure that she'd want to know either. Perhaps this was something to keep to myself after all.

I rubbed my hands along my thighs and pushed myself to standing. The sun came out from behind a cloud as I did and warmed the back of my head. I bent down and moved the gerberas closer to her headstone, then turned and walked away.

9

EMMA

'Come on, just press it,' Rachel said.

I took a deep breath, clicked 'send', then buried my face in my hands. 'Oh God, I already think this is a mistake,' I groaned.

'It's not a mistake, I promise,' Rachel said. 'It's totally the right thing to do.'

I peeled my eyes open and peered at the screen where my profile picture smiled back at me like a girl who didn't have a care in the world. This was *definitely* a mistake.

It was a couple of days since I'd last seen Nick and we'd talked about dating other people. Today, Rachel had just helped me set up my profile on Tinder.

'Men love a widow,' she said, when I questioned whether I should mention it.

'I don't want someone with a weird dead husband fetish,' I said.

She'd put her hand on my arm and given me a stern look. 'Emma Vickers, stop being so negative about this,' she said. 'You don't have to find your next husband. You just need to have a bit of fun and stop thinking about a man you can't have.'

That was easier said than done. Even thinking about Tinder made me think about Nick, and his confusion when I'd mentioned it all those weeks ago. At the time I'd thought he was just cute and old-fashioned. I could never have guessed the truth.

'Fine, fine,' I said, clicking my phone off.

'What are you doing? You might be getting some matches as we speak,' she said.

'I'm not sitting here waiting to see if people like me,' I said. 'I'll check it later.' I frowned at her. 'Anyway, how come you're the dating app expert all of a sudden?'

She shrugged. 'A few people at work use them and talk about them all the time. Apparently when you first sign up you get shown lots of hot men because they want you to keep paying for it.'

'And after that?'

She looked sheepish. 'Well, Suzanne said she now only gets men coming up on her app who look like thumbs.'

'Oh great.'

'But that doesn't mean it will happen to you. Perhaps the algorithm just thinks she likes thumb-like men.'

I tucked my phone in the back pocket of my jeans and stood.

'Where are you going?'

'I need to get off,' I said.

'But I thought we were going for a couple of drinks? Iain's all ready to look after the horrors.'

'Sorry, Rach, I've got a splitting headache, I really just need to go home and go to bed.'

'Have I pissed you off, making you sign up to this? Because you don't have to do it. You can just delete it.'

I shook my head. 'Honestly, I'm fine. I really am just tired. Drinks another day?'

She stuck out her bottom lip. 'Sure. But make sure you check the app every now and then and don't just ignore it, okay?'

'Okay.' I turned to leave.

'Oh, and Em?'

'Yes?'

'Be nice to them, yeah?'

'I'll be charm personified,' I said. I blew her a kiss and left. It wasn't until I'd closed the front door behind me and started walking down the street towards home that I let myself think about the reality of dating other men.

When Nick had suggested it, I'd been sure I would never do it. I hadn't been looking for anyone when we'd met and nothing had changed.

But the more I'd thought about it afterwards, the more I wondered whether Nick was right. Whether dating other people was the only way I was going to be able to move on – from him, and from Greg.

Rachel had jumped on the idea of course.

'Does this mean you're not going to see Nick ever again?' she'd asked.

'Not exactly. We've arranged to meet next Wednesday at the usual time.'

'What for?'

I'd given her a look I'd hoped was disapproving. 'Because we don't want to completely cut off all contact. At least, not until we're forced to.'

'So is he planning to see someone else too?'

I shrugged. 'I think so.'

The truth was I hadn't wanted to ask him directly, or think about it since. Even though it was definitely the best thing for both of us, the thought of him with another woman made me feel empty inside.

'Well at least you can compare notes,' she said.

'Yeah,' I agreed.

Rachel had encouraged me to set up a profile on Tinder. 'It's impossible to find a man out there these days if you don't use the apps,' she'd said.

I'd reluctantly agreed. But I was already unsure.

I waited until I got home before I pulled out my phone to see if anyone had checked me out. To my amazement there were already several messages. Before I read them, I made myself a cup of coffee, then went through to the living room and sat down. I stared at my phone, unsure whether to even open the messages. I mean, was this what I really wanted?

A shiver ran through me and I looked up. I had a sudden overwhelming feeling that there was someone in the room with me. My heart thumped and I stood slowly, and spun round. I glanced out of the living room door and down the hallway towards the kitchen. I checked under the stairs and behind the curtain. There was no one there.

But the sense that I wasn't alone was still with me. And, I realised, it wasn't a frightening feeling. More a comforting one.

Could it be…? No, don't be daft.

But what if it was?

What if it was Nick? Or at least the spirit or the soul of him, in this house where he'd lived and loved. A few weeks ago I would have laughed at myself for even thinking like this. But now? Well, the truth was I had no idea what was and wasn't possible. We'd tried to force it and it hadn't worked – but what if it *could* still happen from time to time, the same way the bandstand portal seemed to exist?

What if Nick was trying to tell me to get on with it?

But then again, what if he was trying to tell me he'd changed his mind?

I sat back down on the sofa and took a sip of coffee, staring at the messages from men who had seen my photo, letting them blur in front of my eyes. Could I do this?

Nick and I couldn't have a future. I had to stop thinking about him.

I needed to choose someone for a date, so I might as well get on with it.

I clicked on the first message.

* * *

It was hard to believe the state of dating these days. As I'd scrolled through some of the messages I'd received, I'd begun to wonder whether there were any normal single men left. Men who didn't offer to send dick pics, or talk about the weights they could lift, or tell me how much money they earned, or list all the dirty, seedy things they wanted to do to me.

I'd been about to give up when I'd read Aaron's message. He'd seemed nice. Better than nice. He looked handsome in his profile picture, a carefully chosen photo of him on a beach somewhere in shorts and T-shirt. Not too showy, but nice enough. He claimed to like surfing, cycling and Italian cinema, and he seemed the most normal of all the men I'd matched with. Best of all, he only lived a few miles away.

And now here I was, about to go into the restaurant he'd suggested and meet him.

I felt a bit sick.

My phone buzzed.

RACHEL

Relax and be yourself and you'll nail it! R x

I smiled at Rachel's message, took a deep breath, and pushed the door open.

It was quiet in here and I spotted Aaron straight away. He stood as I walked towards the table, then held his hand out to shake mine when I got there. So far so good – no awkward fumbling cheek kisses. Plus, he looked pretty similar to his photo, rather than twenty years older and balding.

'Lovely to meet you,' he said, as we sat down.

'You too.'

I noticed a bottle of sparkling water on the table, but nothing else.

'I didn't want to guess what you were drinking,' he said, handing me the drinks menu. 'Do you want to choose something?'

'Thank you,' I said, grateful for something to do so I didn't have to think about what to say.

That had been something I'd worried about on the way here – what if we didn't have anything in common, or there were long, awkward silences? It had been more than a decade since I'd been on a first date with anyone, and Greg had always made it easy, the conversation flowing as he asked questions and told funny stories. With Nick it had been different, an unexpected connection, not something either of us had been looking for but something that had just clicked without us even trying. But a date was something else entirely, and I wasn't sure I even knew what the rules were these days.

Luckily, Aaron was easy company. He admitted to being nervous too, and told me that he had been divorced for two years and was only just starting to date again. He didn't have kids, and he asked sensitive questions about Greg. He was lovely, and seemed genuinely interested in me. He was good-looking too, and by the end of the night I was beginning to think that perhaps Nick and Rachel had been right all along. Perhaps this really was what I needed.

We said goodnight and arranged to meet the following week. He kissed my cheek but didn't push for anything more, and as I climbed into a taxi I realised I was smiling.

Well, that was unexpected.

By the time I pulled up outside my house, though, a sadness had started to descend, and I knew I probably wouldn't see Aaron again after all. Because no matter how lovely he was, he wasn't Nick, and the magnetic pull I felt when I was with Nick simply wasn't there between us. It wouldn't be fair on either of us for me to lead him on.

I paid the taxi driver and let myself into the house. I knew Rachel was waiting for details of the date, but I wasn't ready to dissect it just yet. I had something I wanted to do first. I went into the living room, pulled out my laptop from down the side of the sofa, opened a new window then held my fingers above the keyboard. They hovered there, not moving.

I was itching to look for Nick. Despite what I'd told Rachel and the promise I'd made to Nick, I couldn't stop thinking about him being out there somewhere, right now, and that I might be able to track him down.

And if he was out there, did he think about me? Was he with someone else? If he was still alive in 2019, then he'd be – what? Fifty-one. It was weird to think that. I was only thirty-seven, still young enough to have a baby, if it's what I wanted.

He'd asked me not to look for him, and I understood his reasons. But what if I tracked him down and he'd been waiting for me the whole time, hoping I wouldn't listen to the 1999 version of him? What then? We could be together and there would be no need for dating apps or anything else. Could I really go against his wishes?

What if he never forgave me?

My fingers quivered, undecided.

And then I closed the laptop and went to get myself a glass of wine.

I couldn't do it.

10

NICK

Why on earth had I suggested Emma and I date other people? I had no interest in seeing anyone else, and I didn't think she had either. It had felt like the right thing to say at the time but now, just the thought of her with another man was killing me.

Andy had set me up with one of his colleagues, Katy. She sounded lovely.

But she wasn't Emma.

I picked the phone up and dialled Andy's number.

'I've changed my mind,' I said, the moment he answered the phone.

'Nope. Nah-ah. Absolutely not.'

'I can't go,' I said.

'You're not pulling out now. I've bigged you up so much Katy's really looking forward to it.'

'But I really don't want to go on a date.'

'Nicholas,' he said.

'Oh no, this is serious.'

'You bet it is.' A beat. 'You need to try and move on, right?'

'Not necessarily. I was perfectly happy wallowing in my own misery before all this started.'

'Maybe so. But this *has* started, which means that as well as getting over Dawn, you need to move on from Emma, or whatever this idea is of Emma. Agreed?'

'Well, unless...'

'Nope! Stop it! You know it's no good.'

I sighed and slumped into the nearest chair, defeated. 'I know. I'm just not sure if I'm ready for this. I've never even been on a proper date before.'

'Nicky, you need to relax a bit. This is just dinner with a woman, no pressure. Just talk to her, eat some food and drink some beer. That's it.'

'But she knows about me, right?'

'About Dawn? Sure. But it doesn't mean you need to talk about it all night. Ask her about herself, what she likes, her job, whatever. But just try to enjoy yourself, okay?'

'Okay.'

He hung up before I had a chance to say anything else. I glanced at the clock. I had a couple of hours before I needed to be in town. I grabbed my jacket and paused at the front door and placed my palm flat against it. I'd taken to stopping every time I left the house, or whenever I lay in bed at night or stood in the kitchen waiting for the kettle to boil, and trying to feel Emma in the fabric of the house. It hadn't worked before, even when we'd tried really hard to connect, so I knew it was unlikely to ever happen. But it didn't stop me from hoping.

I opened the door and walked briskly to the park. As usual the bandstand was empty, forlorn and long forgotten. I wondered what made someone decide to spend money on it and bring it back to its former glory in a few years' time. I wished I could see it the way Emma did, surrounded by a beautiful rose garden.

I stepped inside. Even though I hadn't expected Emma to be there it still felt like a blow when I saw the bench was empty. I sat down and stared out into the park, watching the blossom drop slowly from the tree and settle at the base. A woman walked past with her dog. She threw a stick and I watched the dog race away across the grass and return it, tail wagging. Where was the playground Emma had mentioned, and when had it been built? What was life really like in 2019? It was only twenty years away, but it felt like a lifetime.

A gap that felt impossible to close.

I closed my eyes and pictured the first time I came here and saw Dawn. We'd been so young but that had only been fifteen years ago. So much had happened in that time – we'd fallen in love, got married, tried for a baby, and then she'd died. In between all that, we'd had so many happy times – days at the coast where Dawn indulged my love of searching for fossils, Dawn coming to watch me play my violin and me watching her singing in front of crowds of people. So many small things that had disappeared into the stretch and bend of time and were forgotten, but that made up a happy life together.

And then I thought about Emma, and the first time we'd spoken. Had we known even that day that there was a special connection between us? That something in the fabric of time had brought us together?

I'd thought a lot about why we'd met and decided it must be because of our shared grief. Her for Greg, me for Dawn. They say grief is one of the most powerful emotions, and maybe that was the reason this had happened. Perhaps we were never meant to be together forever, but simply for this short period of time, to help each other. To deal with our grief and move on.

I should tell her when I saw her next week that we needed to stop this. That we'd come to the end. Because it wasn't good for either of us to yearn for something that we knew we could never have.

I stood, suddenly aware of the time. I'd promised Andy I wouldn't let Katy down, so I owed it to her to at least be on time for our date. I took one last look at the bench, then stepped back onto the grass.

* * *

'I had such a lovely time,' Katy said.

'Me too.'

Katy and I stood facing each other in front of the restaurant. I shifted my weight from one foot to the other and back again. She looked down at her shoes. We'd had an unexpectedly fun evening and despite my reservations the conversation had flowed well. Now, outside saying our goodbyes, things had turned awkward. I suspected Katy was hoping for a kiss, but I didn't want to lead her on.

She took a step towards me and I held my breath. If I stepped back I'd look rude and I didn't want to upset her. And then, over her shoulder, I spotted a car pull up to the kerb, and relief flooded through me.

'Oh, here's your taxi,' I said.

I saw the disappointment in her eyes as she glanced at it. She hitched her bag onto her shoulder, then stepped forward and planted a kiss on my cheek.

'Goodnight Nick,' she said. Then she climbed into the taxi and left.

I waited until the lights of the car had disappeared round the corner before I started walking. It had turned chilly this evening, and I stuffed my hands in my pockets and put my head down against the stiff breeze. It was still early, only just after nine o'clock and I felt bad that I'd dismissed Katy so quickly after we'd finished eating. Should I have offered to take her for a drink, or go for a walk?

But I needed to clear my head, and the half-hour walk home felt like a good time to do that.

The date had been nice, more so than I'd expected. Katy was lovely, and I could see why Andy had thought we might like each other. I'd even managed to avoid talking too much about Dawn.

But there was no spark, not helped by the fact that I'd spent most of the time thinking about Emma. What would it be like to go for dinner with her, to sit across from each other in a candlelit restaurant, holding hands across the table, gazing into each other's eyes? To leave together, to share a kiss? To go to bed together—

Stop it, Nick.

Poor Katy. She deserved someone who wasn't hung up on a woman he could never have.

I shoved my hands deeper into my pockets. I was almost halfway home when I passed the entrance to the park. I slowed down, wondering whether to go inside. It was pitch black, but I could hear a noise, a rumble of voices, in the distance, and I stopped and listened for a moment. What was that?

I pushed the gate open, my steps quickening as I followed the path towards the sound. I barely glanced at the bandstand on my left, and soon I could see lights shining through the darkness too. I could make out crowds of people, and then a stage, lit up from above. I stopped.

This was the open-air theatre Emma had mentioned. I'd never been here before, at least not when something was playing. I moved closer, the makeshift stage slowly coming into focus.

A sign was propped up a few feet away and I headed towards it, peering down to make out the words.

I knew what it was going to say before I saw it, and my heart stopped beating when I realised its significance.

The Importance of Being Earnest, a play by Oscar Wilde

I played Cecily Cardew in The Importance of Being Ernest.

Emma's words rang in my ears and I felt dizzy. Emma was here, right now, on that stage, just a few feet away from me.

She was right here.

My breath felt tight in my chest as I inched forward, closer and closer towards the back of the crowd, squinting through the darkness. My heart thumped wildly. I shouldn't be doing this. Seeing Emma now, aged just seventeen, would only reinforce to me how wrong this whole thing was.

And yet I couldn't leave either.

I hardly dared breathe as I stared at the stage, glancing nervously at the wings to see whether she was lurking in the shadows. And then, she appeared.

I knew I should leave, but I was rooted to the spot.

My chest felt tight, my pulse thumped wildly as I watched, her pale skin and flaming red hair so familiar to me. I had no idea how long I stood there in the cool night air, but as the play came to an end it took everything I had not to call out her name.

The stage emptied, and the crowd slowly began to leave. A wind had got up and I shivered as it cooled my skin, but still I didn't move.

Emma was here and she was real.

'Excuse me, sir, could you make your way towards the exit now please,' a voice called and I turned with a start. What was I still doing here?

'Sorry,' I mumbled. And suddenly, as though a spell had been broken, I knew I needed to get out of there.

I turned and followed the last of the lingering audience into the darkness of the park. I pulled the collar of my jacket up and started walking – and then stopped dead. Because there was Emma, right in front of me. Standing between two people who were clearly her parents, her dad on one side, her mum on the other.

'I'm so proud of you,' I heard her dad say, and Emma's face lit up. And then she looked at me and our eyes locked and I could barely breathe.

She looked away again, turned back to her dad and walked right past me, as though I wasn't there.

And then she was gone.

* * *

I lay in bed for a long time that night, unable to shake the image of seventeen-year-old Emma from my mind.

As amazing as it had been to see her, it had also brought home to me how wrong this whole thing was. I might not want to date anyone else yet, but I had to end this thing – whatever this thing was – with Emma. I was thirty-one and she was seventeen. Just a girl.

I would tell her when I saw her in a couple of days' time.

It was the only thing I could do.

11

EMMA

'I think we should stop meeting up.'

I stared at Nick for several seconds before what he said sank in.

'What, for good?'

'Yes.' He was looking everywhere except at me, and I felt a spark of anger flare through me.

'You don't get to decide that.'

Finally, he met my gaze. 'It's wrong, Emma. We both need to move on.'

I searched his eyes, his face. 'Did you meet someone?'

'What? No!' He was so outraged it was clear he was telling the truth. But obviously something had happened, and I wasn't letting him off that easily.

'How did your date go then?'

He shrugged. 'It was fine. We're not seeing each other again. What about yours?'

'Pretty much the same.' I shuffled slightly closer to him and he flinched. 'Why are you being like this?' I said.

'I'm not being like anything. I thought we'd agreed that we

both need to move on, that's all, and we can't exactly do that if we're still meeting up all the time. So I just think we should call it a day.'

'Is that really what you want?' My chest felt tight at the thought of walking away from here and never seeing him again, and I couldn't catch my breath.

He didn't reply for a long time and I was beginning to wonder whether he'd heard me at all. I was about to say something else when he finally spoke.

'It's not what I want at all. But I have to.'

I put my hand on his arm and he flinched again. Was it because of the usual spark, or was he repulsed by me?

'Please tell me what's happened,' I said.

Slowly, he turned his head. His eyes were heavy with sadness. 'I made a mistake,' he said. I waited. He looked back down at his lap and drew in a long breath of air. 'I went to see you.'

I felt my heart skitter, and my skin fizzled. 'What do you mean?'

He cleared his throat. 'I walked past the open-air theatre.' He looked at me again and I knew what he was going to say before he said the words out loud. 'I saw *The Importance of Being Earnest*.'

'April 1999,' I whispered, and he nodded. I pulled my hand away from his and wrapped it round myself. 'And now you're freaked out because I'm only seventeen in 1999. Am I right?'

He nodded. 'You were with your parents,' he said. 'You're a *child*.'

'But I'm not. I'm not a child right here, right now, where we are. Together.' A thought occurred to me then. 'I nearly looked for you the other day but then changed my mind because I remembered how much you were against it. But if I did find you now, I'd still be an adult and the age gap wouldn't be weird then.'

He shook his head. 'It just felt so wrong,' he said, softly. 'I shouldn't have gone.'

A silence fell between us. If Nick really meant what he said, that he didn't think we should see each other any more, then he had to be the one to get up and walk away.

But he stayed.

The space between us felt charged with energy. I tried to imagine coming back here one day and him not being here. Tried to imagine him never being here again, never seeing his face again, and it made me feel overwhelmingly sad.

'I came here,' I said.

His head snapped round and I looked at him. The lines etched into his forehead, the dimple in his chin, and I longed to reach out and press my hand to his face. I held myself back.

'What do you mean?'

'I came here the other day just to see how it felt without you. I wondered whether I'd feel you here at all.'

'And did you?'

I shook my head. 'No.'

'I came too.'

'When?'

'A couple of days ago, just before my date.' He shook his head. 'I don't know what I was expecting, but I felt nothing out of the ordinary either.'

'I can't stop thinking about you.' I'd been wanting to say it since we arrived, but Nick had thrown a curve ball into the conversation. But if he did still want to stop seeing me, I needed to tell him how I felt first. That he filled my thoughts all the time, that when I was at work talking to clients he was on my mind; that when I'd been on the date with Aaron I'd wished it was him opposite me instead. That he was the first person I thought about when I woke up in the morning and the last person I thought about as I fell asleep at night.

'I sometimes try and picture you in the house,' he said.

'I do too.'

I felt him shift beside me so that our thighs were almost touching. The air crackled.

'I don't know what to do,' he said.

'Let's have a date.'

'What?'

I still didn't dare look at him, but this was what I'd come here to say today, and I wanted to get it out before I changed my mind.

'We tried dates with other people and they didn't work.' I took a deep breath. 'I kept thinking about you the whole time, which meant that no matter what poor old Aaron did, it would never be enough. Because he would never be you. So, I thought, why don't we have a date together. Right here.'

'Here?'

I finally turned to look at him. 'It has to be here, we can't be together anywhere else. But if we do it one evening when it's dark and everyone else has gone home then we should have the park to ourselves. And I know we see each other here anyway, but a date would be different. It would be more special.' I looked down at where our hands sat beside each other's on the bench and I inched mine closer until our little fingers touched. He moved his on top and linked it through. I shivered at his touch and looked up to meet his eyes. 'So, what do you say?'

He hesitated, and I held my breath, expectant. Then he said:

'I say yes.'

12

NICK

Until a few days ago, I'd never been on a formal date. Dawn and I had been together since we were practically children so it had never even really been something that had crossed my mind. And as I got ready for my date with Emma, I bubbled with an excitement I hadn't felt in a long, long time.

I hadn't told Andy about it. I knew what he'd say – that there was no point, that it couldn't go anywhere, that I was just prolonging the agony of saying goodbye. And even though deep down I knew he was completely right, I wanted to do it anyway.

Because despite what I'd told Emma, I wasn't ready to call this a day just yet. Not until we'd explored all options.

We just needed more time.

I had strict instructions from Emma about what to bring. She was bringing the food and some music, I was bringing the wine and a couple of blankets.

The day passed so excruciatingly slowly that there were a couple of times when I had to check it hadn't ground to a halt entirely. Who knew what tricks time would play with me now?

But finally, seven o'clock arrived. We'd arranged to meet at seven thirty, when we were fairly sure that, in April, most people would have gone home and nobody would disturb us. The last thing we needed was for someone to come into the bandstand while we were there, bringing our date to an abrupt end.

I shoved two blankets into my rucksack – one was a checked one that Dawn had wrapped herself in after chemo and it made my heart ache at the memory – and got the two bottles of champagne I'd bought out of the fridge and put them in a cool bag with a couple of ice blocks. It was still light outside, but clouds were gathering on the horizon. I wondered what the weather was like in 2019.

As I walked towards the park gates, I tried to keep my mind from spiralling. Even though Emma and I had met several times over the last few weeks, this felt like we were taking the next step. Except neither of us knew what that might mean for us. Whether it could even mean anything at all.

I was also trying not to think about kissing her. Since that first time a couple of weeks before, we hadn't kissed again. But I could still remember the explosion in my veins as our lips touched, and feel the electricity spark along my skin. Would we kiss again tonight – and would it be the same the second time round? I shivered in anticipation.

I turned the corner and the bandstand was in sight. I knew now not to feel worried when it looked empty, but I still felt a beat of anxiety in the split second before I stepped up onto the raised platform. What if she'd changed her mind?

'Hey,' she said, appearing instantly. She stepped forward, a shy smile on her face. It was cloudy here, but where Emma was the sun was shining and the low light of the late evening sun caught in her hair so that she looked as though she was illuminated from the inside.

'You look absolutely fucking radiant,' I said, before my mind could even think about what I was saying.

'Thank you,' she said, glancing down at herself as a faint blush rose on her cheeks. She was wearing a long red dress that trailed on the ground and a short leather jacket. Trainers poked out from beneath the bottom of her skirt. I felt underdressed in my checked shirt and jeans.

We stood for a moment, staring at each other. Then she turned and pointed behind her. 'I've put up fairy lights, can you see them?' she said.

'Oh, I can!' I said. The string of lights was strung along the rickety old roof, giving the tired old place a magical look.

'I wasn't sure if you would be able to,' she said. 'I'm still surprised by how this thing works every day.'

'Me too.' I placed my bag on the bench and unzipped it. 'I've got blankets,' I said, handing her one. 'And I have champagne!' I handed her a bottle with a flourish.

'Ooh, you went posh,' she said.

I shrugged. 'It feels like a special occasion,' I said.

'It really does, doesn't it?' she said, quietly.

We bustled about for a few seconds, Emma laying out the rest of the food on the picnic blanket she'd brought, me trying to help. Tubs of houmous, salsa, cream cheese, a packet of smoked salmon, olives, a baguette, packets of crisps in shiny packets, some raspberries, a box of chocolates. 'Thank you, this look amazing,' I said.

'I wasn't sure what you'd like so I just chose a bit of everything,' she said.

'It's perfect.'

'Do you want to sit on the blanket on the floor, or would you prefer the bench?'

I glanced down at the dusty floor, covered in old leaves and bird droppings and a couple of rusty cans. 'Is the floor nice over there?' I said.

'It's not bad,' she said.

'It's pretty gross here.'

She grinned. 'Let's sit here then.'

We sat side by side on the bench. I suddenly felt very shy, and as I stared out into the darkening evening, I tried to work out what to say.

'I haven't been able to stop thinking about this all day,' Emma said.

'Me neither,' I admitted. I turned to look at her and she was already watching me, her eyes roaming over my face. I felt my skin flush.

'I don't really know how to do this,' I said.

'Neither do I,' she whispered. 'But there is something we could do to break the tension.'

'Oh?' I said. And then her lips were on mine and I felt my whole body fill with warmth, a deep, sparkling glow that spread to the very tips of my fingers and toes. I felt like I was alight, as though I could float up from this rickety bench and soar into the sky. I never wanted it to end.

When she finally pulled away, our faces hovered, inches apart. I felt her breath on my skin, could hear her breathing. The air seemed to dance, charged with energy. I held my breath, not daring to break the moment.

'Do you feel it too?' she whispered. I nodded. 'It's different, isn't it?' I nodded again, unable to find any words to describe how kissing her felt.

'Do you think...' She stopped and looked down. I raised my hand to her chin and tilted it gently so she was looking into my eyes again. I felt a pull in my belly, a tug of desire. 'What do you think happens between us when we touch?' she said, her eyes wide and searching.

'I don't know. But it feels...' I searched for the right word, and settled on: 'otherworldly.'

She nodded, a smile spreading across her face. 'That's exactly it,' she said. 'Otherworldly.'

A dog barking interrupted my thoughts and I pulled away. 'Shall we have a drink,' I said, reaching for the bottle. I was glad of the distraction because the tension between us felt unbearable and I needed to take a moment. I popped the cork and watched it fly out across the grass, then filled the plastic glasses I'd brought. Bubbles fizzed over the top and splashed onto the rug and Emma laughed. I held my glass up, and Emma did the same.

'I don't know what's going to happen here, but let's just drink to us.'

'To us,' she said. 'Here. Tonight. Together.'

13

EMMA

Had I died and gone to Heaven?

I'd been excited and nervous about this date all day, and when Nick arrived my stomach had flipped with desire.

I hadn't planned to kiss him but in the moment the urge had been overwhelming. And when I did – oh my God. It honestly felt as though my insides had turned to liquid and my skin was on fire.

And even though I wanted to make this a proper date, all I could think about afterwards as we chewed our bread and nibbled on crisps and talked was that kiss – and about kissing Nick again. My body craved it, needed it.

What was *wrong* with me?

How was I ever going to be able to let this feeling go and get on with a life without it?

'Emma?'

Nick looked as though he'd been talking to me for some time and was waiting for an answer. I swallowed my mouthful of bread. 'Sorry, I was miles away,' I said, feeling my face flush. 'What did you say?'

'I was just wondering whether I should open the other bottle of champagne.'

'Oh, we've drunk a whole bottle already?' No wonder my head felt a little spinny.

'Yep. Shall I?'

'Go on.' I watched him as he popped the cork and poured the liquid carefully into the glasses. The park was in complete darkness now and a quick glance at my phone revealed it was nearly nine o'clock.

I pulled the blanket over my knees. 'Want to share?' I said.

'Sure,' he said, giving it a tug closer to him. My knees went with it and brushed against his and the air left my lungs.

It felt as though the air was charged tonight, as though one spark and it might all go up in flames. Was he feeling it too?

I shifted my weight away from him, trying to concentrate. But then I noticed that he was watching me intently. I caught his gaze.

'What are you thinking about?' he said.

I shrugged. There was no way I could tell him the truth. 'Just how nice this is.'

He raised his eyebrows. 'Nice, hey?'

'Yep.' I grinned.

He took a sip from his cup and looked away, out across the park.

'What's it like?' he said.

'What's what like?'

'In 2019.'

I hesitated. He'd already told me he didn't want me to tell him anything about the future. 'What do you want to know?'

'I don't know. It's weird, thinking about the future. And most of the time I try not to. But it strikes me, tonight, that if we want to spend more time together, I should probably try and at least understand a bit more about the world you're living in.' He shrugged. 'You know all about mine.'

'It's probably not as different as you think,' I said.

'I bet it's changed more than you realise.' He looked at me. 'I mean, your phone, for a start. I have a mobile phone, and honestly it feels pretty miraculous. But yours seems... I don't know. Like something from another planet. So I guess I just want to know what else has changed.'

I let out a breath. What could I tell him? 'Well, everyday life isn't much different, but I guess work has changed a lot.' I paused, thinking. 'Everything is done on computers now, and nobody can imagine how we did our jobs without the internet and emails.' I screwed up my nose, trying to remember 1999. 'I guess that's the same for you though, right?'

'Not so much. I mean, the kids at school have PCs to work on if they want to, but only in the computer suite.'

'God, yes, I forgot about that. We have laptops now. I take mine everywhere with me and can work on it wherever I am. And all the kids have them at school too.'

'Wow. What else?'

I closed my eyes and tried to think. The biggest change for me in those twenty years was that I'd grown from a girl into a woman, but that wasn't what Nick wanted to know. 'The Queen is still alive,' I said. 'Boris Johnson is prime minister, and the UK is about to leave the EU.'

'Wait what?'

'Yep. It's an unmitigated disaster, but that's where we are.' I wracked my brains. 'I told you about Woolworths closing. Loads of shops have closed because people do most of their shopping online.'

'The same way they do their dating then?' he said. I glanced at him and smiled. 'Yep, pretty much.'

'It sounds like a soulless wasteland.'

I shuffled round to face him. 'I guess it does, but it's really not as bad as it sounds. In a lot of ways doing everything online makes life a bit easier. But the dating thing – yeah. It's not for me, I realised.'

'No, me neither.'

We fell into silence.

'Actually, I don't think I do want to know any more,' he said. 'Do you mind? It feels a bit weird.'

'Course not.'

'Do you ever think about whether you would have done things differently if you'd have known Greg was going to die?'

My breath caught in my throat. Where had that come from? I took my time to formulate an answer. 'After he died, I thought about it all the time,' I said, slowly. 'I tortured myself, thinking about what I should have said or done differently, or about the things I wish we'd done but that we'd never got round to. But then I realised that's the way to go mad. Because you can't live with regrets and what-ifs. You can only live with what you've got and what you've done.'

'You're right.' He ran his hand down his face. 'I mean, I knew Dawn was dying, and yet there was nothing I would have changed about our last year together. So maybe not knowing the future is better, because you just live your life the way you want to, and do the things you feel are right.'

His hand met mine under the blanket and our fingers entwined. Heat filled me again and I moved closer to him, unable to think about anything else. He must have moved too because suddenly we were right beside each other, currents running between us, fizzing and sparking, and our noses almost touching. I could hear him breathing, feel the warmth of his breath on my face and I stared deep into his eyes. And then my vision was filled and his lips touched mine and it was everything, just me and Nick and nothing else anywhere in space and time.

Our bodies pressed together but it still wasn't enough. I needed him closer. I climbed on top of him as his hands ran over my arms, across my chest, round my back. I pressed my palms against his chest and heard him take a sharp intake of breath, then slid one hand round the back of his head and pulled him closer. The need for him was urgent, primal, and the rest of the world fell away. I no longer cared that we were in the park, in a public place. I no longer wondered what people might see if they walked past, all my thoughts filled with nothing but him and feeling him closer. Besides, I felt safe in the knowledge that, even if they did come inside to find out what was going on, they wouldn't be able to see both of us.

He pulled his lips away and breathed something into my neck. My body shuddered and I leaned down to hear him better.

'Should we stop?' he whispered, his voice hoarse.

I shook my head and pressed my lips into his neck. He groaned, then ran his hand down over my waist, and pulled my skirt up. He slipped his hand into my underwear and I gasped, and reached for his belt. My long skirt covered everything but I no longer cared anyway.

Because I needed him.

14

NICK

We lay on the floor of the bandstand, side by side. My hand gripped Emma's, and we were both staring up at the roof. My heart was pounding against my ribs and my whole body tingled. I felt as though I'd had an out-of-body experience.

Perhaps I had.

'I never imagined physics could feel like that,' Emma said. A laughed erupted from me.

'Don't you mean biology,' I said, turning to look at her.

'Nope, definitely physics.' She grinned and turned to face me. 'Something about the atoms between you and me – the, I don't know, space and time or whatever is broken. That's how we can be together, and even though I don't have a clue how it works or why, if it feels like that then I want more of it.'

'Me too.' Her eyes sparkled in the glow from the fairy lights. I looked away, back at the stars. I could only see a small slice of the night sky through the gap in the roof where the beams had rotted away, but I pictured them stretching out into infinity, further than we would ever be able to see, distances far beyond our comprehension. Was there life on another one of these infinite planets or stars, somewhere else where something as incredible, as mind-bending – as *impossible* – as what had just happened here, on earth? Surely there must be, because why would we be the only ones who'd been chosen?

It was a blessing and a curse, what Emma and I had found. Because on the one hand it was the most amazing connection I'd ever had with anyone – except Dawn, who I'd loved with all of my young heart. But on the other hand, we both knew we could never be together.

We were impossible.

Life was so unfair.

'Nick?'

I turned my head. Emma was watching me with a smile on her face.

'Hey,' I said.

She shuffled round to face me, propping herself up on her elbow. 'As much as I could stay here all night – actually I could stay here for the rest of my life if it meant I didn't have to leave you – I think I have to go home now.'

She lay her hand on my chest and the space around my heart filled with warmth, radiating outwards like a heartbeat. 'You're probably right,' I said, the words like sawdust in my mouth. 'Apart from anything else if we stay here much longer we might get arrested for indecent exposure or something.'

'If I don't freeze to death first.'

I sat up too, the blanket still covering our legs. Our fingers were still entwined, a pulse beating between us.

'I don't want to date anyone else,' I said.

'Christ, me neither.' She looked at me, her eyes wide. 'So I guess we'll do this again then, shall we?'

I felt heat rise in my face. 'Well maybe not exactly this.'

She puffed out her cheeks. 'I wish...' She fiddled with the blanket, twirling it round in her fingers. 'I wish we could be somewhere else.'

'I know. I do too.'

She lifted her hand and ran her finger across my jawline, down my neck and shoulders to settle back on my chest. 'We'll find a way,' she whispered.

And in that moment, I would have given anything for that to be true.

* * *

Leaving was harder than ever this time, both of us aware of a line we'd crossed, and wondering whether the universe, or whatever was controlling this thing, would let us meet again.

'I can't wait too long to see you again. Shall we meet at the same time on Monday?' she said just before we parted ways.

'It's a date,' I'd agreed.

Now, back at home, I couldn't stop thinking about her. I couldn't get the image of Emma on top of me out of my mind, of her body wrapped round mine. I still tingled from what had happened between us, and I felt as though I was floating above my whole body. We hadn't even known it was possible, and yet in the moment it had felt like the most natural and incredible thing in the world.

But, at the same time, there was a heaviness inside me, pressing down somewhere deep in my belly. Because I couldn't stop thinking about what Emma said, all those weeks ago, about coming to find me in 2019.

If I asked her to look for me at least I'd have the hope that one day, in twenty years' time, we could be together. Because if she didn't, my life would feel empty without her in it forever.

Except the reason I'd begged her not to still stood: if she found out that something terrible had happened to me between now and then – if she found out I was ill, or worse – I didn't know how I'd be able to carry on living my life.

15

EMMA

When Rachel opened the door, I was completely drenched.

'What the hell happened to you?' she said, bundling me inside. I stood dripping all over her beautiful tiled hallway while she ran to find a towel.

'Here,' she said.

I rubbed it over my hair and down my arms, then slipped my soaking wet trainers off.

'Thanks,' I said.

She stood watching me, not making a move.

'Are you going to tell me what's happened or should I try and guess?' she said.

'Can we go inside?'

A frown flitted across her forehead but then she nodded and motioned for me to follow her into the kitchen.

'Iain's taken the kids to soft play so we've got the place to ourselves.' I climbed onto a bar stool and waited as Rachel flicked the kettle on and found some mugs. Then she turned round and folded her arms across her chest. 'So come on, out with it. Are you finally going to spill the details about your date?'

Her question took me by surprise. In the excitement of every-thing that had happened with Nick, I'd completely forgotten about the date with Aaron. Rachel had messaged me for details a couple of times, but I hadn't replied yet, unsure what to tell her. Now, the game was up.

'No,' I said, leaning against the counter. My heart thumped wildly in my chest and I stared down at my hands clenched in front of me. 'It's about Nick.'

'Nick? But I thought...' She let out a sigh of frustration and I looked up at her.

'That we'd agreed to date other people?'

'Exactly.' She peered at me. 'Did you even go on the date with Aaron?'

'I did. And it was fine. He was lovely.'

'So what's happened?'

'I slept with Nick.'

The silence that filled the room was deafening. The kettle reached its crescendo and clicked off, and the rain pounded against the window. Rachel pulled out a stool and sat down.

'I'm sorry, what? When?'

'Last night. And it was the most amazing thing that's ever happened to me,' I said, my voice cracking.

'So how...' She rubbed her hand over her face and shook her head. 'How is that even possible?'

'I honestly have no idea.'

She stared at me, then a grinned spread across her face. 'Oh my *God*.'

'I know.' I felt laughter bubble up inside me and burst out. Before I knew it, we were both laughing uncontrollably, tears rolling down our faces. Just as I thought it was about to stop, I'd look at Rachel and start all over again.

Finally, it began to subside and I tried to regain some control. 'I'm sorry,' I said, wiping away my tears.

She stood suddenly. 'Forget tea, we need a proper drink,' she said, and marched over to the fridge. 'Bottle of Prosecco all right? There's not much else, unless you want a Fruit Shoot?'

'Prosecco is good,' I said.

Drinks poured, Rachel sat back down opposite me. 'Now, what is it you need my help with?'

I took a gulp, preparing myself. 'I want to look for him.'

'But... didn't he ask you not to?'

'Yes, he did. And I understand his reasons. But things have changed now. We slept together, Rach, and it was... it was unlike anything I've ever felt before. It was mind-blowing.'

'That'll be the twenty years between you, it's the best way to have mind-blowing sex. I read it in *Cosmo*.'

'It's not funny.'

She looked at me and shook her head. 'God I'm sorry, Ems. I'm just bloody jealous.'

'*Jealous?* What on earth of?'

She shrugged and didn't meet my eye. 'Mind-blowing sex.' She let out a sigh. 'It's been a while since me and Iain... you know.'

'Oh Rach,' I said, reaching across and covering her hand with mine. 'It'll just be a blip. You're great together.'

'Yeah, I know. I just feel so... deeply unsexy all the time.'

'You, unsexy? You're kidding me right? You're the sexiest woman I know. If I wasn't straight I'd definitely want to screw you.'

She finally looked at me and smiled. 'Thanks, Em. But I definitely wouldn't want to shag you.'

I laughed. 'Charming. I'm serious though. This situation, it's nothing to be jealous of. It's torture.'

'I know. And I'm sorry for making this about me.'

'Don't be daft.'

She pulled her hand away and took a sip of her wine. 'Anyway, tell me more. What exactly do you want to do? What's the aim?'

I knew what she meant. If 1999 Nick had asked me not to look for him, then he was unlikely to be open to me turning up on his doorstep in 2019 either. Chances are he would slam the door in my face or, worse, seeing him in real life now would somehow break the spell between us. Plus, of course, there was the other possibility to consider: if Nick hadn't tried to look for me in 2019, then he was right – there was a strong chance that it was because he wasn't around any more.

And yet I couldn't get the idea out of my mind and I knew that, unless I tried, I never would.

'I need to look for him. I can't live the rest of my life wondering whether we could have made a go of things.'

'What if you do find him and he's angry with you?'

I'd thought about it. Of course I had. 'Then I'll just have to accept that.'

'And if we can't find him? What will you do then?'

Her meaning hung heavy in the air, the elephant in the room.

'Then I'll deal with it.'

Rachel studied me a moment longer, then nodded. 'Then let's do it.'

* * *

An hour later, I closed Rachel's laptop with trembling hands. A heavy weight pressed on my heart, and I took a deep, shaky breath in.

'Drink this.' Rachel put a glass of something amber in front of me and without even asking what it was I tipped it down my throat. It burned, like a fire inside me.

'I should have listened to him.'

She wrapped her arms around me from behind and pressed her cheek against my back. 'I'm so sorry,' she whispered.

A tear tracked down my cheek and I swiped it away. I had no right to cry about this. It was all my own doing.

I'd been so sure I was doing the right thing, looking for Nick in 2019. I'd been so confident that he would be fine, that he'd be living his best life and that I'd find out all kinds of details of what he'd been up to over the last twenty years. Despite what I'd said, the worst I'd imagined was that he'd be happily married and I'd have to live knowing he was unattainable. But I could handle that. It was the not-knowing I couldn't handle.

But that's not what our search had found.

Just like last time, his name didn't bring anything up at all, so we'd narrowed it down, typing in 'teacher' and 'London'.

And then I'd seen it. A few pages down, but there it was.

An article in the local paper, dated 13 March 2006.

Local teacher named as victim of fatal Euston train crash

I'd known even before I clicked on it what I was going to see, but by then there was no choice but to find out more. And when the page loaded, my breath had left my body. Because there was a photo of Nick, smiling into the camera, his hair shorter than now, his face slightly more lined, but undeniably Nick.

It was the caption underneath that took my breath from me: 'Popular maths teacher Nick Flynn died at the scene in the Euston train crash on Sunday.'

I couldn't speak.

Rachel pulled away from me and dragged a bar stool over to

sit beside me. She pushed my hair back from my face and tucked it behind my ear.

'What have I done?' I whispered.

'You couldn't have known.'

'But he specifically asked me not to. He said he didn't want to know. And this is why.'

'You don't have to tell him.'

I shook my head. 'I won't tell him. But I don't know...' I sniffed. 'I don't know whether I can keep this from him. I don't think I'm that good an actor.'

I tried to picture how I would act when I saw Nick again as arranged the following day. Would I be able to pretend nothing had changed, that I hadn't found out anything? I mean, I hadn't mentioned that I was going to look him up again. And if I'd found him and gone to look for him in real life then I hadn't even planned to tell him that either, but just wait for him to discover it when he got to 2019.

But this was different. This was huge.

How could I keep it from him, that he was going to die?

And yet at the same time, I also knew that I could never tell him. Because knowing it would destroy his life.

I realised I was crying, huge, uncontrollable sobs wracking my body, and Rachel pulled me to her and held me and let me cry. I didn't think I was ever going to stop.

Why hadn't I listened to Nick? I'd ruined everything.

* * *

For the first time since I'd met Nick, I was nervous about seeing him. We'd arranged to meet on Monday at 5 p.m. as usual, but I was early, pacing up and down in front of the bandstand trying to work out how to arrange my face.

'You can do this,' Rachel had assured me when she rang before I left.

'I'm not sure I can,' I said.

But if I wanted to keep seeing Nick, which I desperately did, then I had to get this right.

I checked my phone again. Three minutes to five.

I took a deep breath, walked up the path and stepped up onto the bandstand.

He wasn't here.

I sat, my leg jiggling beneath me. I hated waiting, and it was even worse that I had no way of checking to see if he was on his way. My leg continued to bounce and I hung my head between my knees.

That's how I was sitting when Nick arrived. 'I'm sorry I'm late,' he said, bursting onto the bandstand full of nervous energy. He was soaked through, his hair plastered to his head, his shirt sticking to his body. 'It started pissing it down just as I left work but I didn't have time to go home and change.' When he finally looked at me, he frowned. 'Is everything okay? I really am sorry for being late.'

'I'm fine,' I said, forcing a smile. 'I just didn't sleep very well last night.'

'Oh no.' He sat down beside me, water dripping from his hair into his eyes. He looked so handsome I wanted to lean over and kiss him, but held myself back. 'Do you want to go home and get some sleep? We could do this tomorrow instead?'

I shook my head. 'No, I'll be okay. I've been looking forward to seeing you after...' I trailed off shyly.

A flush crept up Nick's face too. 'Yeah, me too. It was pretty... spectacular, wasn't it?'

I nodded, all the words I was trying not to say to him stuck in my throat. I looked down at the floor because looking at him just reminded me of the image of his happy face peering out from the newspaper article, blissfully unaware of his fate.

Nick Flynn died at the scene.

The words kept ticker-taping through my mind, and I shook them away, trying to dislodge them. I had to try and forget what I'd read.

It wasn't going to be easy.

'It was amazing,' I said.

'I wish we could go somewhere else to be together.'

Oh, how I wished the same. Not being able to meet Nick wherever and whenever I wanted; to enjoy days out together, snuggle up together, to be normal – it was hell. I wished with all my heart that we'd met under any other circumstances.

And yet, if things had been different between us, we would probably never have met at all.

I turned to look at him and noticed he was studying me closely.

'What?' I said.

'You seem... different,' he said. He was still staring at me and I turned away, afraid my face might give me away.

'It's just tiredness. Honestly.'

'Are you sure? You seem very down. You haven't... I don't know. Met someone else, have you?'

'Since two days ago?' I gave a sad smile. 'No, I haven't met anyone else. I haven't exactly been looking.'

'Right.' He looked down at his trousers and plucked at an imaginary thread. My stomach squeezed with anxiety. I needed to pull myself together. Perhaps I should ask him what he'd been up to. Yes, that would be a normal conversation opener. I opened my mouth to speak but before I could say a word, he spoke again.

'Something has happened, hasn't it?'

I don't know what my face did, but it clearly wasn't good,

because he took a sharp intake of breath and moved away from me so the gap between us widened. 'You've tried to find me, haven't you?'

'No, I wouldn't—'

'And it's bad news, isn't it?'

'No!' I said, too quickly. But the look on his face told me he didn't believe me. I wanted to rewind time, to go back to five minutes ago when he first arrived and start all over again. I wanted to smile and be happy, not morose and untalkative. Of course he could tell there was something wrong, I had never been like this with him.

And of course there was only really one thing it could be, one thing that I couldn't admit to.

But I had to try and convince him he was wrong, otherwise things would be over between us before they'd even got started. Not to mention what it would do to him, if he even suspected that bad news was coming his way.

'There's no bad news,' I said, hoping my voice didn't betray me. I reached my hand out to take his, but he snatched it away and inched even further along the bench away from me.

'I don't think I believe you,' he whispered.

'But I—'

He shook his head. 'You see, this is why I asked you – *begged* you – not to go looking for me.' He buried his face in his hands. 'I can't... I don't know...'

I couldn't speak. I didn't mean I couldn't find the words, I meant I physically couldn't get my throat to make any noise. Because how could I lie to his face and tell him everything was fine, when I knew it wasn't?

And yet how could I tell him the truth?

He stood suddenly, the air displacing around him. I looked up. He was silhouetted against the sky and I couldn't see the expression on his face. But his body was hunched and tense, his hands in fists at his side. I stood too, facing him.

'Where are you going?' I said.

'I can't do this,' he said, his voice tight.

'Please,' I whispered. 'Don't go. Not like this.'

He didn't answer or move. I took a step towards him. I could make out his eyes from this distance, see the pain in them, and I wanted to reach out for him, to hold him in my arms and beg him to forgive me. But I couldn't so instead I just stood there, arms hanging limply at my sides.

'I've fucked up,' I said, when it became clear he wasn't going to say anything. I stared down at the floor. 'I've fucked up and I'm so sorry.'

I heard a noise coming from him and I looked up sharply. His eyes were filled with tears. He looked broken.

I'd broken him. I'd broken us.

'I should go, shouldn't I?' I said, softly.

He sniffed and swiped his hand across his face. I noticed it was trembling. 'I think it's probably best if we both go,' he said. His voice sounded rough, as though his throat was trying to stop him getting the words out.

I felt my insides collapse, folding in on themselves.

I'd ruined everything, any chance of happiness we might have been able to find, and all because I couldn't stop being nosey. I just couldn't help myself and now, this. This was all I deserved.

I bent down and picked up my bag and he did the same, slinging it over his shoulder.

'I'm sorry,' I said again, the words bouncing off the metal of the railings, barely adequate. I felt my breath catch in my chest.

'Me too,' he said. 'More than you'll ever know.'

And then, before I could say anything else, before I could ask him whether he might ever come back to find me, he turned and stepped off the bandstand and disappeared.

He was gone, and there was no way of going after him.

I dropped to my knees right there and then, curling up in a ball, no longer caring who might see me or what they might think. The pain of what I'd done, of losing him, was too much to bear and it was the only thing I could do.

I don't know how much time passed, but eventually I lifted my head and gazed up into the roof, at the slivers of sunlight slicing through the gaps, and let out a long, shaky breath. I wanted to howl to the sky and scream and shout. But this would have to do, for now.

I stood and lowered myself onto the bench. The air was cooling and I pulled on my cardigan and wrapped it round me. I didn't know whether there was any chance Nick might change his mind and come back, but I couldn't quite bring myself to give up and leave, knowing I might never see him again if I did.

Not now. Not yet.

I wasn't ready.

And so, I waited.

16

NICK

There was a hammering on the door, and I pulled the duvet further over my head to try to block out the sound. But whoever was there wasn't letting up, and eventually I swung my legs off the sofa and dragged myself up to standing. I'd been lying there so long my head spun and I noticed it was getting dark outside.

I had a fairly good idea who I was going to find at the door. It had been two nights since I'd walked away from Emma, and Andy had been trying to ring me almost every hour on the hour ever since. I'd ignored every call, eventually taken the phone off the hook.

Now, though, he was here, and I knew full well he wouldn't take no for an answer. There was no choice but to let him in.

The second I answered he stormed inside and strode into the living room.

'Jesus Christ, Nick, what's going on in here? It stinks.' He turned to me and sniffed. '*You* stink.'

I shrugged. I knew I didn't smell that fresh but that was what happened when you didn't shower for two days. I rubbed my hand over my chin. It felt rough beneath my touch.

Andy shook his head. 'I got a call from Rob from your school. He said you'd taken time off sick but that you wouldn't answer his calls, so I said I'd check up on you.' He stepped towards me. 'What on earth's happened, Nicky?' he said, his voice gentler now.

I shrugged and walked past him and slumped onto the sofa. I hadn't thought I'd cared about my appearance, but now Andy was here I felt ashamed of the way I looked and of the empty bottles and plates congealing around the edge of the sofa. I pushed the duvet to one side. Andy sat in the armchair opposite me.

He folded his arms across his chest but said nothing. I stared at a spot on the carpet, unable to meet his gaze.

'It's...' I started, but my voice was gravelly, my throat rough. I coughed, and tasted the staleness of my breath. I was about to try again when a sob erupted from me and suddenly I couldn't stop, tears pouring from me like a river, sobs wracking my body. Andy jumped up and ran to my side and pulled me into a tight hug and even though it made it difficult to breathe I didn't try to pull away or move at all, just let my big brother hold me as I let out all the tension and terror of the last few days.

When I finally stopped, I sat up straight and looked him in the eye. Even though I was sure Andy didn't completely believe me about Emma, I needed to tell him what had happened. 'Emma found something out,' I said, my voice a whisper.

'What do you mean? About you?'

I nodded, and looked back down at my lap.

'What is it, Nicky?' he said, rubbing his hand up and down my spine.

'She...' I sniffed. 'She looked me up. In 2019.'

'Oh. Didn't you ask her not to?'

I nodded.

'I assume she found out something bad?'

I shrugged. 'I think so.'

A pause. 'Nicky, look at me.'

Reluctantly, I turned to face him. I could see the confusion on his face as I met his eye. 'So you're telling me – what? That you think Emma might have found out something bad happens to you in the future, but you don't actually know for sure?'

'She didn't get a chance to tell me because I left.'

Andy looked at me for a moment longer then shook his head. 'Jesus, Nick.'

'I couldn't stay,' I said, desperate to defend myself. 'It was obvious whatever she'd found wasn't good, and I couldn't wait around to find out.'

'And you know for certain it was bad news?'

I thought about the look in Emma's eyes as she'd looked at me and knew there could be no other explanation. 'Yes.'

Andy laid his hand on my knee. 'Don't you think you should go back there and ask her? Make sure she's not lying to you, that she isn't some madwoman just trying to make you believe this is all real?'

I shook my head. 'I knew you didn't believe me. But it is real, which means that, even if I thought that was a good idea, I've got no way of getting hold of her. This is the first time we've left each other and not rearranged a time to meet again.'

Andy sighed. 'But she's usually there at 5 p.m., isn't she?'

'That's the time we usually meet, yes.'

'So go tomorrow, and the next day, and the next day until she comes. You owe it to her and to yourself to find out the truth.'

I thought about it. Imagined seeing Emma again, seeing the look on her face as she told me I'd died, or had a terminal illness, or whatever else she had discovered. I thought about what life would be like if I knew how long I had left to live, about the pressure I'd feel to make every day, every week, every month, count. How would it feel to know exactly when you were going to die? How would Dawn and I have felt if we'd have known the future when we'd first met? Would we have done anything differently?

'I just can't,' I said.

Andy said nothing for a moment and we just sat there in the darkening room in silence.

'What if I've got a brain tumour?' I said, suddenly.

'What? Why would you think that?'

It hadn't occurred to me before, but now it made perfect sense.

'Think about it,' I said. 'It would explain everything that's been happening over the last few months – the time travel, which you said yourself was impossible, the hallucinations. If this was caused by a brain tumour, it makes sense that Emma discovered I'd died of a brain tumour in a few years' time.'

'Except if that was the case, that would mean Emma doesn't exist, and so she couldn't have found anything out – and you're certain she does.' Andy leaned down and gathered the dirty plates and cups together, then stood. 'Listen, I'm going to clean this place up a bit. Why don't you go and have a shower, and then I'm taking you out for some food.'

'I don't think I can,' I said.

'You can and you will. I'm not leaving you to sit and stew in your own mess any longer. Now go.'

I did as I was told, and as I stood under the jet of hot water, I tried to clear my mind. I had to stop imagining the worst and move on. I had to try to forget the amazing connection Emma and I had, forget the spark and crackle between us even when we weren't touching, and get on with my life as though we'd never met.

After losing Dawn, I had to protect my heart in the only way I knew how.

By being alone.

PART II

17

EMMA

It had been more than a month since I'd last seen Nick, and it had been a month of hell. He hadn't come back to the bandstand that day and eventually I'd had to give up and go home. Back at the house I tried to feel his presence, the way I sometimes had before; listening for the echoes of him in the walls, trying to breathe in the molecules of him in the home where we'd both lived. But there was nothing.

Even though Rachel had told me not to, had told me that I needed to let Nick go and move on, I went back to the bandstand every evening at five o'clock just in case he came back to find me. Every day I'd step up onto the platform, my heart in my throat, my pulse pounding in my ears.

And every day my heart would drop as I'd see that the place was empty.

'I don't think he's coming back,' Rachel said gently, two weeks later.

'But he might. And what if he comes to find me and I'm not there?'

'But what if he doesn't? Are you going to wait around forever?'

I knew she was right. Of course. It didn't mean I had to like it.

It took every ounce of self-control I had to stop myself from going to the bandstand every night after that. But I did manage to stay away, and the more distance I put between me and what had happened there, the more that everything between us began to feel like a dream.

'Why don't you try going on another date?' Rachel suggested tentatively.

'Absolutely not,' I said. I'd cancelled my Tinder membership and had absolutely no intention of dating anyone for the foreseeable future. I needed time for my heart to mend.

But then an idea came to me in the middle of the night and, despite my best intentions, it proved impossible to ignore. I sat up in bed and let the idea roll around my mind, studying it from all angles, trying to work out whether there was any fault with it.

But as far as I could see, if it worked, it could just be the perfect solution. I couldn't believe I hadn't thought of it before.

I leapt out of bed and ran downstairs into the living room. On the bookshelf there were a few old notepads so I grabbed one, found a pen, and settled on the sofa. I hesitated a moment, the pen hovering over the page as I tried to work out what to say. And then I began to write.

I don't know how long I sat there for trying to get the words right, but by the time I was happy with it, sunlight was beginning to filter through the window and the birds had started their dawn chorus.

Dear Nick,

I know you're angry and you don't want to talk to me, and I understand why. But if you've found this letter PLEASE don't throw it away. There's something I need to tell you.

At 10 a.m. on Sunday 12th March 2006, you take a train into London.

Please do NOT get on that train.

I won't tell you why because I know you don't want to know any details about the future. But I wouldn't tell you this if it wasn't vitally important, so you'll just need to trust me on this one.

Don't get on that train.

Emma

I stood, stretched my arms and reread it one last time. I'd considered telling him the truth about the crash, perhaps even asking him to try and stop it happening at all – after all it's what happened in all the time travel stories I'd ever read and watched. But the more I thought about it, the more worried I was about trying to mess with the past too much – not mention that Nick categorically told me he didn't want to know anything. Besides, what could he actually have done to stop a train crashing? If he'd tried to tell anyone his fears, they would just have assumed he'd lost his mind.

Stopping him getting on the train would have to do. Now all I had to do was deliver the letter.

I ran upstairs and threw on some clothes. It was still early, about 5 a.m., but I didn't want to put it off in case I changed my mind or, more likely, Rachel tried to talk me out of it. I ran back downstairs, found an old envelope tucked away in a kitchen drawer and stuck the note inside. I wrote Nick's name carefully on the front of the envelope and sealed it, then grabbed my keys and left the house.

It was warm already, the ghost of yesterday's heat lingering in the early morning air. It was rare to be out this early and there was something soothing about the peace, about knowing that most people were still asleep behind their drawn curtains. It felt as though the world was holding its breath, waiting for something to happen.

At the entrance to the park, I hesitated. Was it sensible for a lone woman to go in here so early, with no one else around? I glanced left and right but could see no one, no strange men lurking in bushes, no one waiting to pounce.

I set off, marching along the path. The bandstand was only a few minutes away, and soon it was in sight. I stopped. My breathing was heavy, nerves stopping me from drawing in enough air. I waited until it had slowed, then started walking again. Slowly, one step at a time, each step weighed down with anticipation. My blood fizzed in my veins.

And then I was through the rose garden and at the threshold. I paused one last time. Did the air feel different here? Was there something that, if you were looking, gave away the defect that had allowed Nick and I to be together? Or was it in the air, in the molecules that surrounded me?

I still had no idea.

I took a deep breath and stepped inside. It was empty apart from some abandoned beer cans in one corner, and a piece of silver foil scrunched up at the back of the bench. I brushed it away and sat down, placing my hands either side of me, palms flat against the grain of the wood. If I concentrated hard enough, would I feel Nick here? Could I somehow conjure him, or send a message that would bring him to me?

I let out a lungful of air and buried my face in my hands. If only I knew the rules of this thing. As it was, I was flailing around in the dark.

I waited a few more minutes. It was so peaceful here this early, just me and the birds. I closed my eyes and tried to relax. When I opened my eyes, I spotted a woman outside the bandstand. Her foot was balanced on the raised floor and she was leaning forward stretching her hamstrings. I coughed, and the noise must have caught her attention because she looked at me and smiled.

'Lovely at this time of day, isn't it?' she said.

'Gorgeous,' I said.

I waited as she finished her stretches, then she gave me a little wave and jogged off down the path. As soon as she was out of sight, I stood. It was my cue to do what I came to do and get out of here.

I looked up to the ceiling. I needed to find somewhere to leave this note where it wouldn't blow away, where it wasn't easily findable, by just anyone, but where there was a strong chance that Nick might eventually see it. I stood on the bench and peered up into the beams, squinting into corners where dust and pigeon droppings gathered. Surely this whole plan wasn't about to be ruined because I couldn't find somewhere to hide the note?

And then I saw it. A little gap between the wooden upright and the balustrade, just about at eye level when you were sitting down. Even better, it was on the side that Nick normally sat on. I tucked the letter inside, making sure it was safe, then sat down and looked over to check it was visible. It was, but only just. I stood and pulled a little more of the envelope out then sat and checked again. I looked away then back. Yes, I could definitely see it. I just had to hope that, even though I was in Nick's future, the time slip somehow still worked for me, and that Nick would find it before someone else did. It was a small chance, but it was at least a chance.

I gave the letter one last tug to make sure it was secure, then I glanced round the bandstand one last time and stepped back into the park.

It was done. Now all I could do was wait and see if it was enough.

18

NICK

So many times over the last few weeks I'd gone to the park and stood looking at the bandstand, wondering whether to step inside. Would Emma be there? Would she ever be there again? Maybe she was there right now, waiting for me, hoping I'd come. Hoping she'd have the chance to explain why she did what she did. If she was, all I needed to do was to take a step, and I'd be with her.

But in the end, I hadn't been able to do it. Because I didn't see how I would ever be able to forgive her for what she'd done.

Even though I didn't know exactly what she'd discovered about me, the thought of what it *could* be haunted me throughout my days. I knew that whatever I imagined could very well be worse than the reality, in which case finding out the truth would help. But there was always the possibility that it was exactly what I feared, and once I knew, there would be no going back.

Every night I lay in bed trying to sleep, and the demons would flood my mind with images I didn't want to see.

Some were memories: of Dawn's last days, of the promises I'd made to her to go out there and live my life. Others were flashes of what might be to come, of me ill, or dying; endless possibilities cycling through my brain on a loop until I'd have to get out of bed and find something to distract me. The lack of sleep was driving me mad.

'You need to go get some help, talk to someone,' Andy told me, over and over.

I knew he was right. But the sort of help he was suggesting felt impossible. There was no way I could tell anyone about my fears – that I was afraid I was going to die some time in the next twenty years, that I was living on borrowed time – without telling them about Emma. And if I tried to explain *that* to anyone, I risked being sectioned.

So instead, I'd agreed to speak to my GP and ask for something to calm my mind and help me sleep.

It had worked too. Because now I had a prescription for three months of antidepressants, and enough sleeping tablets to sink a small ship.

I just had to hope to God it worked, because I couldn't go on like this.

I needed to get better and get on with living the rest of my life – however much of it I had left.

19

EMMA

'Oh my *God*,' Rachel whispered, when I told her what I'd done. 'Do you really think this could change things?'

'I don't know. But I had to at least try.'

She nodded. 'Okay. But now you've done this you have to put it out of your mind and get on with your life. Do you promise me?'

'I promise.'

And I was doing it. I was going to work, enjoying nights out with friends, going to the theatre, booking a holiday. I even joined a local am-dram society and was loving being on stage for the first time in years. I started to feel revived, like I really could do this.

And then, two weeks later, everything changed.

It took me a while to notice that I wasn't feeling very well. A low-level, underlying nausea that felt like I'd been reading in a car for too long. It hung around all day, only clearing by bedtime and starting all over again the next day.

And then I realised that I hadn't had a period for a while.

When I bought the test, I was fairly certain the result had to be negative. Because there was no way I could be pregnant after having sex with someone who didn't even live at the same time as me. As impossible situations went, that would be up there with the best of them.

So I wasn't particularly nervous as I peed on the stick, or as I waited for the blue line to appear, confident there would only be one line, and my sickness would be caused by something else entirely.

There were two lines.

Not once. Not even twice. But three times.

And then I knew it had to be true.

I was pregnant with Nick's baby.

* * *

For the next few days I felt like a ghost, living outside my own life. I had this enormous secret, and I couldn't tell anyone about it. Not even Rachel, because I was too scared of what she'd say. The only person I wanted to tell was Nick, and that was impossible.

But there was something else on my mind too.

There was endless information to be found online about pregnancy. Whatever you needed to know, it seemed you could find someone to help you, and there didn't appear to be a single topic that was off-limits, that hadn't been written about hundreds, thousands, millions of times. If I wanted to know how big my embryo was likely to be at two months old, I could easily find out (the size of a grape, if you really wanted to know). If I needed to find a hypnobirth expert, or a mother and baby class, or a newborn photographer, or advice on swollen ankles during pregnancy, there it was.

But the one thing I desperately needed to know was something that no expert in the world would be able to answer, and I couldn't stop thinking about it.

Would this baby even be viable? Was there any chance that it would form properly and grow into a healthy, normal baby? Would it even be possible for me to have this baby, given that its father was dead at the time it was conceived?

Imagine typing that question into Mumsnet.

I got through the next few days at work on autopilot, then hurried home and locked myself away from the world. Some evenings I stood at the door of the small box room at the top of the stairs and tried to picture a cot in there, a little chair where I would sit and rock a baby to sleep in the darkest hours of the night. Greg and I had talked about it often, had discussed what our babies would be like, what they'd be into.

'Eddie will be an actor like his mum, and Connor will be into sport like his dad,' he said, and I'd roll my eyes.

'No girls?' I said.

'Maybe one day,' he said, and winked.

And although it hadn't been this house we'd envisioned bringing them up in, our old house had had a room just like this that we'd earmarked as the nursery. One day soon.

One day.

Was this the room that Nick and Dawn had imagined as the baby's room? He told me they'd planned the nursery – had they picked out colours, bought a mobile, a cot?

Nick.

I thought about his face when he'd talked about being a dad. About how much he'd wanted a baby, how sad he'd been when he talked about the fact he and Dawn had been unable to conceive before she fell ill. Being a dad was all he'd wanted, and now he wouldn't ever know about this baby. It felt like the cruellest trick of fate.

I pushed myself off the door frame and went downstairs. The nausea had eased a little and I needed to eat something other than the endless packets of spicy Monster Munch that seemed to be the only thing I'd been able to keep down these last few days. I was just stabbing a potato with a fork when the doorbell rang. I froze. I wasn't expecting anyone, and the only person who'd come round at this time of night unannounced was Rachel. I wasn't ready to tell her what was going on yet.

I didn't move, hoping she'd leave. But the doorbell rang again, then the rap of the knocker. I heard the clatter of the letterbox, then Rachel's voice, reedy through the tiny gap in the door.

'Emma Vickers, I know you're in there. Stop ignoring me!'

The seconds ticked by. I held my breath.

'Fine. But just so you know I'll be back tomorrow, and the next day. And I'll ring you every ten minutes until you pick up. You know I will.'

The letterbox clattered shut. I was about to peer round the kitchen door to see whether she'd left when my phone buzzed.

RACHEL

Seriously, darling, I hope you're okay. I hope we're okay. Love you. R x

A wave of guilt washed over me. I knew Rachel worried about me. I should reply.

EMMA

I'm fine, just not up to talking. Thanks for caring. Love you too. E x

20

NICK

Two months was long enough, I decided. Long enough to have stayed away from the bandstand. Long enough for the pain of losing Emma to start to ease, and for the desire to go back to the place I'd always loved to return.

I didn't tell anyone I was going. I especially didn't tell Andy, because I knew what he'd have to say about it.

'You need to move on with your life, Nicky. Stop dwelling on the past and start thinking about your future.'

And although I knew he meant well, I couldn't help thinking that he hadn't said the same thing when I used to come to the bandstand to remember Dawn. For him, that was perfectly normal behaviour. Acceptable. Which told me all I needed to know about whether he'd ever actually believed me about Emma. Although he'd never said it again, he clearly still thought she'd been conning me, or at least lying to me, for whatever reason.

But why would she? And, if she had been, where was she now?

So no, I didn't want to tell him about it, because I didn't want to feel angry about it when he said what I knew he would inevitably say.

The day I decided to return was a warm June day, and as I walked through the park I tried not to think about the last time I was here, almost running in the opposite direction. Away from Emma.

It was quiet here today, hardly anyone around, and I was glad. My rucksack was making my back damp, and the sun felt hot on my head. A dog squatted under a tree, its owner glancing round furtively to see whether anyone had noticed or whether they could get away with leaving their pet's doings on the grass where young children played. When they caught my eye, I looked away, not in the mood for any kind of confrontation, and felt immediately guilty.

It didn't take me long to get to the bandstand and as it came into sight I spotted a woman sitting on the bench and for a moment my heart flipped over.

But of course I knew that, even if Emma was there, I wouldn't be able to see her from here. Which meant that this woman must be real, right now in 1999. The disappointment felt like a rock in my throat.

As I stepped inside she looked up from the book she was reading and gave me a brief smile. By the time I'd smiled back she was looking back down at her book again. I settled on the other end of the bench, the end I usually sat, and looked out into the park. I watched a young mum walking past holding hands with a toddler, a young girl no more than two or three. They were chatting animatedly, the little girl bouncing up and down excitedly and I felt a pang I hadn't felt in a long time. Becoming parents had always been so important to Dawn and me, had consumed our world for the few years before she died. And despite everything, I'd never doubted that it would happen one day. Except now, here I was, aged thirty-one, and I couldn't imagine ever meeting anyone else I'd want to be with enough to start a family with. It felt like a punch in the gut.

As the pair disappeared round the corner I looked the other way, wondering exactly where the playground was that Emma had mentioned. When had it been built? There was a clear space without any trees across the other side of the path close to the toilets and next to where the ice cream van was usually parked, perhaps it was there. I hoped they didn't cut any trees down to accommodate it. And when had they planted the rose bushes to create the rose garden that Emma had been able to see?

I tipped my head back and closed my eyes and tried to conjure Dawn's face. It was safer to think about Dawn, to remember her, than to dwell on Emma. Because although I couldn't have either of them, at least nothing had tainted my memories of Dawn. At least they were still honest and unsullied. Uncomplicated.

A shuffling sound made me open my eyes again. Beside me, the woman was getting ready to leave. I waited while she stuffed her book in her bag and looked around then, as she stepped into the park, I said, 'Have a lovely day.'

She flashed me a smile. 'You too.'

It was as she walked away that I spotted it.

It was just a flash of white at first, so tiny I thought I must have imagined it. But when I stood up and moved closer, I could see there was definitely something there. A piece of paper, wedged into the gap between the wooden post and the metal railing. I reached my hand out and tugged at it, but it didn't budge.

Intrigued, I bent down, peering into the crevice. How on earth had something got caught in there? I stuck my index finger and thumb into the gap and pinched the paper between them, tugging gently so as not to rip it. Slowly, it started to inch towards me, and after a bit more tugging, it came free. I was surprised how big it was – the size of a small letter. In fact, it *was* a letter, it seemed. How had a letter got stuck right down there?

I looked around, wondering whether someone might be missing it. The paper looked clean and pretty new. But of course, it was unlikely to have just been lost, because it had been well and truly wedged into the gap.

I looked down and turned the envelope over in my hand – and that's when I stopped dead.

My name was printed on the front in neat, handwritten letters.

Why was my name on it?

I turned it over and glanced up again. Glanced back. My heart thumped and my vision tunnelled and I slumped down onto the end of the bench, the paper shaking in my hands.

And then it hit me.

It had to be from Emma.

I pictured her, writing this letter, sealing it and bringing it here, looking for somewhere to hide it where I'd be likely to find it, and fury forked through me like lightning. How *dare* she do this. How dare she, despite the fact that I'd walked away from her knowing full well she wouldn't be able to find me again, still take it upon herself to write to me?

Hadn't I made it clear enough that I couldn't do this any more?

Hadn't she understood – even agreed with me?

I stood, searching across the park for a bin. I couldn't keep this. I'd always be tempted to open it, and no matter what she wanted to say to me, I didn't want to hear it.

But there was no bin in sight so instead I stuffed the letter into my rucksack, threw it over my shoulder, and stomped home. I'd decide what to do with it when I got there.

21

EMMA

Rachel had been staring at me for so long without saying a word that I was beginning to wonder whether she'd slipped into an alternate universe too.

I waved my hand in front of her face. 'Er, hello, earth to Rachel?'

She opened her mouth, then closed it again. Rachel and I had been friends for a long time, but I had never seen her lost for words before. Normally, she had plenty to say about everything.

'Aren't you going to say anything?' I said.

'I...' She shook her head. 'I honestly don't know what to say.'

'Congratulations might be a start?' I was beginning to feel a bit irritated, and it came out snarkier than I'd intended.

Suddenly Rachel stood, the stool she was sitting on scraping back loudly across the kitchen tiles, and threw her arms around me.

'Jesus Christ, Emma, I'm so sorry,' she said, squeezing me so tightly it was hard to breathe. She pulled away, tears shining in her eyes. 'Of *course* that's what I should have said straight away. I'm a complete twat.'

'You are, but I forgive you,' I said.

She sat back down and rested her chin in her hand, studying me.

'I just... I mean, I'm thrilled for you, obviously. But what the actual *hell*, Em. Could you have made things any more complicated for yourself?'

'I know.'

I'd left it for three more days but I'd finally got round to telling Rachel about the baby. It was hardly any surprise she'd reacted this way. It was a lot to take in.

'So how do you feel about it?' She nodded at my belly.

'I'm absolutely terrified.'

'If you're worried about doing this alone, don't be,' she said. 'You know Iain and I will always be there for you. In fact, you won't be able to get rid of us.'

'I know, thank you,' I said. 'But it's not just that.'

'Go on.'

I swallowed, unsure how to say the words out loud. 'What if...' I started. 'What if there's something wrong with this baby because...'

'Because its dad died thirteen years ago...' Rachel finished.

'That's exactly it.'

Rachel took a sip of her coffee, thinking. 'But surely if this baby wasn't meant to be, then it simply wouldn't exist. Surely the sheer fact that you conceived in the first place means that it will be fine.'

'Will you come with me, for the scan? Just in case.'

'Try stopping me,' she said, smiling.

'Thank you.' I sighed. 'I just wish I could tell Nick.'

'I know.' She gasped. 'Oh! Do you know whether he found your note?'

I shook my head. 'I haven't dared check.'

'What? Why?'

I shrugged. 'I was... I'm trying to give it long enough.'

Rachel folded her arms across her chest and gave me a stern look. 'I think three weeks is plenty of time, don't you?'

I nodded. 'I know. But even if it's gone, how am I supposed to know whether it slipped through time and was taken by him and not just by someone passing through? I mean, it's a pretty long shot.'

'You'll never know that. But we should go and at least see if it's still there or not.' She stood. 'Come on.'

My eyes widened. 'What, now?'

'No time like the present.'

She grabbed my hand and I reluctantly followed her.

* * *

I dragged my feet all the way to the park. My legs were made from rubber and I felt like I was going to throw up.

At the entrance, I stopped. 'I don't think I can do this.'

Rachel took my hand. 'You can,' she said. 'Otherwise, you'll always wonder.'

My bones thrummed with tension. 'But what if it's still there? What if he didn't find it? I mean, I have no idea of knowing whether he will even be able to see it.'

'Then we'll come back and check again tomorrow, and the next day and the next.'

I puffed out my cheeks and nodded. 'Okay fine.'

We walked the rest of the way to the bandstand in silence. It was a hot day and there was no shade, the sun beating down on our heads. Pockets of people lazed on the yellowing grass, scattered like picnic crumbs. A group of teenagers threw a frisbee back and forth without enthusiasm, the plastic disc slicing languidly through the thick air.

I ignored them all, focused on only one thing.

We arrived at the bandstand, and I hesitated before stepping up. There was a couple on the bench holding hands and laughing at something. They glanced at me and smiled.

'Hi,' they said in unison.

'Hello.' Rachel was so close behind me I could feel her breath on my neck as she spoke. I didn't move, thrown by unexpectedly finding someone else in the place I thought of as mine and Nick's. Then Rachel jabbed me in the ribs and pushed me forward. I took the final step up.

'I'm so sorry, my friend misplaced something the other day so we've just come to see if it's still here,' she said, as we crossed in front of them. 'We won't disturb you for long.'

'No worries,' the man said.

We reached the other side. My heart thumped wildly as I bent down to peer into the gap in the wooden upright where I'd tucked the letter. I couldn't see it. I leaned further forward and stuck my finger in the gap.

I turned to look at Rachel. 'It's not there,' I whispered.

She turned to the couple. 'I don't suppose you've found an envelope in here have you?' she said.

The woman frowned. 'No, I haven't, I'm sorry. Was it important?'

'No, it's fine, I'm sure it will turn up.' Rachel flashed them a smile. 'So sorry to disturb you, enjoy the rest of your evening.' Then she grabbed my hand and tugged me away, off the bandstand and towards the tree. As we reached the shade I glanced up at the initials Nick had carved all those weeks ago, back when we were still discovering exactly what magic there was between us. It felt like only yesterday, and yet also a lifetime ago.

'Do you think this means he's got it?' I said.

'I think you have to assume he has,' she said. 'Otherwise you're going to spend the rest of your life wondering.'

'So what happens now?'

'Now, we go home and see if anything has changed.'

* * *

'I'm not sure this is a good idea,' I said. The screen glowed at me, the search bar empty. I slammed the laptop shut and closed my eyes.

'What are you scared of, Em?' Rachel said, gently.

I opened my eyes and looked at her. 'Everything.' I sighed. 'I'm scared he will have found my letter and ignored it, but I'm also scared that he didn't ignore it, and I might have changed the path of the future.' I rubbed my face. 'And I'm also scared that the letter just blew away or was found by someone else and now I'll never know whether I might have made a difference.'

'I get all of that,' she said. 'But that doesn't explain why you won't look him up again.'

On the walk home from the park Rachel and I had discussed what the next stage of the plan was.

'The thing is, none of us have any idea of the rules of this thing,' I said. 'Nick and I tried to work it out, to control it, but nothing ever worked. So how am I meant to know how this next bit goes?'

'The way I see it is, if he finds the letter and decides to take your advice, then one of two things could happen,' Rachel said.

A trickle of sweat ran down my back as I waited for her to carry on.

'Either the future is changed from right now and he will still be alive and you could go and tell him about the baby. Or nothing will change until the date of the accident in 2006. Which will be 2026 for us.'

'I'm not sure that's how time travel works,' I said miserably.

Rachel raised her eyebrows. '*None* of us know how this works, Em. And besides it's not really time travel, is it? You haven't gone anywhere, and neither has he. It's more that there seems to be a sort of portal between your individual times.'

'I guess you're right,' I said. 'Which means on that basis, I might have to wait seven years to find out whether I've changed anything.' My heart dropped as realisation dawned.

Even though I'd had the rest of the walk home to let it sink in, now the moment of truth had arrived, I wasn't sure whether I could actually go ahead with it. There were too many uncertainties. Maybe I should just forget this whole thing, put Nick out of my mind and get on with my life without him.

'Do you want me to look?' Rachel said.

'I...' I started. I'd been about to say no, let's forget it. But then an image of my baby had flashed through my mind and I knew I owed it to him or her to do whatever I could to make sure their daddy was part of their life. 'Yes please.'

She pulled the laptop towards her and typed. My pulse pounded in my ears as she squinted at the screen. She scrolled and squinted again. It was as though time had slowed down, each second like treacle, stretching out and out and—

She slammed the laptop shut.

'What is it?' I said. My head spun, my vision reduced to a tiny pinprick.

Rachel gave a tiny shake of her head. 'There's no change,' she said.

Nick was still dead.

'Can I see?' I said, the need to see for myself suddenly overwhelming.

'I don't think you should,' she said.

'Please.'

She paused a moment, then slid the laptop towards me. My hands shook as I opened it, my heart was in my throat. And then, there it was. The same newspaper article, the same story. The same photo.

I stared at Nick's picture, and I felt the disappointment like lead in my veins. I shook my head.

'It didn't work,' I whispered.

'It still could,' Rachel said, pressing her hand against my arm. 'It's not over yet. You know that, don't you?'

I nodded. It might not be over, but, if Rachel was right, I could be in for a very long wait.

22

NICK

For months after finding it, the letter haunted me. By the time I got home that day I'd calmed down a little so, instead of tearing it up or burning it, I hid it in at the bottom of my wardrobe under a pile of boxes. I'd decide what to do with it another time.

Except that time never seemed to come.

I still couldn't bring myself to open it: I didn't care what it said because there was nothing Emma could be telling me that I'd want to hear.

But for some reason I couldn't bear to throw it away either. It felt too final.

I wished I could talk to Andy about it. Only, for the first time ever, this was something I couldn't tell him, because I knew what he'd say. That Emma was tricking me. Lying to me.

And so I stewed on it alone, as the thought of it burned a hole inside me, never fully out of mind.

The truth was I missed Emma like a limb, the need to see her like a physical ache. There were plenty of times I almost went back to the bandstand at the time we usually met to see whether she was there. I wanted to confront her, ask her what she thought she was doing, writing to me.

I also wanted to throw my arms around her and hold her forever.

So I resisted going back and slowly, as the days and weeks passed and the memory of that night – of those few amazing weeks we spent together – faded, I began to emerge from my cocoon of grief and start to live again.

I spent time with Andy, Amanda and my beautiful nieces, Ella and Imogen. I went for the deputy head position at a nearby school and got it. I went on the occasional date, usually set up by Andy and Amanda, and although some led to a second date or a third, I wasn't looking for love, necessarily. I just couldn't seem to let myself go, to give enough of myself to someone.

Because all the time I kept wondering how long I had left. I felt like a ticking time bomb, scanning myself for signs of illness, worrying that every little niggle was cancer, or wondering whether today was the day that I'd step off the kerb and get run over by a bus. It was no way to live, and one day, almost a year after walking out on Emma, Andy had a suggestion.

'Do you think you should get some counselling?' he said.

I shook my head. 'No, I'm fine. I'm happy,' I said.

He gave a mirthless laugh and shook his head. 'You used to be the happiest person I knew, but it's like the joy has drained from you and I'm looking at a shell of my baby brother.'

'Thanks for the vote of confidence,' I said.

'Come on, Nicky, you know I'm right. Ever since you made the assumption that Emma had discovered you'd died, it's like you've been waiting for it, not living.'

'I am living. Nothing's changed,' I insisted, but he just shook his head and said, 'That's exactly my point.'

23

EMMA

Even though Rachel was true to her word and was with me every step of the way, coming to scans and buying me folic acid and giving me advice on which buggy, cot or nappies to buy, being pregnant was still overwhelming. It wasn't as though I'd been left alone by someone who wanted nothing to do with being a dad, and there were so many nights when I lay awake, imagining different scenarios in which Nick and I got the chance to bring up our baby together.

'What will you tell the baby about their father when they're older?' Rachel asked one day.

'I honestly don't know. I suppose I'm just clinging onto the hope that by the time they start asking questions, I might have found him.'

She didn't need to tell me it wasn't a great plan. I already knew. It's just that I had no idea what other option there was, and could only pray that I'd know what to do once the time came.

As for telling everyone else, that had been tricky too. Mum and Dad struggled to understand why I didn't want to bring the baby's father into it. We'd always had a strained relationship –

they'd never really approved of Greg, thought he was too flighty, and were never there for me after he died in a way I truly needed – but this just alienated them even further. Everyone else, including my colleagues and boss, simply assumed it was a one-night stand and that I didn't know the father's name. It wasn't ideal but at least it avoided awkward questions.

As promised, Rachel was my birthing partner. And in the days and weeks leading up to the birth, knowing she was going to be by my side calmed me.

Then, on 28 January 2020, almost fourteen years after his father had died, my baby boy was born. And from the moment he arrived in the world, a bright red bundle whose screams filled the hospital room, I felt a wave of love so strong it almost over-whelmed me. My whole body was flooded with it.

Alongside that came relief that my baby was actually here; that he'd made it. He was a little miracle time traveller, and only two people in the world knew about it. And that thought led to an all-encompassing feeling of sadness, which settled like a small rock in the middle of my chest; a constant reminder that my boy was never likely to meet his daddy. It would most likely always be just me and him.

I called him Flynn. It was Nick's surname, and it was at least something to bind them together. It was all I had.

For the first couple of months, things were great. Exhausting, overwhelming and emotional, but great. I'd turned the small front bedroom into Flynn's nursery, decorating it in a beautiful shade of pale green and buying a second-hand cot. A mobile hung above the cot, casting shadows of stars and moons all around the room, and I hung a photo of the bandstand on the wall, a reminder to me of where my little boy had come from.

It was amazing how something so small could change a life so completely. And even though I'd spent seven months preparing for his arrival and becoming a single mum, it still knocked me for six.

Most days Rachel would drop by. Sometimes she'd bring me new nappies or a packet of baby wipes, other times she'd come with a giant bar of Dairy Milk and we'd sit and devour it together while I fed Flynn or rocked him in his Moses basket.

But then the world went into lockdown, leaving Flynn and I all alone, and with the rest of the world on the other side of a window.

It was during those long, lonely days and nights that a thought began to form in my mind. A thought that I tried to ignore, but that proved to be insistent.

I knew – or at least I suspected – that finding Nick was likely to be impossible for at least another six years: even if my letter did have the power to change the future, it appeared so far that I was going to have to wait until at least 2026 – or 2006 in Nick's life – to find out whether I'd saved him.

But there was someone else I could track down. Someone to give me some connection to Nick.

His brother, Andy.

I wanted to discuss it with Rachel, but I knew she'd tell me it was a terrible idea and try to talk me out of it.

And she'd be right of course. There was nothing to be achieved by looking for him. And yet I knew I was going to do it anyway.

Finding him was easy, as it turned out. He had a Facebook page and although he didn't post on it often, there were a few photos of him and his wife and two girls, both now in their late twenties. We hadn't had much time to talk about families, but I remembered Nick telling me how much he loved them, and I wondered how they'd coped when their uncle Nick had been killed.

Although Andy looked familiar from the photo I'd seen alongside his interview in the newspaper back in 2007, a year after Nick's death, he'd aged and his skin was leathery, his hair now entirely white. I tried to imagine Nick at the same age, but it was impossible.

I scrolled back a few posts, and that was when I saw it. A photo of Nick, just a few years older than he was when I last saw him.

It had been posted on 12 March – the fourteenth anniversary of his death – and my eyes blurred as they wandered over the caption, reading about how much he was loved and missed by his loved ones. But it wasn't even that which made me stop in my tracks. It was his eyes.

Because they were Flynn's eyes.

I shut the laptop, shaking. I wanted to keep scrolling through Andy's page, to find more and more photos and torture myself studying photos of Nick before he died. But I knew I had to step away. These people had been through so much grief and pain. I couldn't bring any more into their lives. I couldn't try and find Andy – at least not until after I'd found out for sure whether my letter had saved Nick.

But thinking about Nick's family had shaken me. Because it reminded me that, somewhere out there, Flynn had a family he may never get the chance to meet.

To take my mind off it during the long, lonely days, I got into the habit of taking Flynn to the park. The weather had been freakishly hot and sunny for weeks, as though the weather gods were trying to make up for the fact that nobody could go anywhere or do anything. Usually this part of the park would be packed with groups of friends and families enjoying the sunshine. But today there were only a few people walking alone on the paths that wound between the patches of parched yellow grass, afraid to break the strict rules by stopping for too long. It was an odd feeling, to be so isolated from the rest of the world.

I rounded the corner and the rose garden and bandstand came into view and as always my heart began racing. Throughout my pregnancy I'd come here a few times, even though Rachel had thought it was a bad idea.

'You're just torturing yourself,' she'd said.

And although I knew she was right, because the note I'd left here all those months ago had gone but the news stories about Nick dying in the train crash had remained the same, I couldn't help myself. What if he happened to be there and I didn't go? Seeing him one more time could change everything.

But since Flynn had been born, I hadn't been able to pluck up the courage to step back inside. A deep-rooted fear kept me away. Fear of seeing Nick and him not wanting anything to do with Flynn and me. Fear of him still being angry. Fear of finding out that nothing I did was going to change the course of time.

It became easier for my shattered heart to simply stay away.

Today, though, on yet another hot day in June, something made me steer the pram away from the main walkway and up the small side path towards the bandstand. It was shady here and a relief after the heat of the sun. I adjusted the parasol that had been protecting Flynn's face and gazed down at him. He lay flat on his back, his arms splayed out to the sides, his little cheeks red, long eyelashes spread out across the round apples of his cheeks. He looked so like his daddy, and my heart filled with love as I gazed down at him, fast asleep and totally oblivious to the turmoil I was going through.

'Hey, baby, this is where I met your daddy,' I whispered. I looked up at the bandstand. It was usually fairly clean, but clearly nobody had been around recently to maintain it, and dust and spiderwebs gathered in all corners, empty bottles and cans littered the ground. I stood rooted to the spot, staring at the bench where Nick and I had met, where we'd got to know each other, told each other stories about our lives, confided in one another. Where we'd fallen in love and discovered the impossible; the place where Flynn had come into being.

I bent down and scooped Flynn into my arms. He grizzled at the disturbance, then settled his cheek against my shoulder and closed his eyes again. I loved the feel of him against me, his warm little body moulding itself to mine, his heart beating against my chest. How had I ever lived without it?

'Shall we go and see if we can find your daddy?' I whispered. He shuffled, a little smile forming on his lips, then went still again. I placed my foot onto the platform and paused, nervous. What if Nick *was* here? What would I do?

Before I could change my mind, I took a deep breath and stepped up.

Blood roared in my ears and the world turned fuzzy round the edges, as though someone had added a filter to the scene. I stood still, let out a low, slow breath, and allowed everything to settle.

There was no one here.

I walked across to the bench and sat down, leaning back against the wooden slats. I ran my free hand over the smooth wood of the seat and pressed my lips to the soft roundness of Flynn's head, smelling his sweet, comforting baby smell.

His eyes flicked open and he looked up at me. And then, in slow motion, his little face folded and crumpled, and his mouth opened and a deafening roar filled the air. I leapt up and rocked back and forth trying to calm him. 'Hey hey hey,' I soothed, running my hand up and down his back. But he was inconsolable and the screaming only got louder, his face turning more and more red. I paced back and forth, back and forth, but nothing helped. He'd only been fed just before we left the house, but perhaps he was hungry again. It wasn't as though he could tell the time, and it usually settled him when he grizzled. I sat back down and slipped my top up and unclipped my bra and tried to encourage him to latch on, but he squirmed and turned his face away, his whole body going rigid with the effort.

Tears ran down my face, and I wished I had someone here with me to tell me what to do. I hated making every single decision alone.

I fumbled to do my bra and top back up then settled Flynn against my shoulder and stepped back down to put him in his pram and take him home. But as soon my foot hit the soft earth, there was instant silence. Flynn stopped crying, his sobs became hiccups, and he looked up at me with wide, wet eyes.

'What was it, baby boy?' I said, running my finger gently down his cheek. 'Could you feel something wrong in there?'

I glanced back at the bandstand. Was it really possible that a four and a half-month-old baby could feel something was awry? Could he really detect a shift in the energy, or had the molecules of the universe changed for him when we were inside the only place where I'd ever known his daddy?

Needing to know for sure, I took a step back onto the platform. Sure enough, Flynn's body instantly went rigid again and his mouth opened ready to scream. But this time, before he became too distressed, I stepped back off. He relaxed immediately.

What did this mean? Did it mean anything, or was it just that he didn't like it in there? He'd been known to cry a lot simply walking round the supermarket, only stopping the moment we walked outside. And yet this had felt different. This had felt like a sort of desperation, as though his whole body was rejecting something about the very air he breathed.

Trembling, I placed him gently back in his pram and hurried away as quickly as we could.

* * *

Halfway home I made a detour. By the time I arrived outside Rachel's house I was hot and sweaty and in desperate need of a drink.

'Quick, come into the back garden,' she said, ushering me round the side of the house. By the time I managed to manoeuvre the pram round to the back garden Rachel was standing by the back door, and a cold can of Diet Coke sat dripping on the wooden table.

'I wiped my fingerprints off it,' she said, pulling a chair at least a metre away from the table and sitting down. I settled in the other chair, angling the pram so that it was in the shade of the parasol, and took a welcome gulp.

'I think I love you,' I said.

'Only think?'

I smiled. But before I could stop it, a sob rose up in my throat. I turned away before Rachel noticed, but it was too late.

'Darling, what's wrong?' she said. I couldn't look at her because if I did the concern on her face could very well tip me over the edge.

I shook my head. 'I just...' I wiped my eyes and finally looked at her. 'I just really need a hug.'

She buried her face in her hands than looked back up at me. 'Me too. I want to come over there and give you the biggest squeeze in the world and then give that beautiful boy of yours one too. But you know I just can't risk it, with Iain's mum.'

'I know. I'm sorry, I just needed to see you.'

She leaned forward so her face was in the shade. She looked

tired, I noticed, the circles beneath her eyes darker than usual. A stab of guilt shot through me. I'd been so absorbed in getting to grips with being a mum that I'd ignored how hard all this was for her too. Iain's mum had been having chemo prior to lockdown and had a compromised immune system as a result. The treatment had taken it out of her, so she'd moved in with them while she was still allowed, but it meant that they all had to be even more careful than most not to bring any infection into the house.

'I'm sorry, I've been so selfish I've barely even asked you how it's going,' I said.

'You are not selfish. Everything's fine here, really. It's just different. But at least we've got each other. It's you I worry about, all alone in that house learning to be a mum.' She shook her head. 'I wish there was more I could do to help you.'

I smiled sadly. 'I do too. Flynn needs Aunty Rachel's cuddles. But this will all be over soon and things will get back to normal.' I took another sip of my drink, enjoying the feeling of the cool liquid sliding down my throat. Now I was here and had calmed down a little I felt bad about interrupting Rachel's day. She was trying to do her job as a buyer for a fashion brand from the dining table with the kids running around and Iain working in the spare room. It was a lot to cope with. I stood.

'Thanks for the drink. I should leave you in peace.'

'Absolutely not,' she said. 'I might not be able to hug you, but I can still listen.'

I hesitated, unsure. I really didn't want to burden her with anything more than she already had to deal with. But then again, who else did I have to confide in?

I sat down again, rocking the pram mindlessly back and forth. I suddenly felt bone-weary, every last drop of energy draining away through the cracks in the decking.

'I went to the bandstand this morning.'

Rachel didn't reply, just watched me from across the table. 'I haven't been back since Flynn was born but something was just calling me today.'

'Were you hoping to see Nick?'

'Yes. No.' I shook my head. 'I don't know really. I suppose part of me hoped he'd be there. Of course he wasn't.' I looked up at her. 'Flynn hated it.'

She raised her eyebrows. 'What do you mean?'

'When we got there, he went mad, screaming and crying. I've never seen him like it before. But then the moment we left, he calmed down. I mean almost instantly.'

'Do you think it means something?'

'I think it has to. If it wasn't for that place, Flynn would never have existed. It was as though he could feel something weird about it.'

'Oh, Em,' Rachel said. 'I wish there was some magic wand I could wave to stop you feeling like this.'

'Me too.' My breath hitched in my chest. 'I just really miss him. I think about him all the time. Every time I look at Flynn I see the dimple in Nick's cheek when he smiled, the sparkle in his eyes when he looked at me. His eyes. I just... I'm so fucking lonely.'

Before I knew what had happened Rachel was on her feet and round the table and had thrown her arms round me. Her head was pressed into my shoulder, her face turned away, but the feel of her against me, of human affection, was so overwhelming, something inside me broke, and my whole body gave in as sobs wracked it from deep inside.

We stayed there for a few minutes, just holding each other. Finally, as my sobs began to subside, Rachel pulled away. She stood, arms hanging by her sides, her face filled with sadness.

'I'm sorry. I know I shouldn't have done that, but screw Covid, I couldn't just leave you sitting there like that.'

'Thank you,' I said, my voice gravelly. 'I'm glad you did.'

'I truly wish there was a way we could let Nick know about Flynn. But I think you're just going to have to accept it's impossible and try to move on.'

I knew she was right. It's just a shame my heart didn't agree.

24

NICK

Sometimes I wondered whether I was going slowly mad. Life ticked on, people moved, got new jobs, grew up. I went to work every day, taught the kids, came home. I still met Andy for a curry every Thursday night, and I still spent time with my nieces.

But most of the time I was alone, at home. Eating alone. Sleeping alone. Being alone.

Except that, sometimes, I wondered whether I actually *was* completely alone.

It started one late autumn evening in 2001 a couple of years after I'd last seen Emma. The letter she'd left for me was still buried somewhere, far from view, and I only thought about it from time to time, when it would hit me like a blow to the stomach and I'd have to try and forget about it all over again. A couple of times I came close to going to find it and ripping it open and putting myself out of my misery once and for all, but in the end I managed to talk myself out of it. No good could ever come of opening that letter. And yet I still didn't throw it away.

This particular night, I'd gone into the small spare room at the front of the house, the room Dawn and I had earmarked as a nursery. I didn't come in here very often, but sometimes I liked to stand at the doorway and try to imagine another life – a life in which Dawn hadn't fallen ill, in which she'd fallen pregnant instead and our baby was living here, its cot where my desk now sat, a changing table taking up the space where a small wardrobe now was. This day, I stepped over the threshold into the room and sat down on the chair by the desk. I tipped my head back and looked at the ceiling – and that's when I felt it, and my body froze.

Slowly, I sat up and looked round the room, holding my breath. I stood and walked over to the corner, and the closer I got the more my skin began to tingle, a feeling like a feather was being run across it. I whirled round, looking up and down, my eyes tracing the entire room. What *was* that?

And then it hit me. It was the same fizzing, tingling feeling I'd experienced when I was in the bandstand with Emma. The feeling that I wasn't quite in my body – how had Emma described it? Otherworldly, that was it. It felt otherworldly, and for a moment I couldn't move. I closed my eyes and inhaled deeply, trying to relax into the feeling, to let it spread through my whole body. And then, just as suddenly as it had begun, it stopped, and I was left standing there, wondering what had just happened.

After that night I went into the box room every night, trying to see whether I would feel it again. But for some time there was nothing, just a room with empty air, and I tried to ignore the clench of disappointment in my chest.

I put it down to tiredness, stress. Work had been busy, and everything that had happened with Emma had hung over me like a dark cloud for the last couple of years. It was just my mind playing tricks on me.

Maybe Andy was right. Maybe I did need counselling, to help me move on once and for all.

But then it happened again. This time I was in the bathroom, soaking in a bubble bath, when I felt it. I sat up, water pouring off me, and looked around, searching for something, someone. But, just like before, there was no one there.

After that, it happened at random times, in different parts of the house. Sometimes I'd feel it in the dining room, other times in the bedroom, the kitchen, the living room. Once I felt it in the garden, out by the little apple tree. It was usually only fleeting, but it was definitely there. And while I had no proof of what it was, to me there was only one explanation. It was a connection to Emma in this house, twenty years in the future. And while it should have left me feeling shaken, scared, what it actually made me feel was comforted. A sense that somewhere out there, some time in the future, there was someone that I loved. Someone who loved me.

And for a while at least, it brought me some peace.

25

EMMA

'Mummaaaaaaa!' The yell from the other room had reached a deafening crescendo. I put down the crumpet I was buttering and poked my head round the living room door. I couldn't see Flynn anywhere, but the huge pile of cushions in the middle of the room gave me a clue as to where he was.

'Hello?' I called.

No answer, just a giggle.

'How strange, Flynn must have left for playgroup already. Maybe I'll eat his crumpet instead.'

'Nooooo!' A cushion tumbled and then a little person appeared, clambering over obstacles to reach me. 'My crumpog!' he said, jumping up and down.

'Oh there you are,' I said, bending down to scoop him up. He wriggled in my arms but I managed to force a cuddle before he squirmed back to the ground and raced through to the kitchen. By the time I got back he'd already devoured half the crumpet I'd been part-way through buttering.

'Someone's full of beans this morning,' I said, taking a foil-wrapped sandwich out of the fridge and placing it carefully into his Bluey lunchbox. I added a small box of raisins, some Pom Bears and a carton of blackcurrant juice, and then tucked a box of raw carrots down the side that I was certain would come home again completely uneaten, and zipped it shut.

'Don't break my cave, will you, Mummy?' Flynn said, his blue eyes wide.

'I wouldn't dare, darling,' I said, glad I was going to be in the office today so I didn't have to look at the chaos in the living room.

I'd gone back to work three days a week after my maternity leave. I wished I could be with Flynn every single day, but I needed to earn some money. For a while I'd planned on selling the house because the mortgage was too much on a part-time wage. But then something had happened that had changed my mind.

Flynn was just over a year old the first time.

We'd been in the bathroom, splashing around in the bubbles, and he was laughing like a hyena when he'd suddenly stopped dead and stared at the doorway, eyes round. I glanced over my shoulder but couldn't see anything.

'What is it sweetheart?' I said, tickling him under the chin.

'Man!' he shouted, his gaze never leaving the empty doorway.

I stood, water splashing all over the floor, and poked my head round the doorway.

'There's no man there,' I said, crouching back down beside him and running my hand over his bubbly head. 'It's all good.'

His gaze stayed fixed on the doorway for a few more seconds, then he looked back at me and smiled his gappy grin.

I didn't think anything of it until a couple of weeks later when the same thing happened – only this time we were in Flynn's bedroom. He was on my knee on the little chair beside his bed, curled up against my chest while I read him a story. He was almost asleep when his body had stiffened, suddenly alert, and he'd stared at the open doorway again.

'Flynn, what's the matter, darling?' I said.

'Dada,' he said, the words as clear as day and my heart stopped beating.

Even though I knew there would be nobody there, I stood with Flynn in my arms and walked over to the doorway.

'Who did you see, little man?' I whispered.

'Dada,' he said again, and I thought my legs were going to give way right there and then. I stood still for a moment, trying to feel a presence, sure that if I wished for it enough, Nick would come to me. But after a few minutes I gave up and walked back over to the chair once more.

After that, it happened every few weeks. Sometimes Flynn would stop, stare at a point in the distance, and either smile or shout 'dada'. Other times we'd be out in the garden, collecting apples that had scattered across the lawn from the large tree in the corner and separating the worm-eaten ones from the good ones, when a smile would break out on his face and he'd whisper 'No, not there, that's a bad one.'

And while Flynn was too young to tell me what he was seeing or who he was speaking to, it was clear to me that it was Nick. We might not have been able to force the connection between us, but the link between father and son was obviously too strong, and Flynn could feel his daddy's presence in the house. Although I had no idea what I was going to tell Flynn if he ever started asking about him, it was a comfort to me to know Nick was there, somewhere, looking over us.

How could we ever leave this house now?

'Right, five minutes, mister,' I said now. 'Go and clean your teeth and get your shoes on.'

Flynn slid off the chair and ran upstairs, his feet thundering on the stairs like a small herd of elephants. I checked my bag, grabbed my own sandwich from the fridge, and went into the hall to apply my lipstick in the hallway mirror.

A few minutes later Flynn and I were walking along the street hand in hand, Flynn with his tiny rucksack on his back and his lunchbox swinging in his other arm. He chattered away as we walked, telling me about his friends, about Miss Hardcastle, about the birds in the trees and shouting every time he spotted a yellow car. At one point we had to stop and watch as a fire engine screamed past, Flynn's mouth wide open in amazement.

It was only a ten-minute walk to Flynn's nursery, but it usually took at least twenty, and by the time we arrived this morning most of his friends had already gone inside. Miss Hardcastle was still there, smiling.

'I go now, Mummy,' he said, tugging his hand away.

I crouched down and gave him a hug. 'Be a good boy for Mummy, won't you?' I said.

'Yep!' Then he turned and ran towards the door, disappearing into the darkness beyond.

I was just about to leave when I heard someone call my name. I turned to see Miss Hardcastle walking towards me.

'Is everything all right?' I said, my stomach plummeting to the ground.

'Yes, nothing to worry about,' she said, her bright smile lighting up her face. 'I just wondered...' She glanced over her shoulder then back at me. 'I wondered if I could ask you a rather personal question?'

'I... I guess so.' I was intrigued now.

'It's just, Flynn had never mentioned his daddy before, and I've always assumed he's not around, but I... I wondered if I could show you a picture he drew yesterday?'

'Yes of course.' My heart thumped low in my belly as she went back into the classroom and re-emerged a few seconds later clutching a piece of paper. It fluttered in the breeze as she handed it to me, and it took me a few seconds for my eyes to make out what was on the bright white sheet. But when they did, my stomach flipped over.

On the paper Flynn had drawn a large purple square, with green scribbles underneath it, and blue scribbled above. A yellow scribble sat in the top right corner. But it was what was inside the box that my eyes focused on.

Flynn had drawn three crude figures. One had long orange scribbles around its head which I took to be me. One was smaller with blond hair and our hands were joined so I guessed that was Flynn.

The third one, though, was what I assumed had piqued Miss Hardcastle's concern. The figure was drawn higher than the others, almost as though it was floating above it. It was scribbled entirely in black, and even though Flynn's drawing skills were rudimentary, when I looked back at the stick figures of me and him, we both had tears in our eyes.

My hand had started to shake and I handed the piece of paper back.

'Sorry, I don't know where that's come from,' I said, forcing a smile.

Miss Hardcastle tipped her head to the side and nodded. 'That's okay. I just wanted to make you aware in case... well, in case there is anyone else in his life that he might feel a bit fearful of.' She cleared her throat. 'Not that this always means that. Often it can just point to an overactive imagination, but we always like to mention it to parents, just in case.'

'Yes, thank you. That's very kind but I'm sure it's nothing. He probably just wishes he had his daddy around like his friends do.'

Miss Hardcastle smiled sympathetically. 'Yes I'm sure you're probably right,' she said. 'Well, thank you for your time, Ms Vickers. I hope you don't mind me showing you this.'

'No, of course not. Thank you,' I said, backing away. As soon as the young teacher had turned back to the classroom I turned and scurried away, keen to get out of there as quickly as possible.

I walked the rest of the way to work on autopilot, my mind. My breath came fast and I stopped just before I reached the office to calm myself down. I leaned against a wall and took a couple of deep breaths.

I wished I'd asked to bring Flynn's drawing with me so that I could look at it again. Had I overreacted? It had seemed obvious to me at the time that the purple square represented the bandstand, and that the three figures were me, Flynn and a man... his daddy? I thought back to the only time I'd ever taken Flynn to the bandstand, the place he was conceived, back when he was a tiny baby. His reaction had been so strong I'd never dared take him back there again. But what if something in his subconscious remembered it? What if he'd somehow made the connection between the man he saw in the house and the bandstand? After all, Nick had come to me through some sort of portal – God, *listen* to me – that only seemed to work there.

Maybe the time had come to take him back and see whether the portal was still there – because what better person would there be for Nick to visit than his own son?

* * *

I was about to let myself into the house when a voice stopped me in my tracks. I turned to find my neighbour leaning over the fence.

'Hello,' I said, surprised. We'd spoken a few times over the last few years, but we barely knew each other, and I could count on one hand the number of times she'd stopped me to say hello.

'Hello, Emma. I was just wondering how you were?'

'Me? I'm good thank you. You?'

She tilted her head. 'I'm fine thank you.' She looked at the front door then back at me and I wondered whether she was going to say anything else. I'd just decided that she wasn't when she spoke again.

'It's tough isn't it, when they're little?'

'Sorry?'

'Kids,' she said. 'I mean, it was hard enough with the two of us to get up in the night or taking the kiddies to endless parties, but it must be even harder on your own.'

'Yes. It can be.'

She nodded again, slowly. 'Well, you must let me know if you ever need anything. Any help or just a night off.'

'Oh. Thank you.' I couldn't have been more surprised if the Queen had turned up on my doorstep.

'I know we haven't spoken much, but I've seen you with your little boy,' she continued. 'It's lovely to have children around the place, it can be so quiet.'

Oh. Was this just a long-winded way of telling me Flynn was too noisy? But surely not, he wasn't a rowdy boy.

'I'm sorry if—' I began, but she cut me off.

'I was beginning to think the house was bad luck you know,' she said.

'Oh? Why?' She had my attention now.

She waved her hand through the air. 'Well, you know. The couple who lived here last seemed to argue all the time and eventually they divorced and sold the place. And the couple before that – well, they were lovely, but they never had children either, and then she died. Cancer, I think it was. So sad, she was such a lovely girl.'

I froze, my breath caught in my throat, as I realised the significance of what she was saying. She was talking about Dawn and Nick.

'That's very sad,' I said, my throat tight.

'It really was. I chatted to him occasionally while she was ill, and I know how much they wanted a baby. But it wasn't meant to be.' She shook her head. 'So yes, it's been a while since a child lived here.'

I didn't know what to say. It was as though the past had come crashing into the present, and Nick's presence was right there. I wouldn't have been surprised to turn round and find him standing right behind me.

'Well, I'd better get to work,' I said.

'Of course, you go. But I mean it. If you ever need anything, just let me know, all right?'

'Thank you.' Then before she could say any more and before my legs collapsed beneath me, I let myself into the house and closed the door.

* * *

The conversation with my neighbour played on my mind all day, through meetings and phone calls and conversations with colleagues, my mind kept wandering back to it. I don't know why it freaked me out so much – I knew Nick and Dawn had lived in this house before me. But somehow, hearing about them from someone else had made it all more real.

Finally, it was time to pick Flynn up from school, and I had an idea of something I wanted to do this afternoon.

The sun was still warm by the time I skidded through the

front gates a few minutes late, and Flynn raced out and threw himself at my legs the moment he saw me. I lifted him up and planted kisses on his face.

'Hello, gorgeous, have you had a good day?' I said, as he wriggled in my arms.

'Can we go to the park?'

'Maybe.' He had a smudge of ink on his cheek and I rubbed at it, but it wouldn't budge. 'Have you been drawing again?' I asked as I lowered him to the ground and took hold of his hand we started walking towards the gates.

'Yes! I done one for you.' He bent down, carefully unzipped his rucksack, and pulled out a crumpled piece of paper. My heart thumped as I turned it over to look at it, terrified it was going to be a repeat of the drawing Miss Hardcastle had shown me this morning. But it wasn't.

'It's super,' I said. 'Is this grass?' I said, pointing at a stripe of green scribble along one edge of the page.

'No, it's mud, Mummy,' he said, as though I should have known. I smiled.

'Of course it is. So, this must be our house then?' I said, pointing at the strange shape in the middle.

'No, Mummy,' he said, sighing dramatically. 'It's our *car*.'

I laughed. The car I'd bought was an old red Vauxhall Corsa, which had seen better days but had enough room to fit a pram and buggy in the back and had been all I could afford after Flynn was born. The one Flynn had drawn didn't look far off it. 'It's brilliant, sweetheart,' I said. 'Do you want to put it back in your bag until we get home so it doesn't get ruined?'

'Okay,' he said, and we waited while he carefully folded his drawing and pushed it back inside his rucksack. I took the bag from him and grasped hold of his hand.

'Please can we go to the park?'

'Go on then,' I said, smiling. He clearly wasn't going to give up on the idea.

'Yay!' He bounced up and down, tugging on my arm until it felt like it might come right out of its socket. 'And can we have ice cream?'

'Now you're pushing your luck, mister,' I said.

'Pleeeease, Mummy,' he pleaded.

'Fine. But this is the only time this week, okay?'

'Okay!'

It didn't take us long to get to the park, Flynn dragging me there excitedly. When we got to the little playpark he raced ahead and ran straight up to the slide. He was halfway up the ladder by the time I caught up.

'Be careful,' I said, as he whizzed down the slide. He stood and ran straight back round to the steps again. I went over to the bench and sat down.

I could see the bandstand from here, and I thought about the day I'd pointed out this playground to Nick, and he'd said he couldn't see it. That was the day we'd begun to realise what was going on between us. It felt like a lifetime ago, and yet also like yesterday.

I felt a pang of longing. I'd known Greg for more than ten years and I still missed him being in my life. He was part of me, and always would be, even though the memory of him was becoming a little fainter with every day that passed.

I'd only known Nick for a few weeks, but the hole he'd left in my life felt completely different. More like a gaping wound than an empty hollow; a wound with jagged edges that seemed to get sharper and more painful as time passed, rather than easing.

Perhaps it was simply because there was a tiny possibility that I might see him again one day, whereas I'd always known Greg was gone, and could slowly learn to accept it. Or maybe it was because we had this connection of Flynn, a living, breathing person tying us together forever, through the years.

I didn't know. All I did know was that I missed Nick so intensely, it felt like the place where he should be was burning a hole inside me.

'Mummy, can we get an ice cream now?' Flynn was standing in front of me, silhouetted against the sun, and for a moment he looked so like his daddy that my heart almost stopped beating.

He tugged my arm impatiently. 'Mummy!'

I smiled at him. 'Sorry, love.' I took his hand and stood up. 'Come on, let's go and get the biggest, meltiest ice cream we can find.'

The ice cream van wasn't far away. Flynn chose an enormous 99 with a flake and red sauce which started dripping down his arm the moment he was handed it. I ordered a smaller version, and we started walking away.

The sun was really hot now. I'd been planning to go to the bandstand anyway, and now we were right beside it. As usual it looked empty, almost as though there was an invisible force field round the place that kept people away – although I suspected it was more that it was a bit grubby and off the main path.

'Come on, let's go in there,' I said, pointing at it.

Flynn glanced up and I watched his face for any glimpse of recognition, but there was nothing. We walked up the path together, and when we got close I stopped.

'Do you remember being here before, sweetheart?' I said.

Flynn frowned. 'No.' His face brightened. 'But it's on my wall.'

Of course, the picture of the bandstand I'd put on his nursery wall when he was a baby.

'Have you ever drawn this place?'

But Flynn had already lost interest, too busy licking his dripping ice cream to answer. I shook my head. 'Never mind, sweetheart.'

I stepped up onto the bandstand and Flynn clambered up beside me, almost dropping his cone in the process. I hadn't been back inside here since Flynn was a tiny baby, and it had become scruffier in the last three and a half years. There was graffiti along the top of the railing, and deep scratches and scuffs across the wooden floor. Flynn sat on the bench beside me, in the place where Nick had always sat and my heart thumped, low and heavy.

We sat in silence, finishing our ice creams and staring out at the park. A gentle breeze wound through the trees and for the first time all day I felt cool.

I glanced over at Flynn. His hands were covered in a sticky mess. I took the last few bites of my cone then reached for my bag and pulled out a packet of always-present baby wipes. I thought of the time I'd found a candle in my bag to light for Dawn's birthday, and the sweets Nick always used to carry with him, and smiled.

I turned to wipe Flynn's fingers but was stopped in my tracks. He was frozen, his eyes wide, and he seemed to be staring at something just behind me, just the way he sometimes did at home. I glanced over my shoulder but could see nothing there.

'Are you okay, sweetheart?' I said.

He looked at me, then pointed over my shoulder. 'Is that man my daddy?'

My stomach flipped. 'I...' I started, but couldn't get the words out. I cleared my throat and turned to look in the direction in which he was pointing.

'Can you see a man, darling?' I asked gently.

'Yes, Mummy. Right there.' Flynn sounded cross, as though he couldn't understand why I was being so annoying.

'What does he look like, Flynn?' I said.

'Like the man in the house. Like my daddy.'

My breath caught in my throat. There was no way Flynn could ever have seen a picture of Nick because I didn't have any. If I'd ever had any doubts at all that the man Flynn was seeing in the house was Nick, they'd disappeared now.

I put my arm around his shoulders but didn't reply. He kept glancing over his shoulder as if to check he was still there, but he didn't seem scared so I let him. And, eventually, he snuggled into my side, his cheek pressed against my chest. 'He's gone now.'

I kissed the top of his head, and pulled him even closer, feeling my heart slow. There were so many questions I wanted to ask him, but I didn't want to scare him. Besides, where would I even start?

It seemed that Flynn could feel his daddy's presence in the places that mattered – the house where Nick had lived, and the bandstand where Flynn had been conceived. Was Nick trying to let us know he was here, that he knew about Flynn?

I had no idea. But if it gave Flynn comfort, then it could only be a good thing.

26

NICK

Despite the comfort being in the house brought me, I knew Andy was worried about me. And he had every right to be. Because I wasn't really living. In fact I was barely existing, so acutely aware that, at any minute, my life could be snatched away. What was the point of doing anything, meeting anyone – of being happy – if it could all be gone, just like that?

It was about four years after finding the letter that something occurred to me, and for a few weeks I couldn't get it out of my mind.

Emma would be twenty-one now. Right now, in 2003, she would be an adult. I was thirty-five and, despite what I'd said about the age gap, it wasn't inconceivable that we could be together. And I couldn't stop thinking about going to look for her again.

'You're not serious?' Andy said, when I told him over Thursday curry.

I didn't look at him, just shovelled in mouthfuls of curry like my life depended on it. 'Why not?' I shrugged, aiming for nonchalant, as though going to look for Emma was something that had only just occurred to me, but coming off more belligerent.

Suddenly my arm stopped moving and his hand was on my wrist, fork suspended mid-air. A piece of chicken fell off, dropping back onto the plate. Finally, I looked up and met his eye.

'Don't do this,' he said, sadly.

I lowered my fork and sniffed. 'I don't see why it's such a terrible idea,' I said.

He frowned, folding his arms across his chest. 'Tell me then. Tell me what you're hoping might happen if you go looking for Emma right now. I'm all ears.'

I sighed. 'I don't know, Andy, but I can't stop thinking about her and I don't want to—' I stopped myself. I was about to say I still didn't want to open the letter, but I hadn't told him about it and now didn't feel like the best time. I took a gulp of beer and wiped my hand across my mouth. 'I just want to see her.'

Andy shook his head slowly. 'Oh, Nicky,' he said. 'I really thought you were over this.'

I looked down at my plate. My curry had started to congeal and I'd suddenly lost my appetite.

'You never really believed me about her, did you?'

Now it was Andy's turn to look away. 'I didn't say that.'

'You didn't need to. I wasn't lying though.'

He looked up. 'I never thought you were lying, Nicky,' he said. 'I'd never think that. I just—'

'Just what, Andy? Thought I was going mad?'

'No, that's not fair. I just thought...' He twisted his pint glass round and round. 'I just thought it was the grief. You know, you lost Dawn, and then... well. You know. Emma came along and you wanted to believe there was something amazing between you, and that was fine for a while.'

'But why would I do that? Why would I imagine the twenty-year gap? It would have been easier if everything was just straightforward. It makes no sense.'

'No. I suppose not.' He stabbed a piece of chicken with his fork and held it up to his mouth. 'Except that this way you gave yourself permission to fall in love with someone else after losing Dawn.'

And there it was. This was what he'd believed all this time. I didn't know what to say.

'Can we talk about something else?' I said eventually, pushing my half-full plate away.

He hesitated a moment, then nodded. 'Sure.'

We did move on, but the conversation hung over us all night, and we left early.

When I got home I couldn't stop thinking about it. Not about the fact that Andy didn't believe me, because I knew it was all real. But about finding Emma.

When I got home I went straight up to my office and started up my computer. As it whirred to life, I thought about all the things Emma had told me about the future – about her phone which meant she had the internet wherever she went, about the fact that people found dates online. It seemed so incredible that so much would have changed just a few years from now. It seemed almost impossible.

I pulled up the Yahoo search page and typed in Emma's name, then I pressed search and waited, holding my breath.

There she was. Emma Vickers, age twenty-one, at the opening night of a play at a theatre a few towns away. I clicked on the photo and her young, carefree face filled my screen. I stared at it, taking in her sparkling green eyes, her cloud of red hair, her beautiful porcelain skin. She looked radiant, and carefree. And so young.

With shaking hands, I closed the window, and shut the

computer down, sitting in the dark for a moment with the image of Emma stamped onto my retinas. And in that moment I knew that Andy was right.

No good would come from looking for her. I had to stay away.

I was about to walk out of the room and go to bed when another thought occurred to me and I sat back down again.

In all the films I'd watched and books I'd read about time travel, people who go back in time try to change the past, and that affects the future. And while I knew that going to find Emma would be a terrible idea, there was something I knew about her future that could be within my power to change.

In 2017, Greg was going to fall from a tree and die. Although that was still thirteen years away, I couldn't ignore the niggling idea that I should try to warn him. I turned over the implications in my mind – if Greg didn't fall from that tree, then he and Emma would still be together, and that might mean that Emma and I would never meet. I had no idea what that might mean for me – would the memories of everything that had happened between us these last few years be wiped from my mind because they had never happened? Or would I still remember what could have happened anyway?

I had no idea. But I did know that I would be a terrible person if I didn't at least try to stop it.

I spent a few hours trying to find Greg, and eventually, I did. There had been a news story in the local paper last year about his football team winning their semi-final. Greg was the captain and, alongside a photo of the team was a photo of him, beaming out at the camera.

He was handsome, with dark blond surfer hair and bright blue eyes in a tanned, rugged face. Of course he wasn't a tree surgeon yet, but he looked like the perfect candidate to become one.

I stared at him for a long time, trying to work out ways that I could warn this man about a tragedy that was going to befall him many, many years in his future. I pictured going to the football club and walking into the bar after a match, approaching him and striking up a conversation. How would that conversation go, exactly? 'Lovely to meet you, and by the way, don't become a tree surgeon in case you fall from a tree and die one day'?

Clearly not. But there didn't seem any other obvious way of making him listen either. A letter? Too easy to ignore. A phone call? Too easy to trace.

In the end I closed the computer and stared at my warped reflection in the blank screen for ages, thinking it through.

And finally it hit me that what I was contemplating was exactly what I'd begged Emma not to do to me: telling someone about future events. Of course I couldn't go and warn Greg. Because even if he did listen, I could be ruining his life.

No. I'd just have to let destiny play out and hope that things might still change.

For Greg, and for me.

27

EMMA

I was going on a date.

These were not words I ever thought I'd say again, but here I was.

I stood in the middle of my room, staring into my wardrobe trying to decide whether anything in there was suitable. What did people wear on dates these days? It had been a long time since the thought had even crossed my mind that I might need to impress someone.

Oh God, what was I doing?

I could hear Flynn's giggle from downstairs, followed by the rumble of Rachel's voice pretending to be a monster. She'd offered to babysit tonight – in fact she'd insisted, telling me to stop looking for excuses not to go.

'You can't sit around waiting for Nick for the rest of your life,' she said. 'You need to start living. Plus, Oliver is *hot*.'

'Okay, okay,' I'd said, mostly just to get her off my back.

And although she was right that Oliver was hot, I was already regretting giving in to her. What was I thinking?

Oliver and I had got chatting at the school gates on the day that Flynn started reception class. Flynn had looked so smart in his little uniform of red jumper and grey shorts and I'd been busy taking photos of him with his bookbag when he'd suddenly run off.

'Flynn!' I'd called. I watched as he flung his arms round a girl who was holding hands with a man – presumably her dad – then he turned back to me, his face lit up.

'Mummy, this is Annabelle,' he said, as I approached.

Flynn had been talking about Annabelle all summer after they'd been to a holiday drama club together. 'Annabelle was the princess and I was the prince,' he'd told me one day, and 'Annabelle wants me to go to hers for tea,' another day. I'd hoped I'd meet his new friend once they started school, so was pleased to have done so already.

'Hello, Annabelle, it's very nice to meet you,' I said, giving her what I hoped was my friendliest smile.

'Hello,' she said shyly.

It was only then that I'd looked up at the man attached to Annabelle, and my heart had performed a little somersault. He had blond hair with a light sprinkling of silver, and sparkling blue eyes.

'Hello, I'm Emma,' I said, holding my hand out. 'I'm afraid I think my son Flynn is a little bit smitten with your daughter.'

'I think the feeling might be mutual,' he said, putting his hand in mine. It felt warm. 'Lovely to meet you, I'm Oliver.' His face lit up as he smiled and I felt my face glow. Good grief, what was wrong with me?

We walked back towards the gates together and said goodbye to the children. I felt a lump in my throat as Flynn disappeared into the classroom, but it was tinged with relief that he'd already made a friend.

'Well, that went smoother than I expected,' Oliver said.

'Thank goodness for drama club, hey?'

'Absolutely.' He checked his watch. 'Christ, I'm going to be late. It was lovely to meet you, Emma. Same time tomorrow?'

'Yes, absolutely,' I said, swallowing down the feeling of disappointment that he was leaving already, as he turned and raced off down the road.

To my shame, I'd felt myself looking forward to the next morning more than I should have done, and when I saw Oliver was there again my heart did a little flip.

It's just nice to have someone to talk to, nothing more, I told myself.

But Rachel could see right through me.

'You have a crush,' she said, the moment I mentioned Oliver's name.

'I do not have a crush,' I said, more sulkily than necessary. 'Anyway, what are we, twelve?'

She hadn't been deterred though. 'Okay, you like him. Fancy him? Whatever. I'm happy for you, Ems! He's hot and single and it's been long enough.'

I let out a sigh. 'Fine. He is handsome. I might have been looking forward to seeing him in the morning. Happy?'

'Very,' she said, doing a little dance, and I rolled my eyes. 'So, when are you asking him out?'

'Never!'

She'd looked stern then, crossing her arms across her chest and glowering at me. 'Why ever not?'

'Well for starters I don't even know that he is actually single. And even if by some miracle he is, I'm not looking to get involved with anyone,' I said. 'I'm fine on my own, just me and Flynn.'

'You may be fine, but I'm not suggesting you marry the guy. Just ask him out, go on a date, have a little snog...'

'Fine, I'll find out whether he's single at least,' I agreed, more to shut her up than anything else. But in the end I hadn't had to work up the courage to ask him anything, because he did it for me.

It had been a drizzly day at the end of September and everyone was hurrying to drop the kids off before rushing off again. Oliver had been hovering under a tree near the school gates and after saying goodbye to Flynn I went to speak to him.

'What are you doing loitering around here?' I said, smiling. But he didn't smile back and I worried I'd said something wrong. 'Sorry,' I mumbled, getting ready to walk away and leave him to his thoughts. But then he'd cleared his throat and said, 'Actually...' and I stopped and turned back to face him and his face had gone pink and he was looking down at his shoes. When he looked up at me, he looked for all the world as though he would have liked the ground to open up and swallow him whole right then and there. I took a step towards him, and he pressed his hand on my arm.

'Oliver? Is there something wrong?'

He shook his head and forced a smile. 'I hope not. I was...' He shook his head and laughed. 'God, why am I so bad at this?'

And then before he even said the words, I knew what he was going to say and my heart pulsed and my hands turned clammy.

'Would you like to go for dinner with me one day?' He was staring at a point just over my shoulder and my heart went out to him.

'That would be lovely,' I said. And not just because I wanted to put him out of his misery but because I'd realised I actually did want to go out for dinner with this man. For the first time since Nick, I could imagine spending time with someone else. It was a small miracle.

'Oh, thank goodness for that. If you'd have said no I'd have had to move to a different country just to avoid you,' he said.

'Well, why do you think I said yes? I couldn't put poor Annabelle through that.'

He grinned and it took a few seconds for me to realise his hand was still on my arm. I moved it away, and shoved my hand in my pocket. I was aware of a few mums glancing at us as they passed and I didn't particularly want to be the subject of school-gate gossip.

'So where would you like to go?' he said.

'It's been so long since I've been anywhere, I'm open to suggestions,' I replied.

'Well then leave it with me. Friday night good?'

'Friday night is perfect,' I said. There was no point in pretending I had a busy social life when it was obvious I didn't.

Now, though, I was feeling less certain of myself. Why had I even agreed to this? I didn't go on dates, and there was good reason for that. It was hardly fair to lead someone on when, assuming my plan to save him had worked, I was hoping to find Nick in a couple of years' time.

I ran down the stairs in my underwear and stood in the doorway to the living room where Flynn was lying down with his eyes closed and there was a Rachel-sized bulge in the curtains. Flynn's eyes flew open.

'Go away, Mummy, we're playing hide and seek,' he hissed. I held my hands up in surrender. 'Sorry little man. I was looking for Aunty Rachel.'

Flynn rolled his eyes. 'She's *hiding*, Mummy.'

I grinned, my eyes flicking over to Rachel's terrible hiding place. 'Of course, sorry. Well, when you find her would you please tell her that she can go home because I've changed my mind about going out tonight?'

Two things happened simultaneously: Flynn groaned, and

the curtain was whipped back and Rachel's face appeared. She didn't look impressed.

'I absolutely will *not* be going home, because you are going out,' she said, unfolding herself to her full height.

'I'm just not sure it's a good idea,' I said.

'But, Mummy, I don't want Aunty Rachel to go home,' Flynn said, his voice a whine.

'You see? Flynn has spoken. You're going out. Now go on, go and get dressed before you're ridiculously late.'

I hesitated for a moment trying to decide whether to argue back, then let out a sigh. 'Fine,' I said, and ran back upstairs. I could hear them giggling behind me and I rolled my eyes. Since when had Flynn learned to be so manipulative?

I pulled my favourite trousers and a fitted jumper out of the wardrobe and got dressed quickly, put some make-up on, and studied myself in the mirror. I usually wore my red hair tied back but I'd left it loose tonight and it looked good. It was the first time I'd thought about the way I looked in forever, and it didn't feel too bad.

'Right, you two, be good, and don't let him eat any more ice cream,' I said to Rachel.

'As if I would,' Rachel said, giving Flynn a huge wink. I rolled my eyes as I bent down to give Flynn a kiss.

'Now be a good boy for Aunty Rachel won't you?'

'Of course, Mummy. And be a good girl for Annabelle's daddy.'

'I will,' I said, solemnly, ignoring Rachel's snort in the background.

And then before I could change my mind, I left.

* * *

'So I take it Flynn's dad isn't on the scene?' Oliver said, taking a bite of bread and chewing slowly.

I froze, unsure how to answer. I had to say something. Oliver had just told me all about his divorce, about his wife running off with another man and starting another family and how he had full custody because she hadn't shown much interest in seeing Annabelle.

'I have no idea how anyone could do that,' I'd told him, my heart contracting at the mere thought of walking away from Flynn and never seeing him again.

'Me neither. But it made life easier, in the end, for me at least.' Oliver shook his head. 'I just have to hope it doesn't affect Annabelle too much, long term.'

It was only natural that he would ask me about Flynn's dad, and I couldn't believe I hadn't really planned what to say.

I shoved a forkful of risotto into my mouth as a delaying tactic, and watched him studying me, waiting for me to say something. Finally, I swallowed.

'He's not around. He never really has been,' I said.

'That's a shame,' Oliver said.

I shook my head. 'It's fine. It was just a one-night thing, I didn't need him to stick around. Flynn's never known him.'

I knew I sounded cold, but it was the only way I could get through the lie without it sticking in my throat.

'That must be hard though. Does Flynn ever ask about him?'

'Not really. I'm sure he will one day, but he hasn't so far.'

Oliver took a sip of wine and studied me thoughtfully. 'I still haven't worked out what to tell Annabelle when she starts really asking questions about her mum,' he said. 'I can't tell her she didn't want to know her, but I can't lie either.'

I flinch. Is he telling me he knows I'm lying?

Of course he's not. Why would he?

'If only they'd stay little forever and never ask us any awkward questions,' I said, smiling.

'That would be ideal, wouldn't it?'

We ate our dinner for a while, the hum of the restaurant around us our only soundtrack. Oliver was good company, and even the quiet times when we weren't talking felt comfortable, unforced. It was a relief, to be with someone who didn't ask constant questions, or who knew too much about you. I felt I could reinvent my history, in a way. Or at least not let it define me.

The rest of the meal was lovely, and by the end of the night the attraction I'd felt towards Oliver had started to become something more. I didn't want to try to name it or over-analyse it. For now, I was happy to see where this went.

So when he asked me if I fancied going out again, I didn't hesitate to say yes.

'You know, Annabelle was really excited about me coming out with you tonight,' he said, as we walked home through the dark streets towards my house. I knew he lived in the other direction, but I secretly liked the fact that he'd decided to walk me home.

'Flynn was too,' I said. 'I think he hopes it will mean Annabelle will be his sister.'

The words were out before I realised how they sounded and I was glad it was dark so Oliver couldn't see my face flaming. But then his fingers brushed against mine and I didn't move mine away. The next thing I knew they were entwined, and it felt as though the blood had rushed to all the nerve endings in my hand.

'At least we have the kids' approval,' he said, and I was grateful he'd made it easy for me.

Too soon, we were at my front door.

'This is me,' I said, stopping just before it.

He looked up at the windows. 'Have you always lived here?'

'For a few years,' I said. 'I can't really afford it but it's Flynn's home so I make it work.'

'Ah yes, been there, done that.' He glanced at the windows. 'It looks lovely.'

'Thank you,' I said. I felt suddenly nervous, acutely aware that Oliver's hand was still holding mine and that there were only a few inches between us. Part of me wanted to keep the conversation going, to put off the awkward moment when we said goodbye. But the other part of me was screaming out for him to kiss me, and it surprised me. I hadn't expected to want to kiss anyone until I knew for certain that I was never going to see Nick again.

Oliver was looking at me, his face in shadow. I met his gaze and he moved towards me. Then his lips were on mine and I responded. My hand went to his chest, the other one was still in his hand and I felt like I was floating above my own body.

I was kissing Oliver!

I was kissing the hot dad from school!

When he pulled away, he smiled at me. 'Well, that was nice,' he said.

I raised my eyebrows. 'Nice?'

He grinned, the corners of his eyes crinkling. 'Okay, that was pretty hot,' he said, and a shiver ran through me. 'I'd quite like to do it again next week if you'll let me.'

'I think that can be arranged,' I said.

I wasn't sure whether to ask him in. It wouldn't be fair to subject him to Rachel's scrutiny just yet, but I didn't want him to think I didn't want to either. He made it easy for me in the end, by taking a step away.

'I'd better be off now. I need to get back for the babysitter.' His hand left mine and it felt cold suddenly. 'Night, Emma, thank you for a really lovely evening. See you at the school gates.'

'Night, Oliver.'

Then I turned and let myself into the house.

* * *

'Did you kiss him?'

Rachel was in the living room doorway almost the instant I closed the door.

I grinned. 'I might have done.'

'Yes!' she said, in a half-whisper so as not to wake up Flynn. 'Come in and tell me everything.'

I slipped my shoes off and followed her into the living room. I suddenly felt bone-tired, all the earlier nerves and excitement drained out of me, and I flopped onto the sofa and tipped my head back.

'Come on, out with it.'

I lifted my head and peered at my friend. 'It was lovely, he was lovely, it was a lovely night.'

'And?'

'And we're going out again next week.'

Rachel rubbed her hands together in glee. 'Oh, Em, I'm so pleased for you. I really hoped you might find someone sooner or later.'

I screwed my face up. 'This doesn't mean I'm not going to look for Nick though, when the time comes. You know that, right?'

'But what if you properly fall in love with him? Oliver, I mean?'

I shook my head. 'I can't. It wouldn't be fair.'

Rachel scowled. 'So, what? You're going to let a chance of happiness slip away on the off-chance that you might have saved Nick's life, and that even if you did, he'll want to know you?'

'I don't have any choice,' I said simply, crossing my legs and leaning my elbows on my knees. 'Nick is Flynn's dad, and if I have any chance at all to give Flynn his daddy then I'll take it.'

'Even if it means missing out on happiness?'

I fixed her with a look as a heavy feeling settled in my chest. 'It's not just for Flynn that I want Nick to still be alive, it's for me too. Yes, Oliver is lovely and if things were different I'd be feeling excited about the possibility that this could go somewhere. But Nick was...' I trailed off, trying to find the words to describe how things had felt between me and Nick, even though I'd never been able to before. 'It was as though there was an invisible bond between us, a current that ran from me to him and back again.'

'That sounds more like a circuit board than love.'

I shook my head. 'It's impossible to describe, but you just have to trust me.'

'And you're sure that wasn't just the weird time-slip thing? You're sure that the feelings between you were more than just an electrical pulse, or a tear in the passage of time? I mean, there's all sorts of physics going on there that neither of us understand.'

I shrugged. 'As sure as I can be. And even if I'm wrong, all he ever wanted was to be a dad. I have to at least try to find him and let him know that he is, even if he doesn't ever want to speak to me again.'

'And until then?'

'Until then I'll find it hard to let anyone else in.'

28

NICK

I chewed my food and when I swallowed it felt like I was trying to get a brick down my throat. The silence was so dense I could probably have lifted up my steak knife and cut right through it.

I looked up at the woman opposite me and pulled my face into a smile. She smiled back, looking genuinely happy, and guilt pierced my heart.

What was I doing here?

Andy had set me up on a date with one of Amanda's friends, Lucy. And she was lovely – pretty, with shiny brown hair and a full belly laugh. She was interesting and funny and talked a lot – and clearly liked me. And yet I knew I was being sullen and ungenerous with my conversation, and I hated myself for it.

When we finally said goodnight, I felt nothing but relief. I let myself into the house, stepping into the hallway – and as I did, a shiver ran through me. I stopped and closed my eyes. I hadn't felt Emma's presence in this house for a while, had assumed she'd gone, maybe moved somewhere else. So why did it feel as though she was here now, tonight?

Could she be trying to tell me something?

Trying to tell me the day was nearly here?

A gust of wind slammed the door shut and I jumped. What the hell was I doing? Andy was right, I realised. I was holding back, not really living my life the way I wanted. Because every time I did something I thought, *What's the point, I could die tomorrow?*

Something had to give.

Before I could change my mind, I ran upstairs and pulled the loft hatch down, then clambered up the stairs into the dark, stuffy cavern. As I balanced at the top, slightly tipsy, it occurred to me that it would be ironic if I fell from here and killed myself right now, looking for Emma's letter.

I crawled on my hands and knees across the wooden floor and dragged a cardboard box out of the corner. There was a thick layer of dust across the top, but when I opened the flaps the letter was right there waiting for me, as though I'd left it there knowing this day would eventually come.

I tucked it in my pocket and climbed out of the loft and back down the ladder. In my bedroom I took the letter out of my pocket and lay it on the duvet in front of me.

All these years I'd been so determined not to read what Emma had to say. But what if it could help me move on with my life? What if she was telling me I was wrong, all this time?

I left the letter on the bed and went downstairs to pour myself a glass of whisky, then went back upstairs. My hands were shaking so I threw the drink down my throat. The burn was good, a reminder of the fact that I was still here, still living.

Still able to make decisions.

I picked up the envelope and tore it open before I could think about it any longer. My hands were shaking so much it took three attempts to unfold the piece of paper, and even when I did it was hard to focus on the words.

But then I did.

Don't get on that train.

I stared at the page, the words blurring into each other. It was a warning.

And there was a date.

Sunday 12 March 2006.

That was less than a year away.

The walls of the bedroom closed in on me, my vision blurred.

The air felt too thick to breathe.

I stood suddenly, scooping the letter off the bed, and ran back down to the kitchen. Heart hammering, I found some matches in the drawer, then held the letter over the sink and let it burn until it disappeared. As the last of the embers drifted down, I let my head drop and the tears came, thick and fast, splashing into the sink, my chest heaving.

A while later I was sitting on the kitchen floor. It was chilly and there were goosebumps on my arms. A heaviness sat in my chest and I tried to take a deep breath but I just couldn't seem to get the air into my lungs. Was I having a heart attack? Was Emma wrong, and *this* was the moment I was going to die?

Eventually, I got my breathing under control, and pulled myself slowly up to standing, my head spinning. The only evidence that the letter had ever existed was a couple of scraps of blackened paper by the plughole, and I turned the tap on and ran it until they washed away.

That was it. It was over. I had a date. Now I just had to decide what to do about it.

But while the letter might not exist any longer, the words were imprinted into my mind, and they hung over me like a dark cloud for the next ten months. Some days the cloud was so heavy I couldn't get out of bed, and it was on one of those days that Andy made me an appointment to see my GP and practically dragged me there. I was given more antidepressants and sent home.

But I knew that wasn't going to solve anything.

The cloud wouldn't lift until that date had passed.

29

EMMA

Oliver and I did date, in the end. In fact we dated for more than a year, and he was funny and kind and handsome, and he made me feel special every single day without being cheesy or overpowering with it. He made me tea and toast every morning on the nights we stayed together, one slice with just butter, the other with peanut butter. He booked a surprise weekend away to Rome for my birthday because he knew I'd always wanted to go. He loved Flynn and often took him for days out, just him, Flynn and Annabelle so I could have a day to myself.

He was almost the perfect partner.

And then, Oliver dropped a bombshell.

'I think we should move in together,' he said.

I was painting my nails at the dressing table at the time and I froze, my hands stilling mid-air, my thumb still only half painted.

'Emma? Did you hear what I just said?'

I turned slowly to face him. He was sitting on the edge of the bed and he looked so handsome and excited and I knew I needed to say something, but my throat felt blocked. 'I...' I started, then cleared my throat. 'I don't know.'

His face fell and I felt like I'd just kicked a puppy. 'Oh,' he said, looking down at the floor. I moved to sit beside him and he tipped towards me as I sat, our shoulders touching. I pressed my fingers to his chin and gently turned his head until he was facing me.

'You make me happy, Oliver,' I said, softly. 'I love being with you. I just don't... I don't know why we need to change anything.'

His eyes widened slightly as he opened his mouth to speak again. 'I just... it's been a year. The kids seem happy. We're happy. I thought...' He trailed off.

I didn't know what to say. Of course he was right. We were happy, and moving in together would be the next logical step. And in any other circumstances – in any other life – I would have jumped at the chance.

But this wasn't any other life.

The fact was, it was already almost February and I'd spent the last year with one eye on the calendar, counting down to 2026. Counting down to the date, twenty years previously, that Nick had died.

And no matter how I felt about Oliver, or anyone else, I couldn't fully commit to anyone or anything until I found out whether I'd succeeded in making a difference. Whether I'd saved Nick. It simply wouldn't be fair.

'I'm sorry,' I said, before I could change my mind. 'I think we should take a break.'

I waited while my words sank in, and then he pulled away as though he'd been slapped. 'Sorry, what?' he said. He looked as though he was expecting me to tell him I was only messing around, of course I didn't mean it, of course we should move in together. And in that moment it would have been so easy to have backtracked and saved everything.

Except it wouldn't be fair to lead him on, when a piece of my heart was still elsewhere. A clean break felt like the kindest thing to do.

Oliver, of course, didn't agree. Why would he when I couldn't tell him any of this? When he'd been thinking about us moving in together, and now here I was, telling him I wanted to end it instead.

'I'm sorry,' I said, dropping my hands into my lap. 'I just... I know it will be hard – for the kids as well as us. But I've been thinking about it for a while and I honestly think it's for the best.'

He moved even further away from me, the look on his face one of pure confusion. I wanted to reach out and touch him, comfort him. I threaded my fingers together to stop me doing it.

'I don't get it,' he said. 'Everything's been great.'

I looked down at the floor. 'I don't suppose you'd believe me if I told you that this was as difficult for me as it was for you, would you?'

He gave a laugh so bitter it didn't sound like him at all. 'And yet you're doing it anyway.' He stared at the rug in front of him, not looking me in the eye. I couldn't blame him.

'Have I done something wrong?' he said. 'We can slow things down, if that's the problem.'

'No, you haven't done anything wrong, it's not that. It's... you're...' I searched for the right word to describe him. 'Amazing. It just doesn't feel like the right time for me to be with someone. I think... I think me and Flynn will be better off just the two of us for a while.'

His eyes widened incredulously, and he turned to look at me. 'Now I know you're lying. Flynn loves having me around and you know he does.' He stood, the air shifting around him. His face was in shadow. 'I truly have no idea what's going on here or why, but I'm going to leave now. If you change your mind, you know where I am.'

Then he'd walked out of the house and I'd been left feeling bereft, cracked open.

I didn't feel much better now, more than a month later. I'd spotted Oliver a few times at the school gates, but he hadn't even looked at me and had left before I'd had a chance to speak to him. I felt like a part of me had been rubbed away, leaving a raw, open wound. I wished I could tell him I was doing it for him; wished I could tell him the truth. But I couldn't.

Finally, 12 of March arrived – the date, twenty years before, that Nick had died in the Euston train crash.

Since leaving the letter for Nick and realising nothing had changed, I'd checked the old news reports from time to time over the years, just in case. But of course, Nick was still dead, according to them.

But all that time, in the back of my mind, Rachel's words from seven years before hovered: *Either the future is changed from right now and he will still be alive and you could go and tell him about the baby. Or nothing will change until the date of the accident in 2006. Which will be 2026 for us.*

It made no sense, but it was the only sliver of hope I had to cling on to. And now that day was here, and this was my last chance. If nothing changed today, I'd failed, and I'd lost the chance to tell Nick about his son forever.

Everything rested on this.

I felt like a pressure cooker about to explode.

I'd taken the day off and sent Flynn to early morning breakfast club. Rachel had also insisted on taking the day off to be with me. Although I'd objected, claiming I was fine on my own, I was glad of her presence as the time crept nearer.

'Here, take a glug of this,' she said now, plonking a huge mug of steaming hot milky coffee in front of me. I took a sip.

'I'm not sure plying me with caffeine is the best way to calm me down,' I said, wiping the froth from my lip.

'Maybe not. But we need to focus.'

I took another gulp and looked up at her.

'Do you really think something is going to happen today?' I said, my voice so quiet that Rachel had to lean closer to hear me. She pressed her hand against my arm, her palm warm.

'Having never done anything like this before there's literally no way of knowing,' she said. 'All we can do is wait, and hope.'

Over the last seven years we'd tried not to discuss this day too much, both of us agreeing it was better to just get on with things. And with Flynn to look after and a busy job, it hadn't been as hard as I'd imagined for me to put it out of my mind most of the time. But it was during the dark hours of the night when I was feeding Flynn, or when I just couldn't sleep, that I'd tried to imagine this moment: tried to imagine that, somehow, Nick had found the note, not got on the train – and that, from today, the newspapers would tell a different story.

That Nick would still be alive.

I checked the time on my phone – 9 a.m.

There was still over an hour until Nick got on that train twenty years ago and the minutes were groaning by like hours, days, weeks.

I stood, unable to sit still.

Rachel looked up at me. 'Where are you going?'

I rubbed my hand over my hair. 'I can't just sit here. Can we go for a walk?'

Rachel stood and walked round to my side of the table, took my hands in hers.

'Take a couple of deep breaths,' she said, and I did as I was told, filling my lungs and breathing slowly out. I felt the tension drop from me like a rock as I looked at my best friend. 'Whatever happens today, I'm here, okay?'

I nodded.

'I know there's a lot at stake here. But if Nick still dies, you've got Flynn. And me. You've been perfectly fine for the last seven years, and you still will be.'

Her eyes searched my face and eventually I looked away.

'I know,' I said, my voice crackly.

I sat back down. My coffee was cooler now and I took a long gulp. 'Thank you,' I said.

'Don't be daft.' She clapped her hands. 'Now I know you won't be hungry, but I'm going to make you something to eat anyway. At least it'll keep you distracted.'

I didn't argue, and as I watched her make scrambled egg and toast some bread I tried to calm my heart.

Rachel was right. Flynn and I were just fine. He was already six years old and as much as I would love him to know his daddy, I had no idea whether Nick would want to meet him even if he did survive the crash. I just knew that, whatever happened, I would give Flynn the best life I could. That was all that mattered.

Somehow the next hour passed. We ate eggs, which felt like chewing fuzzy felts, and forced down more coffee.

10 a.m. arrived. Almost time.

I stared at the laptop, paralysed, my throat thick with fear.

10.05 a.m.

A bit longer.

10.08 a.m.

The time the trains collided.

I looked at Rachel. She was studying me and gave me a small nod. I pulled the laptop closer and opened it with shaking hands.

Clicking on the news sites I'd left open, I skimmed over the now-familiar details on the BBC, the *Guardian*, *The Times*: 'two trains collided just outside Euston at 10.08 a.m.... emergency services were on the scene within minutes... rescue operation took days...'

All archived stories, all so familiar to me I could have recited them off by heart.

Then I took a deep breath and pressed 'refresh'.

As the words in front of me swam into focus, my breath caught in my chest.

I leaned closer, my whole body shaking, and read the words again.

Then I looked up at Rachel.

'The headline's changed,' I whispered.

'What? What does it say?' She scooted round and leaned towards the screen.

Then together, we read the story, now changed from the familiar one we'd read so many times over the last seven years.

No longer did it say 'popular teacher dies in Euston train crash'.

Now, it read: 'Popular family man dies in Euston train crash'.

And below it, was a picture of someone else.

Someone familiar.

The air was knocked from me as realisation hit me.

It was Andrew Flynn.

Nick's brother had died instead.

30

NICK

A few days before the 12 of March, my mum rang.

'Your grandad's been taken to hospital with pneumonia,' she said. 'I don't like to leave him on his own but I'm away this weekend. Your brother said he'd go on Saturday, so would you pop to see him on Sunday?'

Sunday, 12 March. The day of the crash.

So that was why I was on a train on a Sunday morning.

'Of course,' I said. What else could I have said?

Besides, there were so many things I could do to avoid that particular train if I chose to listen to Emma's warning. Get an earlier train. Get a later one. Drive, take a bus. It would be fine.

When the day arrived I got up and dressed. I packed my rucksack and left the house, planning to catch an earlier train. Surely that would shift the narrative enough to change whatever was about to happen?

But, halfway to the station I stopped dead, inexplicably. It was as though an invisible force had physically stopped me from going any further, and my legs just wouldn't take me there. I perched on a nearby wall and took a couple of deep breaths. Was

I being stupid, considering getting on *any* train this morning? No matter my views on interfering with the future, Emma had sent me a warning for a reason.

Was I a fool to even consider ignoring her?

I sat there for ten minutes trying to decide what to do. The train I was planning to catch left, and I knew I wasn't going to go. I stood and hurried back to my house and climbed into bed.

A text from Andy came through at 8.52 a.m.

ANDY

Give Grandad my love, he seemed a bit better yesterday.

NICK

Sorry I'm ill today so I haven't gone. Don't want to give Grandad anything. I'll pop and see him tomorrow instead.

ANDY

FFS, Nick, Mum only asked you for one thing. You need to pull yourself together.

'Fuck you!' I screamed into the air, then I popped a couple of sleeping pills and pulled the duvet over my head.

I woke up to the sound of my phone ringing. I picked it up and saw Amanda's name on it. Half-asleep, I answered it and put her on speaker phone.

'Hello?'

But she didn't say anything and for a minute I wondered whether she'd hung up before I answered. But the call was still connected. And then I heard it; a strange, strangled sound.

'Amanda, are you there?' I sat up, my head pounding.

She made a sound but there were no clear words. And then I heard one:

'Andy.'

My stomach plummeted. Suddenly, I was agonisingly, terrifyingly alert.

'Amanda, has something happened?'

'Andy... hospital... train... news...' The words came out in gasps as though she couldn't catch her breath. Heart thudding, I clambered across the bed and snatched the remote from the bedside table and switched on the TV. Images of a mangled train filled the screen, a ticker-tape of doom racing across the bottom and a reporter standing near the scene.

The train I was supposed to get on.

A sense of dread filled me as I said the next words, ice filling my veins.

'Amanda, did Andy get on the train this morning?'

'Yes. He said he was going to see your grandad again because you couldn't. I... I can't get hold of him.' The words were more a strangled sob, and in that second my world fell apart.

Angry with me, Andy had gone to see Grandad instead of me.

He had got on the train.

And it was my fault.

Bile rose in my throat and I swallowed it down. I needed to stay strong, help Amanda get through this. I needed to step up and help her get hold of her husband. My brother.

'I'm coming over,' I said.

I was on her doorstep within minutes, and she fell into my arms. When she looked up at me her face was red and blotchy, her eyes puffy. 'I don't want the girls to know there's anything wrong,' she whispered, glancing behind her.

'Let's get inside, I'll sort them out,' I said, leading her back in. Always so capable, she seemed frail now, as though the life had been sucked from her. I sat her down at the kitchen table and poured her a glass of water.

'Drink this. I'll go and see to the girls.'

I ran up the stairs and knocked on Imogen's door first, not wanting to just walk in on her now she was fifteen. She didn't answer so I pushed the door slightly open and peered round. She was sitting on her bed, headphones in, listening to music on her MP3 player. She looked up and smiled when she saw me.

'Hi, Uncle Nick,' she said, pulling her headphones off. 'I didn't know you were coming round today.'

'I wasn't. I just came to ask your mum something.'

'Ah right.' Thank goodness for uncurious teenagers.

'Anyway, get back to your music, I just wanted to say hi,' I said, backing out of the door.

'See you later,' she said, and I closed the door behind me. At least she was fine.

Ella's door was slightly open and I could hear pop music, tinny, as though it was being played through a computer. I tapped a couple of times and stepped inside. Ella was standing in front of the mirror practising a dance move and her face lit up when she saw me, and she threw her arms around me.

'Hey you,' I said, kissing the top of her head.

'I'm just practising for the show next week,' she said, pulling away from me. She loved dancing and I'd been to see her countless times in shows over the years. I felt guilty that I'd been so self-absorbed that I hadn't known she had one coming up.

'Ah right. Am I coming to see it?' I said.

She shrugged. 'Dad didn't know, but I think he got you a ticket.'

'Oh good, I'll definitely come then,' I said.

'Do you want to see my routine?'

'Tell you what, let's keep it as a surprise for the show, shall we?' I said.

'Yeah, okay.' She turned away and I took it as my cue to leave.

'I'll see you in a bit then.'

'Bye, Uncle Nick.'

As I walked down the stairs I could hear Amanda's voice and I hurried back to the kitchen with my heart in my throat to find her ending a call. The look on her face sent a chill down my spine.

'Who was that?' I said, collapsing into a chair opposite her.

'The police,' she said. 'They've found Andy's phone.'

I stared at her for a minute, trying to process it. 'You mean...?'

'They think he might still be in the train.'

'Alive?'

Her face crumpled before she could speak and I stood on shaking legs and rushed to her side, wrapping her in a hug. I was desperate to find out more, to know whether Andy had made it, but for now all either of us could do was wait.

'This is my fault,' I whispered into her head.

'No,' she said, forcefully, looking up at me. Her face was red and blotchy.

'He was angry with me. I should have gone.'

'He was never angry with you, Nicky, not really. He was worried about you. *Is* worried about you.' We both noticed the correction but said nothing.

The next few hours were like a nightmare unfolding. By the end of the day police had called back and confirmed that Andy's body had been pulled from the wreckage of the train. They sent someone round, a family liaison officer, but Amanda and I had already broken the news to the girls before they got there. It was the worst thing I'd ever had to do, watching the look on those girls' faces as they realised that their dad was never coming home.

'Uncle Nick?' Ella said, looking to me for some sort of reassurance. But all I could do was wrap my arms around them both and let them cry until there were no more tears left to cry.

31

EMMA

I felt as though I might pass out. Beside me, Rachel opened her mouth as if to say something but then closed it again, and peered back at the screen. Her forehead was pinched into a frown. Finally, she looked at me and shook her head. 'But I don't understand. Surely if Nick didn't get on the train and he told his brother why, then Andrew wouldn't have got on either? I mean, even if you thought it was probably bollocks, you wouldn't, would you? Just in case.'

'Maybe.' I wracked my brains to remember what Nick had told me about his brother. They were close, I was sure of that. And I knew Nick had told him about me, at least some of it. But it didn't necessarily follow that he'd told him about my letter. 'I don't know,' I said, rubbing my temples which were beginning to throb. 'I just... I don't know what to think.'

Rachel laid her phone carefully on the table and stood. 'Let me make us a cuppa.'

While Rachel bustled round, I tried to put my thoughts in some sort of order. When I'd thought through the possible outcomes of my actions, not once had this crossed my mind. I'd imagined that Nick had never found the letter and he'd still died; I'd imagined that he had found it but refused to read it, and nothing had changed. And of course I'd thought about what might happen if he had found it, read it and decided to believe me. Would he be grateful to me for saving his life and try to find me?

This outcome though. His brother dying instead of him? I couldn't even begin to untangle the feelings he must have about it.

But there was one thing I was sure of. Whatever had happened, I blamed myself.

And I was certain Nick would blame me too.

* * *

'Look at this,' I said, pointing at the screen. Rachel placed a mug of tea in front of me and peered at the screen.

'You know that interview Andy gave on the first anniversary of Nick's death?'

'Yes?'

'Look at it now.'

I waited while she read it. Then she looked back at me, her eyes wide.

'It's him,' she said. 'It's Nick.'

'Exactly,' I said. The interview with Andy about Nick had now been replaced by an interview with Nick about his brother. There were the same photos of the boys together, growing up, huge grins for the camera, and later, photos of Andy with his family, his kids. And while all of it made me feel even worse, it was the photo of Nick I couldn't tear my eyes away from.

He was older than the last time I'd seen him, but that was hardly surprising given that this had been written in 2007, eight years after the last time I saw him. But it was more than that; until this moment I'd forgotten how much Flynn looked like his daddy.

Given that I'd never been able to take a photo of Nick, I'd relied on my memory of him, of the angles of his face, the tilt of his eyes, the dimples in his cheeks when he smiled. But as the years had passed, that image had become blurry, unfocused, until I couldn't be sure whether it was accurate at all.

But now, here he was, staring out at me from 2007 – and he looked just like I remembered. He looked just like his son.

* * *

'He's six years old and he's been perfectly fine without a daddy in his life until now,' I said, folding my arms. 'You said it yourself.'

Rachel said nothing, just raised her eyebrows.

'What? He has. We're happy, just me and Flynn.'

'Maybe you are. But don't you think you're being a bit selfish refusing to even consider giving Flynn the chance to know his daddy – or Nick the chance to know he's a dad – given what you know now? I mean, this is what you wanted all along, isn't it?'

I shook my head. 'I can't do it,' I said. 'I've thought about nothing else from the moment Flynn was born, and I've dreamed about him knowing his daddy. But this is... I don't know. It feels wrong. Andy *died*. I'm not sure it's fair to anyone.'

'Except Flynn is already starting to ask questions that you can't answer, isn't he?'

I looked down at the table. Rachel was right. At six years old, Flynn had been asking questions about his daddy for a while, but they were becoming more specific now. The other day he had asked me whether his daddy was in heaven like Zara's in his class, and a few weeks before he'd asked whether his daddy had run away because he didn't love him. I didn't know what to say to that, so had rapidly changed the subject, the way I always did.

But I'd never wanted to outright lie to him. I couldn't tell him his daddy was dead, because what if I did find him? How on earth would I explain that to a six-year-old? Besides, not having any photos of him would have made that weird. What sort of mother doesn't keep photos of their child's dead father?

And although I'd got away with being slightly vague about it so far, I knew it couldn't go on much longer.

'I'm scared,' I said, looking up at Rachel.

'What of?'

I shrugged, trying to work out how to explain it. 'Nick rejected me once, when he thought I'd gone against his wishes. What if... what if I find him but he rejects me again?' A heavy weight pressed against my heart. 'Because it would mean he was also rejecting Flynn and I'm not sure I could bear that.'

Rachel's hand slid across the table and she threaded her fingers through mine. 'Just tell him you're sorry for what you did, but you hope he'll forgive you, and see whether he replies.'

'And if he doesn't?'

'Then you won't have lost anything. But if he does – well, then you can decide what you want to do. Either way, you'll never stop wondering if you don't even try.'

* * *

It had been fairly easy to find Nick, in the end. Although Nick Flynn wasn't an uncommon name, the fact that he'd spoken to a newspaper made him easier to trace. The things I'd discovered about him so far were that he had a Facebook profile but never posted, didn't have Instagram or TikTok or any other social media, and he still worked as a maths teacher. About two years after the crash he'd moved away from the area and now lived up in Suffolk. There were very few photos of him and none that seemed very up-to-date, so I had no idea what 58-year-old Nick might look like.

But the mere fact that he existed was a miracle.

Eventually I found his email address on the school website, then I wrote him an email.

Dear Nick

I've rewritten this email so many times because I don't have a clue where to start. Sorry is probably a good place. So, I'm sorry. For everything.

If you're reading this then I'm assuming you found and read the letter that I left for you in the bandstand. I hope you understand why I left it. I never wanted to leave things like that between us.

I know a long time has passed but I'd really like to see you. I wondered if it's something you'd be interested in, with absolutely no pressure?

Thank you for taking the time to read this. I hope to hear back from you soon.

Emma

I clicked send. Now all I could do was wait.

PART III

32

NICK

After Andy's death, as the days had turned to weeks and the weeks into months, we all slowly started to heal. At least, the girls did, and Amanda, eventually. But the guilt felt as though it was eating me up from the inside, and apart from my work, I stopped engaging with the world. I stopped seeing friends, I saw the girls and Amanda less and less often, the pain of knowing what I'd done to them too much to bear. Eventually, I moved away, to Suffolk, and found a job in another school, far away from everything I'd known before. Ten years after his death I finally felt strong enough to set up a charity in Andy's name, to help people who had unexpectedly lost a loved one to access grief counselling, and that kept me busy, but apart from that I led a quiet life, alone. It felt like all I deserved.

Now, in 2026, twenty years had passed since that fateful day. And although I'd learned to accept what I'd done and slowly started to forgive myself, it didn't take much to set me back again.

And then, Emma's email had appeared, and it was as though the last twenty years had never happened.

Emma Vickers.

The woman who had made me fall in love with her, then broken my heart.

The woman I had never truly got over. Or forgiven.

I'd shied away from checking up on her, from looking her up online. My grief was too raw and my heart too fragile. It was easier to let the memory of her face fade in my mind with the passing of time.

In a few weak moments more recently I had contemplated knocking on the door of my old house on one of my infrequent visits to see Amanda and the girls. I'd tried to picture Emma's reaction, to imagine how it would feel to see her face again; whether she would be pleased to see me, or whether she would simply slam the door in my face.

Would I be pleased to see her, or would I only be able to see the face of the person I blamed for my brother's death?

In the end, I hadn't dared to do it. I'd made peace with the fact that she'd never be part of my life again and there was no point in stirring up the hornets' nest.

But now, here she was, splitting my life apart like an axe through a log, and I couldn't ignore it any longer.

She wanted to see me, and I had to decide whether to pull that loose thread one last time and risk my whole, safe life unravelling – or leave it alone and live with the knowledge that being here, in my life, was enough.

33

EMMA

How long do you wait for someone to reply before you give up on them? Although email was great for so many things, one of the worst things about it was the uncertainty: did Nick get my email, or had he changed his email address? Had he read it? Had it gone into his junk folder? Or had he seen it and decided to ignore it?

After six weeks had passed, I was fairly certain I wasn't going to get a reply from him no matter what the reason. The question was, should I try to find him another way, or did he simply just not want to know?

'You have to at least give him the chance to decide whether he wants to be part of Flynn's life,' Rachel said.

'I don't want to trick him into anything,' I replied. 'If he's not interested in seeing me, then that's that.'

Rachel knew not to push me on it, but her words stayed with me. Perhaps she was right. Perhaps Nick did deserve to know about Flynn no matter what. Maybe I should have told him about his son in the email, rather than being opaque about it.

But I hadn't wanted to frighten him off. I had no idea what Nick Flynn's life had been like since we'd last seen each other, and I had no idea whether he was even in a fit state to see me. Besides, this was pretty big news I had to tell him, not something to just drop into an email.

'We need to look him up,' Rachel said. 'There must be more about him online.'

'There really isn't,' I said. 'I've tried everything, but he doesn't seem to have an online presence.'

'What, not at all?'

'Only a couple of local news stories from when he took his new job as deputy head at that school in Suffolk, another one where he's quoted saying how proud he is after the school received an excellent OFSTED inspection, and a couple of articles in the local paper about a charity he's set up for grieving relatives.' I shrugged. 'It makes me worry that he's deliberately hidden himself from the world.'

Rachel peered more closely at me. 'What are you really worried about, Ems?'

I tried to ignore the burning sensation behind my eyes, blinking back the tears before they escaped. I sniffed. 'He must blame me for what happened to his brother,' I said, my voice wobbly. 'He must hate me. I'd hate me.'

'It's not your fault. You must know that?'

'Of course it is,' I said, as the tears streamed down my face. 'If I hadn't written that letter then his brother would never have died!'

'But Nick would have done.'

I shook my head. 'But that was the way it was meant to be. This is why he told me he didn't want to know anything about the future, because nothing good can ever come from interfering with it.'

'You don't know for certain that he even found your letter.'

I looked up. 'What do you mean?'

'I mean, you have no idea whether he found it, or whether the fact that Andy got on the train rather than Nick was just a coincidence.'

I stared at her. That had never even occurred to me. I'd just assumed that Nick's brother dying instead of him was down to me. But what if Rachel was right, and it *was* just a coincidence?

'Maybe. But that still doesn't change the fact that he hasn't replied to my email.'

'Then let's go and find him,' she said.

'Find him?'

'You know. In real life.'

'No!' I shook my head. 'Absolutely no way. I am not just turning up out of the blue, I'd give the poor man a heart attack.'

'Fine, fine.' Rachel held her hands up in mock surrender. 'But you need to think of something, otherwise you could spend the rest of your life sitting around worrying about it and that's no good for you or Flynn.'

I agreed. The trouble was, I was still no closer to coming up with a solution.

Luckily, the universe came up with one for me.

The next morning after dropping Flynn at school I logged onto my emails as usual, fully expecting the same result as always. But this time as I scanned the screen, the breath left my body.

There was an email from Nick.

I stared at it for ages, the words blurring in front of my eyes until I couldn't see anything at all.

Nick had replied, but there was no subject, and no clue as to what the email might contain.

My hand hovered over the mouse, ready to click. But I couldn't do it. What if the words he had written made my whole world implode?

I picked up my phone and called Rachel.

'Can you come?' I said, my voice small.

'Darling, I can't right now I'm at work,' she said. 'What on earth's happened?'

'It's Nick,' I whispered, almost breathless. 'He's replied.'

'Oh my God.'

'I know.'

'Okay, open it now. I'll stay on the phone.'

'I can't,' I said. I was completely paralysed with fear.

'I'm here,' she said. 'It'll be fine. It's just words. Words can't hurt you.'

I sat, frozen, with my mobile pressed against my ear, my other hand poised, ready to click. And then, I did it.

And I read the words that were about to change my whole future.

34

NICK

It took me a long time to decide whether to reply to Emma. On the one hand, how could I face her, after everything that had happened? The ripple effect of the letter she had written was so far-reaching it felt as though it would be impossible to look her in the eye.

On the other hand, just seeing her name got me thinking about her again, and all the feelings I'd spent so many years suppressing came flooding back.

In the end, it was the thought of what Andy would have told me to do that got me to reply. *It doesn't matter what's happened in the past. You still love her. Go and see her.*

And I knew he was right. I'd adored Dawn, she'd been my childhood sweetheart, the love of my young life. But there had been something special between Emma and I, something magical – and in all the intervening years since we'd been together, I'd never met anyone else like her.

I needed to know what she wanted to say to me.

Even then, though, it took me a long time to get the tone of the email right. These were the first words I'd said or written to Emma for twenty-seven years. They needed to be perfect.

In the end, I kept it simple and emotionless.

Hello Emma

Thank you for your email. I'm sorry it's taken me a long time to reply. As you can imagine, hearing from you has come as quite a shock.

I did find your letter and have thought about you often since.

I would be happy to meet you. Let's arrange a time and a place.

Yours

Nick

* * *

Of course there was only ever one place where we would meet up, and when Emma replied to my email the very next day, she had the same idea.

If you can bear to, let's meet at the bandstand, she wrote.

I hadn't been back there for so many years, and at first the thought made me feel dizzy with fear. But the more I thought about it, the more it made absolutely perfect sense. And so I said yes.

Over the next three days I worried about it constantly. Had I made a huge mistake, letting this woman back into my life, even briefly? Would seeing Emma again send me spiralling back down a rabbit hole of depression or, possibly worse, would all my old feelings resurface, and I'd risk going through heartbreak all over again?

But now, the day was here. The day that I never thought

would come and that I'd spent the last twenty-seven years trying (and sometimes succeeding) not to imagine.

I hadn't told anyone about meeting Emma. The only person I had ever told about her was Andy anyway, so there really wasn't anyone I *could* tell. But that meant I had no one to talk to, or to reassure me that I was doing the right thing.

I woke up so early that morning that it was still dark outside. I went downstairs, made myself a coffee and stood at the kitchen window looking out into my small back garden. I thought about the kitchen in the old house, the house where I had lived with Dawn, and where Emma had lived since. It was strange to think about Emma being in that kitchen, that house, after I left it to move here.

Finally, it was time to leave. I dressed carefully, climbed in my battered old Ford Focus, and set off. The drive was a couple of hours, and those two hours felt like a lifetime as doubts and memories crowded my mind, jostling for attention. But finally, I arrived in the place I still thought of as my hometown, and pulled into the car park round the corner from the park. I hadn't told Amanda and the girls I was here and, as much as I loved seeing them, I hoped I wouldn't bump into them.

Today, I needed to focus on this.

I climbed out of the car. My legs felt shaky and I realised how nervous I was. The sun was warm but a gentle breeze stopped it from feeling too hot, and as I set off towards the park I let myself think about what it would be like the first time I saw Emma again after all these years.

What would she think of me now? I knew she'd be older – forty-three, forty-four? – but at fifty-eight, I was twenty-seven years older than the last time she'd seen me, almost old enough to be her father. I was going grey round the temples and the lines on my face seemed to deepen by the week. I wasn't fool enough to imagine that Emma would still find me attractive, and yet I couldn't fully extinguish the tiny flame of hope that burned inside me that there could still be the same spark between us.

As I approached the gates of the park my footsteps slowed.

I was here, and the moment I had tried not to imagine for so many years had finally arrived. I stopped to gather my thoughts. The blood roared in my veins and my head spun. I caught a glimpse of myself in a car window. I looked old and tired. What was I even doing here?

Come on, Nick.

I took a deep breath and stepped inside the park. I turned the corner, and the bandstand loomed into sight – surrounded, just as Emma had described all those years ago, by a beautiful rose garden, pinks and yellows and peaches bursting all around. My heart hammered and my breath came in gasps.

And then, there she was. Sitting inside the bandstand with her back to me, red hair flaming in the bright midday sun.

It was Emma.

My world imploded.

35

EMMA

When I turned round and saw Nick approaching, I felt as though I might pass out. I took him in, feeling a jolt of surprise at how much he'd aged. But of course he was now twenty-seven years older than he had been when we'd first met. As he got closer, though, I could see that he was still handsome. His hair was shorter, and going grey round the temples, and his face was more lined, his chin less defined. But he was still Nick, and he still set my pulse racing, despite the years that separated us.

And then he was there, in front of me, and all the words left my mouth.

'Hello, Emma,' he said, and I smiled, unable to reply.

He stepped up onto the bandstand and sat beside me, on the same side of the bench that he'd always sat. Finally, he looked at me and his piercing gaze nearly knocked the breath from my lungs. I looked away.

'This has changed,' he said. 'It's nice.'

'Yes,' I said, looking out at the roses which were in bloom now, the riot of colour a beautiful backdrop to this... whatever this was.

'It's weird knowing we can see the same thing,' he said, as a couple strolled past hand in hand.

Of course. This was the first time we'd ever been here together and been able to see the same view. I felt dizzy at the thought.

We fell into silence, the tension between us growing with each passing moment. Finally, I had to speak.

'I read about your brother.'

He gave small nod, his lips pressed together.

'I don't know how to begin to tell you how sorry I am.'

'It was a long time ago.'

'I know. But it was my fault—'

'No!' The word exploded out of him, and even Nick looked surprised at the force with which he'd said it. He pressed his hands against the slats of the bench. 'It wasn't your fault, it was mine. I didn't...' He stopped, swallowed. It was clear this was difficult for him to say. 'I didn't tell him about your letter. I should have done, but I wasn't in a good place, and I... I should have told him. But he was angry with me for not going to visit our grandad, which was why he didn't tell me he was getting on that train instead of me that morning.'

Saying the words out loud seemed to have taken everything from him and it was as though his body had deflated as he finished. Without thinking, I reached out my hand and pressed it against his. A spark ripped through me and I gasped, pulled my hand away. I looked up at him.

'Did you...?'

He nodded, but said nothing. I put my hand back on his, prepared for the jolt this time. 'I hope you haven't spent the last twenty years blaming yourself for Andy's death?' I said gently.

'Of course I have.'

I shook my head. 'But it was down to me. It was me who wrote that letter telling you about the crash, even though you'd told me you didn't want to know anything about the future. But I was selfish, and I... I just wanted to save you, if I could.'

He pulled his hand away and clutched it in the other one in front of him. He didn't look at me for a long time but when he finally did there was unbearable pain in his eyes.

'I spent so many years blaming you. I hated you for what you did,' he said, and his words sliced through me. I said nothing though, because I deserved it. 'But as the years have passed that anger has faded, while my anger with myself for just not being honest with him, for not telling him the truth about the letter, grew.'

'Why didn't you tell him?'

'I don't think he ever truly believed me, about you,' he said. 'I also thought he might try and convince me to open it, and for a long time, I didn't want to. I put it away in a box and tried to forget about it and get on with my life. But it ate away at me, knowing it was there. Knowing that there was something you needed to tell me. Something important.' He scratched the back of his neck. 'It took me six years. And when I finally did read it, I wished I could go back in time and erase it all. But it was too late, because I *had* read it, and I did know that something was going to happen. And it ruined everything for me.'

I didn't know what to say, couldn't speak. What do you say to a man who thinks you've destroyed his life – especially when you know he's probably right? Sorry didn't even seem to touch the sides.

'Do you realise this is the first time we've been anywhere together at the same time?' Nick said, suddenly.

My heart skipped a beat at the memory of our time together here, which was still relatively fresh in my mind. While for him, it was almost a lifetime ago. I wondered whether the memory of what we'd shared, how amazing it had been, had faded over the years. Whether it had morphed into something else, just a fleeting memory.

'I know,' I said. 'It was what we always wanted, wasn't it?'

'More than anything,' he said.

When I looked up Nick was studying me and I held his gaze.

'You haven't changed,' he said.

'Oh I have,' I said, Flynn popping into my mind. It wasn't the time to mention him yet. I needed a little longer before I told him, in case he left and I never saw him again. I just needed a little longer.

'I must look ancient to you,' he said, running his hand self-consciously over his hair.

'You don't,' I said, and I meant it. I'd expected him to look older, of course. But I'd been worried he would look completely different – that life would have been so hard for him after everything that happened that who he was would have fundamentally changed. But against all the odds, he was still the same Nick.

And he still set butterflies off in my stomach.

'You look amazing,' I said, my face flushing.

'Well now I know you're lying, but I'll take it.' He swivelled round and hitched his knee up onto the bench so we were just inches apart. His eyes sparkled. 'Do you remember the night of our picnic?' he said, suddenly, a smile playing on his lips.

'Oh, er... yes, of course,' I stammered.

The picnic. The one date we managed before I ruined everything.

The night we made Flynn.

'Sorry, I didn't mean to make you feel uncomfortable,' Nick said.

'It's fine,' I said. My hands were shaking, and I hoped Nick wouldn't notice. 'It was an amazing night,' I said.

'It was,' he agreed.

This was my perfect chance to tell him about Flynn.

You have a son.

We have a son.

You're a daddy.

Except the words still wouldn't form in my mouth.

'So, did you ever meet anyone?' I said, changing the subject swiftly.

This time it was Nick's turn to look uncomfortable.

'No. I never really found the right person,' he said.

'That's a shame,' I said, even though I was secretly relieved that meant he wasn't with anyone.

'After losing Dawn and then you, I was happier alone. It was safer that way, given that I knew something bad was coming. Less chance of getting hurt, or of hurting someone else. And then when Andy died, I...' He trailed off. 'Well, I wasn't really in a fit state to meet anyone at all, so I threw myself into helping other people instead. At least his death meant something that way.'

We'd gone full circle again, back to me feeling the need to apologise for wrecking his life. It was clear from what he'd told me so far that the last twenty-seven years hadn't been easy for him. That he'd closed himself away from life, let his world become smaller and smaller, and I blamed myself for that. I'd known he was still grieving for Dawn, and I'd known it was one of the reasons he didn't want to be told anything about the future – because he never wanted to think about what could have been different. And yet I'd looked anyway, and ruined any chance we had of being together – and any chance Nick had of trusting anyone else.

I couldn't keep saying sorry though.

'I didn't either,' I said.

'You're still young though,' he said, softly. 'It's all a bit late for me.'

'That's not true.' I wanted to reach out and touch him, to feel the connection between us again, but I didn't dare. Instead, the air shimmered between us, thick with tension and longing. At least, it did for me.

'I didn't mean to ruin your life,' I whispered.

For a moment I wasn't sure that he'd heard because he didn't move or say anything. But then he slowly looked up at me and gave a tiny shake of his head.

'No matter what has happened since, I will never regret meeting you,' he said.

'Me neither,' I said, my chest hot, a fire burning in my belly.

It was time.

I had to tell him.

I leaned forward, closed the gap between us. And then I opened my mouth and said, 'Nick, I have something I need to tell you.'

36

NICK

'Why do I get the feeling this is not going to be a good thing?' I said. My hands had begun to shake and I took a deep breath to calm my nerves. It didn't work.

'It is a good thing,' she said. 'It's just... well, it's quite a big thing.'

'Right.'

The air thinned and my lungs felt like they couldn't pull in enough oxygen. I watched as Emma opened her mouth to speak, but before she could get any words out, I stood, suddenly overcome with the urge to get out of there.

She looked up at me, surprise in her eyes, then stood too.

'Nick?'

My blood felt icy in my veins. 'I don't think I can do this,' I said. 'Last time you had something to tell me it didn't end well. I told you before and I believe it even more now. Nothing good can ever come of knowing about the future.'

'But, Nick,' she said. 'I don't know anything about the future. We're here, both of us. Right now.'

I stared at her, at her beautiful flaming hair that hung in

waves around her face, at her sparkling green eyes, the handful of freckles sprinkled across her nose, and all the fight went out of me, deflating like a leaky tyre. I dropped back onto the bench. Beside me, Emma sat still, saying nothing.

'I'm sorry,' I said. 'Of course you don't know anything about the future.' I rubbed my face with my hand, feeling the prickle of stubble against my palm. 'So, what do you need to tell me?'

She paused a moment, then I watched as she bent down and pulled her bag onto her knee and rummaged around in it. She pulled out her phone and a white envelope, and lay them both on the bench beside her. She pressed the flat of her palm against the top of the envelope and looked at me. She looked absolutely petrified.

She opened her mouth, closed it again, then pushed the white envelope towards me.

'Open it,' she said.

I looked down at it. It was plain white, A4 size, and I thought back to the last time I'd found an envelope from Emma, telling me about the train crash, and how much the contents of that had changed my life. For a moment, I couldn't move, paralysed by fear and indecision.

What if the contents of this one turned my life upside down too? I wasn't sure I could handle that. And yet, it was clearly important to Emma.

I took a deep breath and picked it up and pulled the flap open. Glancing up at Emma, I could see her watching me, frozen. Her hand holding her mobile was shaking. I looked back down and peered inside. There was a sheet of paper and a couple of what looked like small photos and, trying to keep my hand steady, I pulled them out and lay them in front of me, face up.

They were all photos, one grainy, printed out on plain paper from a computer, the other two on proper photo paper and clear as day. From all three, the faces of small children grinned out at me. I frowned.

'Who are they?' I said.

A smile flickered across her face. 'It's not they,' she said, softly. 'It's just he. One boy. Flynn.'

'Flynn?' I said, a flicker of something deep in my belly.

'Look at him again,' she said.

I did as instructed, spreading the three photos out beside each other. Now I looked again I could see it was the same boy at different ages. The same smile, the same wide, blue eyes.

And then I saw it and the world stopped spinning.

I looked up at Emma, then back down at the photographs.

'This is... this is your son, isn't it?'

She nodded. 'Yes, it is.'

'And he's...' I swallowed. 'You named him after me? Flynn?'

She nodded. I held her gaze. 'I named him after his daddy.'

Images flashed through my mind like old video footage; the one night Emma and I had together; the day I knew she'd found out something bad about my future and I walked away from her; the letter she left me; the spiralling after I opened the letter; the day of the crash, and Andy dying; the last twenty years, closing myself away from the world. All of it, every single moment of it, had been leading to here, right now, this moment.

The photos swam in front of me, blurring and warping. But when I focused again, I knew she was telling me the truth.

'He has my eyes,' I said. My heart was racing so fast I only just had the breath to say the words.

'And your smile,' she said.

She was right. He did. He looked like me, and he looked like Emma, and it was all I could do to hold it together right now.

Finally, I looked up at Emma. She was watching me worriedly.

'I can't believe it,' I whispered. 'I can't believe this could even happen.'

'I could never believe any of it. But it's true,' she said.

And she was right. It was.

It was all I'd ever wanted, and now it had happened. I just needed some time to truly let it sink in.

I jumped as Emma's hands wrapped round mine on the bench. They felt warm and so real.

'Would you like to meet him?' she said.

I looked up and met her gaze.

'I can't think of anything I want more,' I said.

37

EMMA

I'd been terrified and excited about meeting Nick today, unsure how he'd react to seeing me. I'd expected him to be furious, had even been fully prepared for him to tell me to leave and never come back. And if he had, I would have respected his wishes.

But from the moment we were together again, the connection between us was there, as strong as ever – if not stronger. Perhaps it was because, for the first time since we'd known each other, we were living in the same time.

I hadn't been sure whether I was going to tell him about Flynn today.

'Just see how it goes,' Rachel had said. 'I'll bring Flynn along, and if you do end up telling him and he wants to meet him, then let him. If not, we can just go home again.'

In the end, telling Nick about Flynn had been the only thing I could have done. And his reaction was better than I could ever have imagined.

As I showed him photos of his son on my phone – Flynn being born, Flynn's first steps, in his first school uniform, on holiday, in his armbands at the side of a swimming pool, on his first bike in the park – Nick wanted to know everything about him. What he was like, what he liked to do, was he funny, was he clever, was he good at sport, did he play any instruments. I told him everything, about all the milestones he'd missed, a quick snapshot all in one go. I couldn't even begin to imagine how much this was to take in, but he didn't seem to want to stop.

And then, it had been time to go and get our little boy.

'Wait,' Nick said, as I stood. I stopped. 'Does... does he know who I am?'

'I've told him you're his daddy, but I haven't worked out the rest yet, how to tell him where you've been all this time. I didn't want to confuse him any more. But listen, we can work that out. Let's just let you meet each other first, shall we?'

Nick nodded. I pointed to the playground across the way, the playground that hadn't existed last time Nick had been here, and told him Flynn and I would meet him there in half an hour. And then I stepped out of the bandstand into the bright sunshine and walked on wobbly legs to meet Rachel, feeling as though I'd been hollowed out.

'We're getting ice creams,' Rachel told me when I called her.

As I turned the corner and saw the pair of them, I smiled. Chocolate ice cream dripped down Flynn's arm, and his face was smeared with it.

'Mummy!' he said, running towards me.

'Hello, gorgeous boy,' I said, crouching down to hug him. 'What have you got here?'

'Aunty Rachel bought me two scoops, and she said I could have sprinkles and chocolate sauce too,' he said, breathlessly.

'Did she now?' I said, grinning at her as I stood up.

'Well, if his Aunty Rachel can't spoil him then who can?' she said.

'He's a very lucky boy,' I said, ruffling his head.

I moved closer to Rachel and she raised her eyebrows. 'I assume it went well?' she said.

I nodded. 'Better than I could ever have dreamed. Am I doing the right thing?'

'Of course you are, darling. Flynn is excited, he hasn't talked about anything else all morning.'

'Thank you,' I said. 'I couldn't have done this without you.'

'Don't be daft. You can do anything you set your mind to,' she said, hooking her arm though mine. I held out my other hand for Flynn to take. 'Now, shall we go back to the park?'

'Will my daddy be there?' Flynn said, and I glanced at Rachel. She gave a small nod.

'Yes, he will. Shall we go?'

'Yes!' he said, and stuck his sticky hand in mine.

* * *

I could see Nick sitting on the bench by the slide as we walked towards the park. He looked nervous, his leg bouncing up and down. Every now and then he glanced at his phone in his hand, then looked left and right.

I pushed the gate open, Flynn still clutching my other hand.

'I'll leave you here,' Rachel said.

I turned. 'Are you not coming with us?'

'I think it would be better if it was just the three of you, for this part,' she said.

I nodded. 'Thank you.'

Flynn and I started walking across the playground, hand in hand. Nick looked pale and kept raking his fingers through his hair. He looked up as we stopped in front of him, his face pale.

'Flynn, there's someone here I'd like you to meet,' I said, crouching down to Flynn's level.

Flynn pressed himself into me, suddenly shy.

'You're my daddy,' he said, his voice almost a whisper. He stuck his thumb in his mouth, something he hadn't done since he was two years old.

'I am,' Nick said, his face finally breaking into a smile. Flynn seemed to relax then and smiled back. Then he peeled away from me and pulled himself onto the bench beside Nick.

'I'm Flynn,' he said.

'It's lovely to meet you, Flynn,' Nick said, his voice rough. He coughed.

Flynn looked puzzled. 'But I've met you before,' he said.

Nick looked up at me, a question on his face.

'You've seen your daddy in our house haven't you, sweetheart,' I said, gently.

'Yes.' He looked back at Nick. 'But you've never spoken to me before.'

I sat down beside Flynn and took his still-sticky hand.

'Nick – that's your daddy – didn't know about you before because Mummy didn't know where he was, so he couldn't have spoken to you,' I said. 'But now I've found him and I hope you can get to know each other. Does that sound good?'

Flynn hesitated a minute as though weighing up what I'd said. Would he question the logic of me saying I didn't know where Nick was when Flynn himself believed he'd seen his daddy in our house? But to my relief he simply gave a nod and jumped off the bench.

'Can Daddy come and push me on the swings?'

Nick looked to me and I gave him a small nod.

'Sure thing,' Nick said, a smile spreading across his face. And before he even got the chance to stand up, Flynn was racing off, arms pumping back and forth.

'I guess I'd better go then,' Nick said.

'He won't wait around for long,' I said.

I watched as Nick made his way over to where Flynn was already on the swing, pushing himself back and forth, his trainers scraping along the ground. Then Nick went round behind him and started pushing him, sending him higher and higher into the air.

And as I watched the pair of them, I felt a sense of calm settle over me, and a feeling of happiness that I hadn't felt for many years.

Because, I realised, it no longer mattered what the future was going to bring. Nick was here, and Flynn and I would do whatever we could to keep him in our lives.

And no matter what happened between Nick and me, it was clear that, this time, I had done the right thing, bringing Flynn and his daddy together. Now, we could muddle along together in a messy future that neither of us could predict, and hope it would bring us the happiness we'd waited so long for. And who could ask for anything more than that?

* * *

MORE FROM CLARE SWATMAN

Another emotional, heartwarming read from Clare Swatman is available to order now here:

https://mybook.to/ClareSwatmanBook11

ACKNOWLEDGEMENTS

This is now book 12, and you would have thought I'd have something original to say by now. But the truth is, there are always the same brilliant people I want to thank, some for helping me with the actual book, and others for supporting me and allowing me to do this job.

Firstly, to my mum and dad, who always get excited every time a new book comes out, I'd like to say thank you for everything and I love you. The same goes for my baby brother Mark, although to him I say muchos gracias pequeno. I also want to give my husband Tom and brilliant sons Jack and Harry a mention for being there for me and driving me mad in equal measure. And no, I'm not making you any more toast Jack.

I think this has been my favourite ever book to write. Although the details about the time slip and time travel drove me mad at times, I adore stories with time slips, so writing one has been such good fun. I also need to say thank you to my editor Rachel for pushing me to make the timelines make sense, and for doing everything to help me make this book the best it can be.

Thank you to Serena, as always, for always championing me, and to writing buddies Rowan Coleman, Laura Pearson, Julie Cohen and Kate Harrison for giving me pep talks when I needed them!

A HUGE thank you also goes to fellow author Becky Alexander. Becky was working on a book and needed someone to read it and give her some feedback – so we agreed a swap. I read hers, and in exchange she read an early draft of mine. Her feedback was both encouraging and invaluable, and gave me the confidence to realise that this book actually DID make sense after all!

There is one very special person I need to thank, and that's the wonderful Linda Hill. Linda is a fabulous book blogger and such a champion of authors. Last year she bid on a charity auction and won the chance to name a character in my next book. Well, this was the next book, and it's thanks to her that Emma Vickers came into being. I know this is a very special name to both Linda and Emma's parents, and I so hope I have done the name proud.

Finally, thanks to you, my lovely readers. Every time I write a new book, there are loads of you who get excited and preorder it and read and review it, and I am always so, so grateful. I never take it for granted, and I will continue to try and write the best books I can. Thank you!

ABOUT THE AUTHOR

Clare Swatman is the author of bestselling women's fiction novels, which have been translated into over 20 languages. She has been a journalist for over twenty years, writing for *Bella* and *Woman & Home* amongst many other magazines. She lives in Hertfordshire.

Download your exclusive bonus content from Clare Swatman here:

Visit Clare's website: www.clareswatmanauthor.com

Follow Clare on social media:

facebook.com/clareswatmanauthor

instagram.com/clareswatmanauthor

tiktok.com/@clareswatmanauthor

ALSO BY CLARE SWATMAN

Before We Grow Old

The Night We First Met

The Mother's Secret

Before You Go

A Love to Last a Lifetime

The World Outside My Window

The Lost Letters of Evelyn Wright

Last Christmas

A Chance Worth Taking

The Garden of Shared Stories

Clare Swatman writing as C.L. Swatman

No Son of Mine

After the Party

Boldwood

Boldwood Books is an award-winning fiction publishing company seeking out the best stories from around the world.

Find out more at www.boldwoodbooks.com

Join our reader community for brilliant books, competitions and offers!

Follow us

@BoldwoodBooks

@TheBoldBookClub

Sign up to our weekly deals newsletter

https://bit.ly/BoldwoodBNewsletter

Printed in Dunstable, United Kingdom

74497460R00170